Natsume Soseki

The Tower of London

Tales of Victorian London

Translated and introduced by Damian Flanagan

PETER OWEN

London and Chester Springs

Translated from the Japanese by Damian Flanagan
Calligraphy by Kosaka Misuzu

PETER OWEN PUBLISHERS
73 Kenway Road, London SW5 0RE

Peter Owen books are distributed in the USA by
Dufour Editions Inc., Chester Springs, PA 19425-0007

This collection first published in Great Britain 2005 by
Peter Owen Publishers

'Rondon Shosoku' (1901), 'Jitensha Nikki' (1903)
first published in *Hototogisu*;
'Rondonto' (1905), 'Kaarairu Hakubutsukan' (1905)
published in the collection *Yokyushu* (1906);
'Geshuku', 'Kako no Nioi', 'Atatakai Yume', 'Insho',
'Kiri', 'Mukashi', 'Kureigu Sensei'
published in the collection *Eijitsu Shohin* (1909)

'Kiiro Geshukunin' first published 1953
© Yamada Keiko 1997

Translations, introduction and notes © Damian Flanagan 2004

ISBN 0 7206 1234 9

Printed in Singapore by
Excel Print Media

Contents

Illustrations

These translations are dedicated to my mother,
with love and gratitude
– Damian Flanagan

Introduction

WHAT do geniuses do with themselves before they are famous? How do they conduct themselves when they are down on their luck, isolated, impoverished; when they have time on their hands, indeed all the leisure in the world to fret, dream, weep; when they have yet to glimpse their destiny but more than enough scope to imagine a life of hopeless frustration? When they have few friends, only a vast, lonely city and an ocean of obscurity in which to wander, what happens to a mind that will later change the way a whole nation will think about itself? What mundane events and persons shape such a future?

In their most intriguing manifestation, these questions pre-occupy the Japanese in the guise of the man who would one day raise up the country's literature to heights never seen before or since. He has left generations of scholars from the other side of the world pacing the modern streets of London trying to discern for themselves the areas where once he was lost in the fog, or left them casting their eyes across the river Thames to sights – and not the most expected sights – that now burn themselves in the Japanese literary imagination. This is another London, one quite unknown to the British themselves, a boarding-house trail and visionary pilgrim-age in search of the sights and sounds of the early twentieth-century megalopolis most special to the Japanese for having traumatized, eviscerated and energized their greatest literary genius.

It was in May of 1900 that an outstanding but largely unknown 33-year-old professor of English working at an institute of higher education in Kumamoto was asked by the Japanese government to leave behind his pregnant wife and child and embark on two years of foreign study in London. Previously he had been an accomplished composer of haiku, but now he would be given only a meagre stipend, insufficient to pay for both books and comfortable lodgings, and have to endure great loneliness and unhappiness in an unknown land.

Passing out of Japanese waters on his long sea passage to the West, the scholar, a certain Natsume Kinnosuke, noted in his diary that he could not bring himself to write haiku any more in such alien surroundings. For two years in London and two years as university lecturer afterwards in Tokyo, Kinnosuke wrote scarcely anything at all, but struggled with the concept of the fundamental nature of literature itself. He suffered repeated nervous breakdowns. He would be thirty-seven before his professional writing career even commenced.

Yet it was a very different presence that, within twelve years, would lie dying on a tatami mat in Tokyo. By then the finest collection of novels, memoirs, criticism and short stories the Japanese language has ever seen had tumbled forth in one *annus mirabilis* after another. He had assembled around him a coterie of adoring acolytes known as 'the mountain range' (*sanmyaku*), which included some of the most precocious literary, scientific and philosophical talents of the century: Akutagawa Ryunosuke, Terada Torahiko and Watsuji Tetsuro to name but a few. With his works, indisputably recognized today as the zenith of Japanese literature, the man who boarded that boat to Europe passed out of this world transformed into the most fiercely blazing meteor across the sky of Eastern literature, Japan's millennium man: Soseki.

If you seek his monument, look around you. The most featured writer by far in Japanese university entrance examinations; the most widely read of Japanese authors (even in today's unlettered age it is comparatively rare to meet a Japanese who does not claim to have read at least one of his novels); the man whose life and works have been so endlessly analysed and argued over that no bookshop in Japan is complete today without a good two shelves filled with criticism of his works. And then, for twenty years (1984–2004), that deceptively mild-mannered, moustachioed visage looking out at you from every thousand-yen note. National fame does not get any bigger than this.

Yet it was London that was to be the crucible and crossroads of his life, the place where Soseki was faced with the intense cultural shock and social alienation that led to the eventual tumultuous release of his pent-up creative urges. It was in London that he decided to attend the lectures of Professor Ker, a specialist in medieval literature at University College. For Japan's greatest expert in English literature to have travelled around the world to attend lectures with a leading professor of literature in London, how exciting the prospect must have been. Yet how disappointing these lectures turned out to be. Not much different from the lectures in Japan, and so much time wasted in commuting to them. So Soseki stopped attending after only two months, but instead, through Ker's introduction, made arrangements for weekly tutorial sessions with one of the editors of the Arden Shakespeare, a reclusive scholar called William Craig.

He restlessly moved from one boarding-house to another, repeatedly unsettled by the domestic tensions of the families with whom he lodged, and, generally isolated from British society, roamed across the seemingly vast metropolis. During two years, Soseki made no friends with any English people and, apart from a few other Japanese acquaintances in London and the families running his boarding-houses, held court with nothing but the hundreds of books he acquired from second-hand bookshops. He preoccupied himself with solitary and intense study, but reading countless literary works to try to delve into the nature of literature was, he later said, like 'washing blood with blood'. So instead, stimulated by conversations with Ikeda Kikunae, a Japanese scientist (and, incidentally, later to become the inventor of the food additive monosodium glutamate) who stayed with him in London for two months, he nurtured the concept that literature, too, might be treated scientifically and objectively and turned his attention to reading a whole variety of scientific, psychological and historical works. Hoping to produce a revolutionary, quasi-scientific 'theory of literature', he set about the daunting task of producing the copious notes that would be eventually published as his monumental and complex *Bungakuron* (*Theory of Literature*) in 1907.

His research was pursued with such single-mindedness, however, that he quickly began to suffer from acute mental health problems. By September 1902 another Japanese studying in London was said to have passed rumours on to the Ministry of Education that Soseki had gone insane, and, shortly before his return to Japan at the end of 1902, he was in for more trauma, receiving news that his best friend, Masaoka Shiki, Japan's foremost haiku poet, had died of consumption. It must have been in something of a dejected condition that Soseki commenced the long journey home.

But impressions of Britain remained vivid, painful and precious. Just as cultural shock caused him acute neurosis in England, even leading him to believe he was being followed and spied upon, and provoking outbursts of rage against the hypocrisy of the British that lasted until his death, so, too, that culture silently oozed into his pores. Upon his return to Japan, Soseki appeared obnoxiously Europeanized to his Japanese students. Now he sported a fashionable Kaiser moustache, ate beef and toast and wore a frock-coat. And for all his vitriol against the British, when the First World War broke out, he found himself deeply concerned over the fate of British liberalism under the threat of German militarism.

Soseki had arrived in Britain at the very close of the Victorian era and had witnessed such events as troops returning from the Boer War and the funeral procession of Queen Victoria; he had also visited London's renowned Tate Gallery only three years after it had been opened. His writings on Britain are contained in: 'Letter from London' (1901) and 'Bicycle Diary' (1903), both of which were published in the literary magazine *Hototogisu* (*The Cuckoo*); the stories 'The Tower of London' and 'The Carlyle Museum', published in January 1905 and later included in the *Drifting in Space* (*Yokyoshu*) collection of 1906; and extracts from *Short Pieces For Long Days* (*Eijitsu Shohin*), serialized in the *Asahi* newspaper in 1909.

The pieces in this collection, which comprise all Soseki's memoirs of Britain and associated fiction, form a very small but extremely important part of his complete works. They are here arranged in the order in which they were written. Thus Soseki's 'Letter from London', written in 1901, describes contemporary events in his second boarding-house in south-west London, whereas sections of *Short Pieces for Long Days*, written eight years later, describe events antecedent to this, recalling his first boarding-house in West Hampstead. The early works, 'Letter from London' and 'Bicycle Diary', are contemporary accounts of Soseki's day-to-day life in London, with, in the case of the former, events unfolding as he was actually writing about them. In contrast, when, at the end of 1904, Soseki penned 'The Tower of London' and 'The Carlyle Museum', he had already been returned from England for two years and based most of the factual detail on guidebooks to the Tower and the Carlyle House that he had brought back to Japan with him. *Short Pieces for Long Days* takes this process of transforming actual experience into literary art a stage further, intercutting various memoirs of Britain with stories of Japan (not presented here) to produce from a seemingly haphazard montage of tales something like the consciousness of its creator. The pieces exist on the borderline of memoir and dream as sentences continuously switch from past to present tense and back to past again. Whereas Soseki's Britain in 'Letter from London' is an alien place whose external appearance is faithfully described by the author, we can observe how it was internalized through the mechanism of memory into something that ultimately exists primarily in the mind of its author.

Soseki's London

Today we might tend to think of Tokyo as being the world's ultimate phantasmagoric, disorientating urban landscape compared with the relatively gentle scale of London's buildings, but, in Soseki's day, exactly the reverse was true. London was a vast, dark, foggy maze where one street and house was often indistinguishable from the next and the dizzy heights of the grey buildings seemed overwhelmingly oppressive.

When Soseki first arrived in London, Japan and Japan's problems were still uppermost in his mind, and he was busily writing letters home to his wife's family about the laxity and arrogance of Japanese 'gentlemen'. Yet on the street he was being constantly mistaken for being Chinese, or even Portuguese, and uncomfortably viewed his short form in shop windows as a 'Tom Thumb' in shabby clothes in a world where on a Sunday even butchers' boys appeared to don silk hats and frock-coats. Outside of his small boarding-house world, he is conscious, through intense scrutiny of the *Daily Telegraph* and the *Standard*, of world events: the rising tension between Japan and Russia over Manchuria; the excommunication of Tolstoy; the struggle in the Transvaal.

From his private correspondence of the period, we know that he was obsessed with not wanting to waste time or money, and, having no confidence in his ability to make confident conversation with Londoners, convinced himself that buying and reading books was preferable to going to lectures or socializing with Westerners. Outside of his boarding-houses, his main social contacts were Mrs Nott and her consorts, all bent on converting him to Christianity. He consoled himself by busily writing letters home to his wife, worried about the progress of her pregnancy. Regrettably, he received little correspondence in return and had to wait a full six weeks after the birth of his daughter, on 26 January 1901, to learn that mother and daughter were well. Still he continued to dish out endless advice to his wife back home about her comportment, her teeth and the way she was to bring up their daughter. He even spent one entire letter lecturing his wife on the necessity of getting up early.

He wandered across London searching for cheap second-hand books and later recalled once eating tinned biscuits on a park bench for lunch to try to save the money to pay for them. Over a two-year period he appears to have spent a third of his entire salary on books and bought as many as five to six hundred volumes, all crammed on to the shelves, table and floor of his boarding-house room until he could ship them safely back to Japan with him. For the first year he also kept a diary, and from this we know that he was a keen theatre-goer and went at least ten times during that period, including trips to variety performances at the Hippodrome and pantomimes such as *Sleeping Beauty* at Drury Lane, the sumptuous sets of which he described with enthusiasm in his letters.

Even as he tried to shelter away from the world and lose himself in intense study, the ordinary world of his boarding-houses crowded in with their human dramas and intrigues. Although subject to some important elements of fictionalization, Soseki was later to recall his first boarding-house in *Short Pieces for Long Days*. In 'Lodgings' the narrator finds himself caught between the dark secrets lurking between his French landlady, her German stepfather, the father's son by a previous marriage and the young maid, Agnes, who herself suspiciously resembles the son. As Japanese critics have pointed out, this household is a microcosm of the tensions between the major European nations – British, French, German – that would eventually explode into the First World War. The German father even has a face resembling that of President Kruger, the Boer leader against whom the British were currently engaged in a bitterly internecine war.

In Soseki's second boarding-house – described in the straight-forwardly factual 'Letter from London', the first piece in this collection – Soseki is reduced to being the last lodger of a pitiful pair of sisters who have fallen on hard times. They used to run a girls' school, but it had to close after an outbreak of fever amongst the students, and now they are so far behind with the rent that they must smuggle out their belongings in the middle of the night for fear the landlord will impound them. Soseki is reluctantly persuaded to move to their new home (their 'new paradise') with them but finds it much less attractive than described. To his dismay, he discovers that the housemaid, Penn, so memorably caricatured as a typically garrulous cockney girl, has been dismissed, and he is left alone with one sister who is 'exceptionally devout' and another who addresses him in the most inadvertently patronizing terms, asking him – Japan's leading expert on English literature – whether he understands the word 'tunnel'!

Perhaps, not surprisingly, after Soseki reached his fourth and final boarding-house and began to confine himself constantly to his room, his mental health deteriorated to the point where those around him – his doctor, landlady and fellow lodgers – encouraged him to take urgent remedial action. One part of this was to leave London altogether and take a short holiday at a house in the Highlands of Scotland, a soothing experience that Soseki recalled seven years later in the 'Long Ago' section of *Short Pieces for Long Days*. The other solution, urged on him by his new landlady – about whom Soseki wrote approvingly in his private correspondence that she spoke fluent French and read Shakespeare and Milton – was that he should take up riding a bicycle as a form of therapeutic exercise. In a typical turn of Chaplinesque slapstick and satirical brilliance, Soseki dressed up the whole episode in terms of a humiliating peace treaty. In 'Bicycle Diary', written shortly after his return to Japan, his battle to retain his own sanity is transformed into a battle (ultimately lost) to establish mastery over a bicycle.

The Tower of London

Throughout his time in London, Soseki appeared to be in withdrawal from the real world, losing himself in a hallucinogenic world of literature and books. In 1906 he published a collection of seemingly disconnected, eerie fantasies entitled *Drifting in Space*, all of which represented a withdrawal from modern life into mystical places. Two of the stories were set in the Arthurian past, three in contemporary Japan and the two presented here – 'The Tower of London' and 'The Carlyle Museum' – in London.

A recurring motif throughout much of Soseki's fiction of this period was that of the Lady of Shalot, the woman condemned to live atop a tower spinning her tapestry of the world, which she perceives not directly but through a magical mirror. The doomed Lady appears in person in one of his Arthurian stories, allusively titled 'The Shallot Dew' (*Kairoko*; not presented here), and the motif helped to link many of the pieces in the collection. In 'The Tower of London' Soseki contemplates the lives of all those imprisoned inside a 'tower' as the narrator walks around touching walls oozing blood-like dew. And in 'The Carlyle Museum' we find Carlyle, too, in a supposedly sound-proof study at the top of a tower-like building in Chelsea, living with a wife who looks 'like a prime shallot'. Carlyle even sits in the basement silently smoking a pipe with Tennyson, the author of 'The Lady of Shalot'.

In both these London stories mystical places are first approached from across the river Thames, a boundary like the river Styx, which takes the narrator out of the present and into a dream-like world dominated by the spirits of the dead. The Tower of London becomes a place where 'visions' are summoned into being, whether the Delaroche paintings (*The Princes in the Tower* and *The Execution of Lady Jane Grey*) that Soseki had seen in books he brought back from London (such as Cassell's *The History of England*) or that he remembered seeing in London's art galleries, or else are visions inspired by literary excerpts such as the grim executioner's song found in William Ainsworth's historical novel *The Tower of London*, which provided much of the historical information for Soseki's story.

As with Ainsworth's novel, at the heart of Soseki's piece is the story of Lady Jane Grey, the accomplished and beautiful fifteen-year-old placed on the throne of England by her ambitious father-in-law, the Duke of Northumberland, in 1553. Champions of the Protestant cause after the death of Edward VI, Jane and her husband Guildford Dudley were deposed after a mere nine days following popular unrest in favour of Edward VI's Catholic sister

倫
敦
塔

Mary, and, after a further unsuccessful rising by Sir Thomas Wyatt on Jane's behalf, both she and her husband were put to death. Such is a bare outline of the plot of Ainsworth's novel, but Soseki handles this material highly allusively, first encountering other visions based on Shakespeare's *Richard III*, before the narrator spies a young woman observing the ravens that seem to guard the place of execution. Amongst many other inscriptions carved with bare fingernails and metal scraps on the wall of the Beauchamp Tower is, he discovers, the single word 'Jane'. The mysterious woman then appears again to elucidate the elaborate crest of the Dudleys also inscribed on the wall but stops short when she comes to her husband's name, Guildford. Suddenly we switch to the scene of the executioners in the cellar cheerfully singing while sharpening their axe (chipped while beheading a woman's 'stupidly hard neck'), before being whisked into the grand finale: the moment of Jane's execution itself, based on Delaroche's painting in the National Gallery.

Soseki's story is an elaborate amalgam of material from highly disparate sources – history books, Shakespeare, Ainsworth's popular novel, Delaroche's paintings – source material whose usage he gleefully deconstructs in his coda. All of this is entertaining enough, but behind the prose Soseki is playing with some very large concepts indeed. Some are technical problems: to what extent can paintings be fused into the fabric of literary prose; are literature and painting really, as Horace claimed, sister arts? (And here we should bear in mind that the whole *Drifting in Space* collection was itself accompanied by sumptuous illustrations and designs by distinguished artists such as Nakamura Fusetsu and Hashiguchi Goyo and represented an elaborate fusion of the visual and literary arts.)

Other aspects of the story draw our attention to how literature can combine seemingly irreconcilable or incongruent subjects and moods. The main thesis of Soseki's *Theory of Literature* was to be that literature is made up of two components: the narrative theme and the artistic mood associated with this theme. In 'The Tower of London' we have a classic example of incongruous subject and mood (which Soseki referred to again in his *Theory of Literature*) in the form of the executioner chirpily singing while sharpening his axe. Rather than attempt to build up a sense of dread by piling up layer upon layer of clichéd terror in grim seriousness, Soseki constantly overturns our expectations by an infusion of the comic and the mundane. After the vision of the assassins in the courtyard discussing the murder of the young princes, we are returned to reality with the sound of the sentry marching as he mentally frolics with his lady-love. In the scene where the executioners are singing in the dark cellar, the lantern illuminates the side of a face that appears 'the colour of a mud-coloured carrot'. The comic elements are inseparable from the ghoulish, but, as with the Porter scene in *Macbeth*, the effect is to heighten not lessen the sense of dread. This is not some distant Gothic fantasy but a real-life world with things readily familiar to us in it.

Soseki leads us through the series of seemingly disparate subject matter by means of a gentle fugue of imagery. The Princes in the Tower wear tunics as 'black as ravens' wings', which foreshadow both their tragic fate and the later eerie appearance at the place of execution of three ravens. Looking at these ravens, the narrator senses that 'the rancour of a hundred years of blood has congealed and taken the form of a bird so as to guard this unhappy place for ever', whereupon the young woman, whom we do not yet know to be Jane Grey, appears with a child and remarks cryptically that there are not three but five ravens, implying that she and the child, too, are 'ravens' doomed also to share a tragic fate.

After going to all this trouble to induce us towards a direct vision of the execution of Lady Jane Grey – whence we have been incrementally led through the indirect telling of the murder of the Princes in the Tower, the appearance of the mysterious woman, the singing of the executioners – Soseki then sets about inverting the supposed reality of it all. First, his landlord dismisses all the elements of his fantasy – the five ravens, the epigraphs on the walls, the beautiful woman – as nothing more than things that can be explained away in the most banal twentieth-century terms. Then, in the coda appended to the story, Soseki explains where all the 'visions' came from in the first place. He strips away any lingering sense of reality, making the artifice of the piece, its 'unreality', manifest. He even goes so far as to tell us that in terms of describing the Tower's features (had this been his objective, which it clearly is not), then the story is unsatisfactory as he cannot now remember exactly what it looks like anyway, and he tosses us a final throwaway line, 'But what's written is written and that's that', as if the whole story has been carelessly dashed off.

If the story is not about describing the Tower, then what is it about? What does the Tower represent? The answer is surely to be found at the beginning of the tale when the narrator makes his way across the bewildering maze of modern London, replete with all its diverse modes of transport: trams, carriages, steam trains. This world is modern, mobile, constantly changing and ultimately completely forgettable. The narrator observes of his journey to the Tower that:

> If I say, 'I came not knowing from whence I came, and left not knowing from whence I left,' it will sound Zen-like, but even now I have no idea which roads I passed along to arrive at the 'Tower' or what districts I crossed over to get back to my house. However much I reflect on it, I cannot recall them. Ask me about beforehand, and I am at a loss; question me about afterwards, and I cannot give you an answer. Only the middle part, which has forgotten beforehand and taken leave of afterwards, is unadorned and clear.

In contrast to the hurly-burly of this ever-changing outer world the Tower itself is ancient, immobile and unforgettable. On Tower Bridge the rushing blur of the outer world is transformed into the stillness of the river, where nothing appears to move and 'everything is the feeling of the past'. On this bridge between past and present, between this world and the next world, the narrator, too, does not know if he is a person of present or ancient times. In the outer world his mind was becoming 'gluey'. Only within the Tower does it achieve clarity as objects acquire material presence and all the narrator's senses suddenly become activated. Not only does he see and hear 'visions' with perfect composure but his senses of touch and smell become stimulated, too. He feels the damp walls with his fingers; remarks of Jane Grey that 'the fragrance from the pistil of a trampled rose does not easily disappear, but distantly stands'; and even fears that the blood spurted out at her execution will splatter his trousers.

Time itself undergoes a transformation when the narrator enters the Tower. Before reaching the Tower, while still in the present-day world, things were generally referred to in the past tense. Yet, within the Tower there is a marked shift from past to present tense. Time within the Tower, the place that contains 'the mysterious things called the past', is a kind of eternal present. The past has present substantiality, while the present-day world outside is shown to be nothing more than an accumulation of particles which every second disappear. And because of this, the visions from the past, whether the apparitions of Archbishop Cranmer ascending from a boat at the Traitor's Gate, or of Wyatt and Raleigh, or of the Princes that appear on the 'stage of imagination', or of the executioners and Jane Grey, have ultimately a deeper sense of reality than those of the sentry or beefeater from the present – and certainly more than the shadowy landlord who appears at the end of the piece.

At the heart of this drama is the question: how in our increasingly rationalized world does one come to terms with a place that contains within it 'the mysterious things called the past'? Should we, like the narrator's landlord (described at the end of the piece as 'a Londoner of the twentieth century'), be numb to the generations of agony stored up in the walls of the Tower of London? Or should we allow the place rather to lead us into a Zen-like contemplation of the fleetingness of this world, so that we finally come to understand that it is the supposed rational solidity of the outer world that is illusory, that this is itself a 'vision', while it is the repository of the ghosts of a 'hundred generations' that is ultimately permanent, that remains unmoving, unchanging and all-knowing, as steam trains and electric trains rush by it.

The Carlyle Museum

In much the same way, the former home of the historian and essayist Thomas Carlyle (1795–1881) in Chelsea becomes the 'Carlyle Museum'. This is not a house like any other but an eternally unchanging place, a museum fixed in the past. It contains all the relics of a dead man: his books, medals, furniture, even his death mask. In 'The Tower of London' the narrator reflected on such relics by remarking that 'Whether graves or monuments, whether medallions or cordons, these things are . . . nothing more than a means of making one recall through a futile object bygone days.' Now, in 'The Carlyle Museum', we are told that all such items 'blithely' remain while the 'smoke-like life' of the man who owned them has long since disappeared. The house itself, despite having welcomed and bade farewell to many masters, 'remains just as it always did'.

To explore this house is to feel what it must have been like to have been Carlyle himself. When Carlyle moved to Chelsea from Scotland in 1834, we are told, he did not himself think that he was living in London. 'He believed himself to be living in the quiet countryside and viewing the cathedrals of the city centre from a great distance.' But when the narrator puts his head out the window:

> neither Westminster nor St Paul's are visible. Tens of thousands of houses, hundreds of thousands of people, millions of noises are standing, floating and moving in the space between me and the cathedrals. The Chelsea of 1834 and the Chelsea of today seem to be completely different places.

The house may have remained unchanged, but the outer world has been rapidly transforming itself about it. It was the multitude of 'noises' from this outer world that worked on Carlyle's nerves, causing him to attempt to build a sound-proof study on the third floor of the house, and it is the ascent to this third-floor room up in the sky – as far removed from the real world as possible – that forms the climax of the story. When the narrator reaches this level, he feels 'vaguely happy without knowing why', and, when he begins his descent, he has 'a feeling of approaching a lower world'.

Yet, just when Carlyle thought that he had escaped the noises of the mundane world below, he discovered that other previously inaudible noises from the outside world now plagued his nerves.

> Yes, the sound of the piano stopped, and the dog's voice stopped, and the cocks' voices and the parrot's voice became inaudible as planned, but things not worth considering when on the lower levels, the church bells and the train's whistle, and then quite unknown voices coming from the distant world below pursued him like a curse and tormented his nerves as of old.

In Tennyson's poem 'The Lady of Shalot' the lady attempts to devote herself to her artistic pursuit, spinning her tapestry of the outer world viewed through a magical mirror, but is distracted by the noise of the approaching Lancelot and is tempted to look directly outside. This brings the 'curse' upon her which causes the mirror to crack and her tapestry to unravel. And so, for Carlyle, too, attempting to devote himself to his art at the top of his tower, 'unknown voices coming from the distant world below' pursue him 'like a curse'. If the construction of the sound-proof study represents a wish to leave the mundane, ephemeral world behind and reach for the infinite, the unchanging and the absolute, the 'noises' of the world below ultimately prove inescapable.

While then this story acts as a companion piece to 'The Tower of London', it also stands in sharp antithesis to it. The Tower of London is 'a great magnet of the past, in excess of one hundred and twenty thousand square yards', which absorbs the narrator like 'a small speck of iron floating in the present age'. The Carlyle House, in contrast, is merely a 'four-storeyed, square house built on the roadside so that one can knock the door directly from the street' and has a garden that is only 'forty square yards'. The Tower of London is a dominating presence, standing haughtily indifferent to the noises of the outer world, saying, 'Steam trains may run along, and electric trains may run along, too, but as long as there is history I alone will be like this.' In 'The Carlyle Museum', however, the emphasis is on the impossibility of escaping 'the train's whistle' and other noises emanating from the outer world.

Thus there are no poetic, dramatic visions as in 'The Tower of London'. 'The Carlyle Museum' is not about encountering visions but, rather, something more personal and intimate, about entering into the spirit of a man tormented by noises from the outer world. It is not, like 'The Tower of London', concerned with activating the narrator's exterior senses but, rather, with activating internal imaginative empathy. And, indeed, the narrator is pre-eminently well disposed to sympathize with how 'noises' grated on Carlyle's nerves, for at the beginning of 'The Tower of London' the narrator, too, confessed that 'If I have to live for two years amongst this noise and these crowds . . . the very fabric of my nerves will eventually become as sticky as a gluey plant in a cooking pot.'

The Carlyle House is also, we should recall, the former home of a most famous historian and visionary thinker, one who has himself, through his books on Frederick the Great and Cromwell, entered into communion with 'the mysterious things called the past'. He is someone who, despite his success, denounced the public as 'forty million fools', recognizing only too well the folly and triviality of the world. Despite being sent a Prussian decoration by Bismarck, and medals being struck to commemorate his birthday, he 'turned down the pension offered him by Disraeli, and led a straight, upright and purposeful life'. Carlyle's humility and lack of self-assuming airs is evidenced in the very opening exchange with the speechmaker at Hyde Park Corner. Having no desire to be acclaimed as the 'Sage of Chelsea', he laughs along with the boorish speechmaker who teases him that 'sage is a bird's name'. 'Although we are all human, calling one person in particular a sage *does* seem to be the same as saying they are a bird. Humans are better off being left as ordinary humans,' Carlyle laughingly retorts.

Carlyle devotes himself not to the acquisition of meaningless baubles but to keeping his gaze on the great scheme of things. It is for precisely this reason that the distractions of the everyday world work on his nerves. Looking up at the sky from his garden, he cries out:

> Hah, in a little while I shall have seen you also for the last time. God Almighty's own Theatre of Immensity, the INFINITE made palpable and visible to me . . . And I knew so little of it; real as was my effort and desire to know!

If the message of the 'Tower of London' was that the great Zen-like truth that the present, everyday world around us is illusory, then the message of 'The Carlyle Museum' is that it is a very different matter for an individual to close himself off from the distractions of this mundane world. The Tower of London may be 'a distillation of the history of England', a collective representation of the dominance of the past that mocks the ephemerality of the present; but the Carlyle House is a 'hermitage', the personal retreat and mindset of a single man, and it is no easy thing for a single man to transcend the outer world.

As with 'The Tower of London', however, Soseki does not allow the narrative to fall into heavy-handed sombreness but takes us by surprise with a host of comic elements and revealing similes. Every time that the narrator contemplates the items left behind by the dead man, he is returned to normality by a guide who is delivering her tour on autopilot, oblivious to whether the visitor is listening or not. He is amused by the desultory thought that he might be the first Japanese to visit the house and remarks in a matter-of-fact way that Carlyle's face looks as if 'the middle of a cliff had collapsed and lay flat on a grassy plain', and that his bathtub is just like a 'big cooking pot'.

Beneath the surface of the story is at work a subtle symbolism. Because the house is dominated by the aura of a dead man, a recurring motif is the number four. This number is highly inauspicious in both Japan and China because the word for four (*shi* in Japanese, *si* in Mandarin) is a homonym with the word for death. Thus the house and gardens in this story are repeatedly described as being square (four-sided); the narrator recounts that he visited and recorded his name four times; he puts his head out the windows four times; and slowly climbs to the fourth floor of the house (the Japanese count the ground floor as the first floor, thus making the story's climax, the sound-proof study, the fourth floor).

This insistence on the narrator's *four* visits (which not a few critics have somewhat incredulously believed to be how many times Soseki actually visited the Carlyle House) emphasizes that the story is not a factual account but a carefully conceived piece of fiction. It is clearly intended to signal a craftily ironic contrast with the opening of 'The Tower of London'. There it was emphatically asserted that:

> During two years of study abroad, I visited the Tower of London only once. Afterwards there were days when I thought I might go again, but I decided not to. I was even invited by other people, but I refused. Destroying memories of that single visit with a second visit would be a shame, and wiping them away completely with a third visit would be most regrettable of all.

Yet here we are told that the narrator visited the Carlyle House *four* times and yet that this is a precise account of the *first* visit as distinct from any other. The story is obviously therefore about much more than an account of Soseki's own visit.

Short Pieces for Long Days

To Soseki, who displayed a deep affinity for Zen throughout his life, the distinction between 'reality' and 'dreams' was becoming illusory. All existence was dreams and illusions; walking itself was a form of dreaming and dreaming a form of walking. In both 'The Tower of London' and 'The Carlyle Museum' we are presented with mysterious, dream-like places that represent a Dantesque passage into the Underworld: the realm of the dead, their spirits and the past. By the time that Soseki wrote *Short Pieces for Long Days* the whole of London has been transformed in his mind into a vast dreamscape, with only snatched glimpses of the foggy 'reality' in which Soseki lived for two years. All of Soseki's memories undergo dream-like transformations, and all the pieces incorporate elements of careful fictionalization.

Soseki describes London's streets as dark valleys where tall buildings blot out the sun and – developing the theme of the narrator's fear from the beginning of 'The Tower of London' that he 'might be swept away in a human wave' – the people who rush along the streets are now a 'human tide'. Everyone appears to know exactly where they are headed and are pressed for time, caught up in the maelstrom of furious capitalist activity. In the whirlpool of human souls milling around Trafalgar Square, the narrator looks up and sees a small figure motionless above a column in the centre (it is, of course, the statue of Nelson) and appears to feel that this is a representation of himself in the currents of humanity around him. He is directionless, lost, moving phantom-like and forlorn at a speed different from everything around him, loitering on the margins, exploring forgotten spaces and seeing everything with somnambulant vision. In this dream-like world even the stone lions in Trafalgar Square are said to be 'sleeping in the midst of crowds pulsing in waves around them'.

Cab drivers, beating their chests in the cold and raising their index fingers to offer a ride, seem almost like apparitions, as does the sight of a gull in the fog from Westminster Bridge and the horses' heads appearing out of the mist at the bus stop. Everything exists on a silent continuum, interrupted, as in dreams, only by the sudden interruption of specific noises, such as the chimes of Big Ben. Step out of this hallucinatory world, and a different dreamscape appears as the narrator winds up the stairs to the gallery of a theatre where hundreds of people sit silently in the darkness peering over the edge into the void as, slowly, chinks of light appear from a stage that gradually transforms itself into a Mediterranean scene.

In the dark valleys of the outer world, the narrator feels as if he is drowning in this human sea, where little figures, buffeted by the wind and shivering in the blackness, scuttle along 'like small fishes slipping out of the meshes of a net'. But, upon entering the theatre, he discovers 'a place of spring-like warmth', where every face is relaxed and quietly composed. He looks down from the balcony into the 'valley' below to see another human sea, bedecked in 'every bright colour imaginable, like ripples on a great ocean . . . in an assemblage of multi-coloured scales'.

Because the outer world is so cold and grey, the narrator is con-tinually drawn towards such points of warmth and colour, and, as everything is now dream-like, it is not just any dream that casts its spell, but specifically 'warm dreams'. In 'Lodgings' the narrator sits in a sunless room with his landlady, being told that Britain is 'terribly cloudy and cold'. Even the daffodil placed in a glass bottle behind her is wilting. He observes 'the trickle of colourless blood pulsing across this woman's shrivelled cheeks and imagined what warm dreams they might have seen in distant France'. He is attracted instead towards the welcoming fire of K's room and to K himself in his bright maroon dressing-gown. He shivers to think not only of the landlady's colourless blood, her craggy throat, fierce visage and black clothes, but also that 'if one was to inadvertently touch her flesh, the blood of the person touching her would turn cold at that spot'. Concurrent with this search for repositories of bright warmth in a frigid, monochrome world are the unexpected appearances of colours out of the darkness and the grey: whether the sumptuous stage costumes in 'A Warm Dream' or the multi-coloured buses emerging out of the mist in 'Fog'.

The time sequence within the series of memoirs is constantly inverted. 'Impression', Soseki's account of his first day in London (though the city's name itself is now never mentioned), is interposed between accounts of wanderings that must have occurred while at his second and fourth boarding-houses. Chronology is itself shown to be an illusion, for all things in 'the past' have, through the medium of consciousness, the potential to break into the present at any time. If in 'The Tower of London' we discovered visions of the Princes in the Tower from the fifteenth century, Jane Grey from the sixteenth century and Guy Fawkes from the seventeenth century all coexisting within a dream of 'the past', now, within Soseki's own memories, the chronology becomes almost incidental to the impression left behind. Within 'the past' itself we may reach further back into other currents of time in a kind of infinite recession. The landlady in 'Lodgings' recalls her own history, while the boarding-house and its family reek of the dark secrets from the past. Walking the streets in 'Fog', the narrator remarks that only about four yards ahead is visible and wonders whether the world has shrunk to four yards square. This is the 'present world' that we are all walking in. We are all contained within the fog of the past. As the narrator walks, a new four square yards constantly appears and 'the world I have walked through passes into the past and continuously disappears'.

In this largely soundless, chilly and colourless world senses of hearing, touch and sight are dulled, and a sense of the past is most readily activated by the sense of smell. Flowers are its most redolent symbol. They wilt in cold, cloudy London, with the drooping flower in 'Lodgings' symbolizing the landlady's 'sad history of a fragrant springtime that had vanished many years ago'. Now, far from being associated with fragrant springtime, the boarding-house smells not of flowers but of something connected with altogether more unpleasant memories. When the narrator revisits his former lodgings he discovers that 'the smell of my past boarding-house, which in the last three months or so I had forgotten, assailed my senses like a flash of lightning'. And what the smell reminds him of is 'a dark hell'.

As with 'The Tower of London', Soseki links a wide diversity of subject matter by means of common themes and imagery: cold and warmth; darkness and colour; crowds and solitude; speed and stillness; present and past; smells and scents. In his superb description of Pitlochry in autumn Soseki captures an entire world that is totally steeped in 'the past'. No longer, as with 'The Tower of London' and 'The Carlyle Museum', does 'the past' exist as small, discrete, mysterious pockets contained within 'the present'. Now 'the past' has completely taken over. We recall the metaphorical description of London's streets as 'dark valleys' and the welcoming warmth of the bright 'valley' of spectators at the theatre in 'A Warm Dream'. Now it seems as if all this was but to prepare us for the transformation of image into real object that occurs when we are transported to the magical Vale of Pitlochry. In contrast to the constant oppressive commotion of the crowds in London's fog, here the autumn sun (not seen at all in London) is calm and, in a throwback to the stillness seen from Tower Bridge in 'The Tower of London', 'perfectly unmoving'. In *Short Pieces for Long Days*, mobility is again associated with forgetfulness: to receive a lasting impression, to enter into the past, requires stillness.

In Pitlochry everything has returned to its natural state. The valley's peaty water 'has turned an old colour' and everywhere is tinged 'a warm colour'. Even the clouds overhead are described as 'old clouds'.

> The Vale of Pitlochry is deep into autumn . . . Like something bitter suddenly turning into something sweet, the whole valley acquires a patina of age. The Vale of Pitlochry returns to the past of a hundred years ago, to the past of two hundred years ago, and gently mellows. Everyone turns world-ripened faces to look at the clouds passing over the backs of the mountains . . . Whenever one looks, one always senses that these are old clouds.

In this 'old' world, not only is the scene – the house, the valley, the master's kilt and sporran – consistent with the past, but the intense fragrance of the flowers, absorbed in the warmth of the autumn sun, activates the narrator's sense of smell and links it with recollection in a way already prefigured in 'The Smell of the Past'. In 'Fog', we should recall, it seemed as though the visible world (the present) had shrunk to four square yards, and that, moving through this, only another four square yards appeared as everything else flowed into the past and disappeared. Now in 'Long Ago', we are told that the scent of the flowers is detectable in a space that is precisely defined as being 'four yards around'. The narrator must stand within those four square yards of the present to inhale the smell of the past.

This 'old world' of Pitlochry is a rural idyll, bright and colourful in contrast to the cold and grey of London. Yet even here historical memories of the battle of Killiecrankie, four miles to the north, flow downstream through time and space and menace the landscape from afar. In 'The Tower of London' we were told in relation to Jane Grey that 'the fragrance from the pistil of a trampled rose does not easily disappear, but distantly stands'. And now, in a characteristic Sosekian transformation of metaphor into real object, after describing the stream of blood that once passed through the Vale of Pitlochry, the narrator discovers in the last line of 'Long Ago' that 'two or three beautiful rose petals are scattered beneath my feet' as poetic symbols of past bloodshed.

Professor Craig

When Soseki writes with affection about his tutor, Professor Craig, he writes of one already dead, one who has already passed over the River Styx, but who still exists in vivid detail in Soseki's mind. Soseki revisits his spirit as if in a dream: there are the 'startled eyes' of his housekeeper, Jane, as she opens the door to his flat; the bare drawing-room with row upon row of books; and Professor Craig himself in all his Irish eccentricity – his 'retiring' hand, his flannelled clothing and slippers, his fleshy nose and overgrown beard, his habit of tapping his knee, his rambling discourses.

Significantly, we are repeatedly told that Craig's apartment was, like Carlyle's study, situated on the third floor (the 'fourth' floor by Japanese reckoning and thus again associated with death). It would appear from a letter written by Soseki while in London that Craig actually lived 'at the back of the first floor', and therefore the shift to a third floor setting is another subtle piece of fictionalization. Moreover, we should recall in the opening of 'The Carlyle Museum' Carlyle being teased that 'sage is a bird's name'; yet now we are told that 'Professor Craig is nestled *like a swallow* on the third floor'. It is intriguing, therefore, to consider this piece in comparison with Soseki's earlier depiction of the Carlyle House. There, the narrator slowly ascended to the third floor and discerned the 'smoke-like life' of Carlyle through the objects he left behind. He reflected how Carlyle attempted to devote himself to his studies up in his third-floor study but how he was distracted by the noises of the 'lower world'.

In 'Professor Craig', the narrator makes the ascent from ground floor to third floor within the first few lines. While the housekeeper fulfils much of the same comic function as the guide at the Carlyle House, now the narrator encounters a dead man, not distantly through the objects he has left behind but by direct observation of the man himself. The whole story is contained within the third floor, the realm of death that transcends the 'lower world', and, by living on such a floor, the suggestion is that, more so than Carlyle, Professor Craig in life escaped the 'noises' emanating from this lower world. He pursues his studies in near total obscurity and with complete indifference to the opinions and encouragement of others. His entire living quarters form one great study devoted to the pursuit of literature. Like Carlyle, he writes 'of things which only he seems to understand', hoarding away his notebooks and turning their pages black with his scribblings. Indeed, his handwriting is so illegible that he needs the services of his servant Jane to write notes for him in order to communicate with the outer world. And his discourses, too, are 'rambling', as if only he understands the train of thought behind them. On the one occasion when he is sighted by Soseki on the street he appears like 'a cabman who has forgotten his whip', someone entirely indifferent to how he is perceived in the 'lower world'.

The all-consuming, lifelong quest of Professor Craig's life is the compilation of the Shakespeare dictionary that he has been working on since the 1870s and the ten blue-covered notebooks in which he stores away references 'like a miser storing away small coins'. The incremental increase of their contents was, we are told, his lifetime's pleasure. Yet, when Soseki learns of his death, he wonders whether the dictionary was left unfinished and ended up as wastepaper.

In fact, Craig's Shakespeare dictionary was never finished (although his scholarship was not in vain, for it formed the basis of much of the annotation to several plays in the Arden Shakespeare series). In this sense, Craig could appear as an almost tragic figure, one, like Causabon in George Eliot's *Middlemarch*, who was futilely in pursuit of a *Key to All Mythologies*, a grandiose project that would never – could never – be completed. Yet Japanese critics have rightly taken a different view. Soseki tells us that 'morning and night, this dictionary is the sole preoccupation of the professor's mind', and it is as well to see the very pursuit of the dictionary as something which gave purpose, meaning and comfort to Craig's life and inspired others. Craig's lifelong quest to produce his Shakespeare dictionary was a reflection of – quite possibly an inspiration for – Soseki's own obsessive, intense research for his *Theory of Literature*. And so, whereas Craig might have been portrayed just as a lonely, forlorn middle-aged man, instead we see a figure imbued with the intense purity of the poet. 'When reading poetry, the area from his face to his shoulders oscillates like a haze of heat,' we are told. And it is this poetic 'haze of heat' that is the 'warmth' that draws Soseki towards him, even if his tutor's treatment of him was 'extremely cold'. (A now forgotten figure in English literature, Craig was incidentally cherished by other literati of the day, and a notable short essay by E.V. Lucas, 'The Funeral', would later describe the scene at the graveside of a little-known literary scholar that was none other than Craig himself.)

In a whole variety of ways, Professor Craig may be seen a strange mirror image of Soseki himself. Both Craig and Soseki are rank outsiders in Imperial English society – Craig by virtue of being Irish, Soseki by being Japanese. Craig tells Soseki that they are both remarkable in being able to savour poetry, unlike the hundreds of English passing by on the streets below. Both men are unworldly figures, dressed in shabby clothes (Soseki's attire being so poor that his fellow Japanese lodger has to lend him the money to buy some new clothes), and both men are desperate for money to buy books: Soseki impatiently waits for his next pay cheque; Craig carelessly forgets that his Japanese student has already paid him the week before, announcing, 'Now there are a few books I wish to buy so I was wondering . . .'

Craig was nevertheless exactly the kind of Westerner with whom Soseki appeared to want to spend time. When looking to move from his second boarding-house, Soseki wrote in 'Letter from London' that 'I would like to be in the house of someone capable of speaking with a little learning, and would not even mind the house being dirty or cramped if I had the pleasure of their constant companionship.' Disappointed with the people he had encountered at his boarding-houses, Soseki recorded with amazement in his diary that, when he went to see a production of *Robinson Crusoe* at the theatre, he was asked by his landlady's husband, Mr Brett, whether this was a true story or fiction. So Soseki approaches Craig with the idea of moving into his apartment, but Craig turns him down and starts rambling on incoherently about Walt Whitman instead. Yet, behind the seemingly absent-minded façade of Craig we can also discern that Soseki must have made a favourable impression on him also, for the professor implores Soseki to use Craig's commentary on Shakespeare when he returns to his own country and, shortly before Soseki stopped coming to him for tuition, even expressed a wistful desire to take up a university post in Japan.

A Note on Soseki and the Art of Translation

Natsume Soseki had very set views on the art of translation. He did not much care for it. (Witness his piqued refusal at the end of 'The Tower of London' to translate the executioner's song.) Despite being Japan's greatest contemporary expert on English literature, immensely well read and capable himself of writing highly sophisticated passages in flawless English, Soseki, in sharp contrast to most of the other leading Japanese writers of the day, published no full-length translation of any Western literary work.

The art of translation did, however, play a seminal role in his life and works. His novels are riddled with key phrases in English and reflections on their meaning, such as the line 'Pity's akin to love', taken from Thomas Southerne's play *Oroonoko*, which features prominently in Soseki's novel *Sanshiro*. And even in 'The Tower of London' Soseki amused himself by translating a few lines from Dante and inscriptions from the Beauchamp Tower into Japanese. Soseki also guided others in their translation labours. Yet he himself showed no desire to be seen as the translator of any other writer's work – rather, it was odd lines from diverse sources which caught his attention that were freely adopted and absorbed into his own literary output.

The reasons for this approach were two-fold. First, Soseki had an innate dislike of undertaking lengthy translations, as, by the very nature of the process requiring a slavish devotion to another's ideas, it opposed his own fiercely creative yearnings. Soseki's desire was not to put English literature into Japanese but, rather, to filter it through the prism of his own personality into his own distinctive works. Second, Soseki poured scorn on the contemporary Japanese vogue of employing a host of Western cultural references, such as allusions to Greek gods, which meant absolutely nothing to the bemused Japanese public. Soseki perceived that the West was only comprehensible to the Japanese if presented within their own sphere of familiarity. Thus, time and again in his writings on Britain we note the skill with which Soseki compares something in Britain with more familiar things back home. In 'Letter from London' Soseki equates the area of London where he is living to a down-at-heel part of Tokyo and comically describes himself descending into the London Underground as the reverse of a Kabuki character being lifted up on the stage. The Tower of London is said to be like a vastly magnified version of a shrine building in Tokyo, and the guide at the Carlyle House is said to have a face that resembles a Japanese bean-jam bun. Japanese cultural references are constantly interwoven with the sights and sounds of the West as a kind of familiarization technique to keep the Japanese reader from being bemused by it all.

In this sense, Soseki's writings on Britain ultimately served the purpose of translating Western culture into something more readily understandable by the Japanese reader. In translating these works into English, however, one is faced with the reverse dilemma of having a text peppered with Japanese references that are completely unfamiliar to the Western reader. The complexity of Soseki's prose is such that occasionally translators have felt justified in playing fast and loose with its rendition in English, on the grounds that a precise translation would be unreadable. Recent translations of his works have tended to range from the satisfactory to the woeful and have not been aided by flimsy analysis and being adorned with dust-jackets depicting cartoon characters. All of this has left the most outstanding of modern Japanese novelists lagging far behind lesser writers in terms of appreciation in the West.

I have attempted in this volume to stay as close as possible to the original text in all instances and not attempted to tamper with the style or content. Although these are a collection of disparate pieces linked by a common theme, all the works in this volume are extremely familiar to the Japanese and have been highly influential both in Japan and other countries (see appendix). Every one is, in its own way, a tiny masterpiece. One might argue that the literary quality steadily rises, but then, even in his first writings, the sophistication of Soseki's prose is remarkable. If just a little of the quality of the original peeps through the shadow of these translations, they will perhaps not be in vain.

A Note on the Text

As is the Japanese custom, Japanese names are presented here with family name followed by given name – thus the author's family name was Natsume and his given name Kinnosuke. Soseki was a 'literary name' (*bungo* in Japanese), something many Japanese writers adopted, and it is by this name that they will usually be referred. (The *bungo* is not intended in any way to mask the writer's identity, however.)

All ages in the stories have been kept as they are in the original. Because of the traditional Japanese method of determining a person's age as being one at birth and becoming two the following new year, there is occasionally a discrepancy between the Japanese and Western systems – so, for example, the ages given for the Princes in the Tower and Jane Grey in 'The Tower of London' are not as they would appear in British history books. This should be borne in mind for all ages used in these stories.

Natsume Soseki
A Brief Biography

1867 (9 February) Natsume Kinnosuke, later known by his pen-name Soseki, is born in the city of Edo, shortly before it is renamed Tokyo. He is the eighth child of a family of moderate means, but, having been born when his father is over fifty and his mother forty, is regarded as something of an embarrassment to his parents and promptly farmed out to a foster family and only returned to the Natsume home when aged nine. At first he studies Chinese classics at school, but later, in order to study something of more contemporary importance, turns his attention to the study of English.

1881 Age 14 Soseki's mother dies.

1884 Age 17 Soseki's enters the preparatory college (later known as the First Higher School) of the Imperial University.

1888 Age 21 Two of Soseki's older brothers die.

1889 Age 22 Soseki forms a strong friendship at the First Higher School with Masaoka Shiki, later to become Japan's leading haiku poet.

1890 Age 23 Soseki enters the highly prestigious Imperial University in Tokyo to study English literature. He will be only the second Japanese ever to graduate in the subject there.

1893 Age 26 Soseki obtains his degree and begins working as a lecturer in the English language.

1895 Age 28 After unexpectedly abandoning the capital, Soseki accepts a position as an English teacher at Matsuyama Middle School on the rural island of Shikoku. In August his friend Masaoka Shiki, who has been working as a reporter on the Sino-Japanese war, returns to Japan ill and comes back to his home town of Matsuyama to recuperate. He shares lodgings with Soseki for two months, and, with Shiki's encouragement, Soseki starts publishing haiku and Chinese verses in newspapers and magazines.

倫
敦
塔

1896 Age 29 In April Soseki takes up a new teaching position at the Fifth Higher School in Kumamoto, Kyushu, in the far south of Japan, and on 10 June marries Nakane Kyoko, daughter of the Secretary General to the House of Peers in the Japanese Parliament.

1897 Age 30 In June Soseki's father dies. During the summer Kyoko suffers a traumatic miscarriage and becomes increasingly prone to severe bouts of depression and hysteria. At one point the following year she even attempts suicide by throwing herself into a river and has to be hauled out by local fishermen.

1899 Age 32 In May a daughter, the first of their seven children, is born.

1900 Age 33 The Japanese government initiates a programme to send outstanding Japanese scholars overseas for two years of study so that they will be able to assume university positions presently occupied by Westerners on their return. When informed that he is one of the three people handpicked by the government for the pilot programme, Soseki is unenthusiastic. With great misgivings, he sells off most of his belongings, takes his pregnant wife and daughter back to Tokyo and the care of her family and, on 8 September 1900, sets sail for England on the German passenger ship *Preussen*.

The vessel calls at Kobe, Nagasaki, Shanghai, Hong Kong, Singapore, Colombo and Aden. Soseki suffers from diarrhoea and seasickness, and records in his diary just how uneasy he is with this gradual immersion into foreign climes. After brief calls at Naples and Genoa Soseki takes a train to Paris, where he remains for a week, marvelling at the 1900 World's Fair. Then, on 28 October, sails from France to England.

1901 Age 34 Writes 'Letter from London', published in *Hototogisu* (*The Cuckoo*).

1902 Age 35 In September Masaoka Shiki dies. In December, after a full two years in London, Soseki begins the trip back to Japan.

1903 Age 36 In April Soseki is duly appointed lecturer at the First Higher School and takes over the lectureship at Tokyo Imperial University from Lafcadio Hearn, but continues to suffer from severe bouts of paranoia that play havoc with his family life. In June publishes 'Bicycle Diary' in *The Cuckoo*. In July Soseki and Kyoko separate for two months. In October a third daughter is born.

1905 Age 38 To distract Soseki, the editor of the magazine *The Cuckoo*, his old friend Takahama Kyoshi, persuades him to write some fiction, and Soseki produces a sparkling piece of self-parody entitled *Wagahai wa neko de aru* (*I Am a Cat*) which he initially intends only as a short story. The story is so well received when it appears in January that Soseki continues with it, gradually transforming it into a fiery critique of contemporary Japanese society.

Soseki soon proves that he can assume mastery of almost any literary form he attempts. He begins to write densely poetic Arthurian tales, stories set in modern Japan and two stories based on his overseas experience, 'The Tower of London' and 'The Carlyle Museum', all employing common themes and motifs. The stories appear in a variety of magazines throughout the year and are collected together the following year under the title *Drifting in Space* (*Yokyoshu*).

1906 Age 39 Soseki produces two early masterpieces: *Botchan*, a brilliant comedy inspired by his year in Matsuyama, and *Kusa Makura* (*Pillow of Grass*; translated as *The Three-Cornered World*), which describes an artist escaping to a mountain spa to paint in a world free of emotion, only to find himself bewitched by a local beauty. He also writes *Nihyakutoka* (*The Two Hundred and Tenth Day*).

1907 Age 40 Having already been approached with an offer of a prestigious academic position at Kyoto University and yet another to take charge of the *Yomiuri* newspaper's literary column, Soseki instead amazes the academic world by announcing that he will be leaving his teaching jobs altogether and taking employment with the *Asahi Shinbun*, Japan's leading daily newspaper. The terms are to write at least one novel a year for serialization and do no writing of any sort for any other papers. The public response is so exuberant that, when the paper advertises that Soseki is to publish a novel called *Gubijinso* (*The Poppy*), Mitsukoshi and other department stores start selling a variety of merchandise with poppy designs. Also publishes *Nowaki* (*The Autumn Wind*), his long-delayed *Theory of*

倫
敦
塔

Literature and writes *Kofu* (*The Miner*), a stream-of-conscious narrative.

1908–14 Age 41–47 Having already conjured into being some unforgettably poetic prose, Soseki now begins to strip it back to a starkly clear, bare style and create the two great trilogies of novels for which he is today perhaps most remembered. In *Sanshiro* (1908) a naïve young student from Kyushu arrives in Tokyo and experiences the first inklings of love; in *Sore Kara* (*And Then*; 1909) and *Mon* (*The Gate*; 1910) the disruptive power of more mature love triangles is explored. In *Higan sugi made* (*To the Spring Equinox and Beyond*; 1912) Soseki moves off in another totally new direction, beginning with an intriguing detective fiction that is transformed into a multi-narrated exploration of familial relationships. In *Kojin* (*The Wayfarer*; 1913) a reclusive intellectual is obsessively suspicious of his wife's fidelity and tries to persuade his own brother to make a trial of her love. In *Kokoro* (*The Heart*; 1914) a lonely intellectual strikes up an unusually close bond with a young student and reveals a guilt-ridden past.

Meanwhile, a steady stream of other works in different genres continues to pour out including *Yumejuya* (*Ten Dreams*) and *Eijitsu shohin* (*Short Pieces for Long Days*) in 1908; *Manchu Tokorodokoro* (*Here and There in Manchuria and Korea*), a travel journal, in 1909; and *Omoidasu koto nado* (*Recollections*) in 1910.

1910 Age 43 Soseki's health problems markedly worsen. He suffers intense stomach pain while writing *Mon* (*The Gate*), spends over a month in hospital and then moves to an inn at Shuzenji hot springs to recuperate. There he again suffers a major stomach haemorrhage, lapses into a coma and only just survives.

1911 Age 44 Soseki is caught in the midst of public controversy when the repressive government of prime minister Katsuro Taro attempts to wield a wider influence over the Japanese literary world by announcing that a select number of writers, Soseki included, are to be awarded honorary Doctor of Letters degrees. Soseki not only indignantly declines the government's offer but vehemently repudiates their attempt to proclaim one artist more worthy than another. Instead he launches into a famous series of public lectures in which he criticizes many aspects of modern Japan, cogently arguing that the strains of coping with the rapidity and intensity of modernization are emotionally torturing the Japanese people and causing them to suffer the collective equivalent of a nervous breakdown.

During the lecture tour, Soseki once again falls ill with ulcers and is hospitalized in Osaka. His condition is not helped by the fact that in November his fifth and last daughter, Hinako, born in March 1910, unexpectedly and inexplicably dies.

1915 Age 48 In the last years of his life, Soseki begins to turn the novelistic scalpel directly on to himself, dissecting his own autobiographical experience in *Michikusa* (*Ramblings*; translated as *Grass on the Wayside*). He also publishes *Garasudo no uchi* (*Within Glass Doors*).

1916 Age 49 Soseki embarks on his most ambitious work, the psychological analysis of the pressures impinging on, and motives within, a modern marriage in *Meian* (*Light and Darkness*). The longest of his novels, it remains tantalizingly unfinished. On 22 November Soseki takes to his sickbed again, suffers major stomach haemorrhages over the following fortnight and dies on the evening of 9 December.

Soseki (aged twenty-seven) in 1894 and his future wife, Kyoko, (aged eighteen) in 1895. These photographs were exchanged at the time of their betrothal in 1896.

Soseki (aged 45) in September 1912. The black armband was worn
as a mark of respect for the passing of the Emperor Meiji

Soseki in London

28 October Soseki arrives in London and stays initially at apartments at 76 Gower Street near the British Museum.

31 October Sightseeing in London, takes in Tower Bridge, London Bridge and the Tower of London and goes with another Japanese to see *A School for Scandal* at the Haymarket Theatre.

1 November In Cambridge, bearing a letter of introduction from the formidable Mrs Nott – the mother of a Christian lady missionary in Kumamoto – whom Soseki encountered aboard ship. He meets Charles Freer Andrews, vice-principal of Westcott House, an associated college of Cambridge University, but returns to London the next day, having abandoned the idea of studying at Cambridge on the grounds that on his scant salary of £15 a month he simply cannot afford the flamboyant lifestyle of Cambridge's aristocratic students.

12 November Moves into a boarding-house at 85 Priory Road, West Hampstead, run by a woman he refers to as 'Miss Milde'.

22 November Calls round to the chambers of William Craig with a view to employing him as a personal tutor. Subsequently attends one-hour lessons with Craig every Tuesday until October 1901.

December Moves into a boarding-house at 6 Flodden Road, Camberwell, in south-east London. His new landlord and landlady are Mr and Mrs Harold Brett.

1901

22 January Death of Queen Victoria. Soseki wears a black necktie to show his 'respectful sympathy'.

21 February Soseki starts taking Carlsbad salts to alleviate the onset of stomach ulcers (the condition that was eventually to kill him).

9 April Begins writing 'Letter from London'.

25 April Soseki is reluctantly persuaded by Mr and Mrs Brett to move with them to 2 Stella Road, Tooting Graveney, in south-west London.

26 April Completes the third part of 'Letter from London'.

20 July Moves to his fourth and final boarding-house at 81 The Chase, off Clapham Common.

3 August Accompanied by the chemist Ikeda Kikunae, visits the Carlyle House in Chelsea.

1902

30 January Anglo-Japanese Naval Alliance signed in London.

September Takes up riding a bicycle as a form of outside exercise to assuage his mental problems brought on by intense study and constant confinement in his room.

October Accepts the invitation of John Henry Dixon, a prominent lawyer and Japanophile, to pass some time at Dixon's home in Pitlochry in the Scottish Highlands.

5 December Departs from England on the Japanese ship *Hakata-maru* and commences his journey back to Japan.

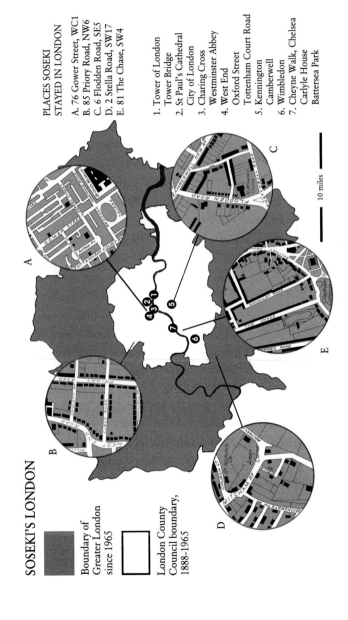

SOSEKI'S LONDON

Boundary of
Greater London
since 1965

London County
Council boundary,
1888-1965

10 miles

PLACES SOSEKI STAYED IN LONDON

A. 76 Gower Street, WC1
B. 85 Priory Road, NW6
C. 6 Flodden Road, SE5
D. 2 Stella Road, SW17
E. 81 The Chase, SW4

1. Tower of London
   Tower Bridge
2. St Paul's Cathedral
   City of London
3. Charing Cross
   Westminster Abbey
4. West End
   Oxford Street
   Tottenham Court Road
5. Kennington
   Camberwell
6. Wimbledon
7. Cheyne Walk, Chelsea
   Carlyle House
   Battersea Park

From *The Cuckoo* (1901–3)

Letter from London (1901)

So I think I will devote the whole evening of today, 9 April, to telling you about various things here. There are actually many things to tell you about. For some reason I have become terribly serious since arriving here. Looking and listening to everything around me, the problem of 'Japan's future' incessantly springs to mind. Do not tease me by telling me I am acting out of character. That someone like me is thinking about such problems cannot be entirely due to the weather and the beefsteak but must, I suppose, be providence. Many things have caught my attention: how literature and the arts are flourishing in this country and how the flourishing of literature and the arts is influencing the national character; to what extent this country's development has advanced materially and what trends lie behind that advance; that there is in England no word for samurai but the word 'gentleman' and what meaning the word 'gentleman' has; how the ordinary person is generous and hard working . . . Yet, at the same time, many irritating things crop up. Sometimes I find myself hating England and desiring quickly to return to Japan. But then again, when I reflect on the state of Japanese society, I feel it to be pitifully unpromising. Japanese gentlemen are, I fear, extremely lacking when it comes to their moral, physical and artistic education. How nonchalant and self-satisfied our gentlemen are! How foppish they are! How inane they are! How satisfied they are with modern Japan, and how they continue to lead the ordinary populace to the brink of degeneracy! They are so short-sighted as not to even know that they are doing these things. Many such grievances occur to me. The other day I wrote a long letter about Japan's upper classes and sent it to my relatives. However, these are merely superfluous things that I have come to feel since coming to England, and as such talk is not remotely connected to England and something that there is no need for me to relate to you nor something you are likely to want to hear about, I will straight away skip over it and talk about something else.

Unfortunately, when I try to come up with something better to talk about, nothing comes to mind. That being the case, I thought I might present to you today's events from my getting up until writing this letter now, written in the style of the diaries solicited by *The Cuckoo*. I say 'events', but in a loafer's life like mine there is nothing interesting or amusing, only extremely ordinary things to report. It might be interesting to say I lost Ann on Oxford Street or saw a fight at Charing Cross, but really my life is pitifully dull. However, I can tell you what I have been doing since coming to London. And, as you both know me, you might be a little interested in that.

Last Friday was 'Good Friday', the first day of the 'Easter' holiday. All the shops in town take a holiday, and shopping is completely forbidden. The following Saturday is the same as ever, but the following day is 'Easter Sunday' and shopping is again forbidden. The next day one imagines it's all over, but this day is called 'Easter Monday' and the shops are again closed. Only on the Tuesday do things finally revert to normal. The husband and wife here have gone over the holiday to the wife's family in the countryside. Tanaka said he would search for Shakespeare's old haunts and went off to a place with the long name of 'Stratford-upon-Avon'. Left behind were the wife's younger sister, the maid, Penn, and my good self.

When I open my eyes, the morning sun streams brilliantly through the gaps in the shutters. Thinking I have overslept, I drag out the nickel watch from under the pillow and see that it is still 7.20. It is not yet time for the first gong of the day. There is no point in getting up, yet I do not feel particularly sleepy. So, turning away from the wall in bed, I look at the window. Some nondescript, calico or hemp curtains are perfunctorily drawn back on both sides of the windows, and behind them the shutters have been pulled down. The sun shines through the gaps between each one. Ha-hah, the weather has thankfully finally become worthy of spring. I had been thinking I would never witness such weather in London but have discovered that, as one would expect of a place where people live, they do occasionally get some sunshine. I look at the ceiling. It is, as ever, cracked and in poor condition, and above it I could hear a kind of thudding sound. The maid probably has her shoes on in the third-floor room. My room becomes increasingly bright. There is still no sign of the gong ringing.

I drop my eyes from the ceiling and look around the room, but there is nothing worth looking at. I am actually quite ashamed of this room. In front of the window there is a chest of drawers. They are really just painted boxes hardly worthy of being called a chest of drawers. In the upper drawers are my underpants, collars and cuffs and below them my tailcoat. The tailcoat was cheap, but I have never worn it, thinking what a worthless thing it was. Above the boxes is a mirror about one foot square and to the left of that my bottle of Carlsbad salts. At its side my dirty brown-leather gloves are half visible. Below the left-hand side of the boxes are two pairs of shoes, one red and one black. The shoes I wear every day are polished by the maid and left in front of my door. Apart from these I have some sparkling shoes for formal wear kept in the wardrobe. At least as far as shoes are concerned, I feel like I could be a wealthy man and am mightily pleased with myself. I start to think how I might take these four pairs of shoes with me if I moved house. I would probably wear one pair and stuff two pairs into my suitcase, but the final pair, would I throw them into the carriage or carry them? One pair will certainly wear out before I move anyway.

Still, it doesn't matter about the shoes, but my precious books are going to be a major problem. These will take some moving. I look around at the books lined up on the floor, the books over the fireplace, the books on the desk, the books on the bookshelves. There was a Dodsley collection in the second-hand book catalogue sent from Roche's the other day. At seventy yen it was expensive, probably because it was leather-bound, but I would love to have it.

Warton's *History of English Poetry,* which I bought previously, is an antique set bound by Kalthoeber and a really cheap find. But there is no point fretting that I cannot buy books, since my money order has not come anyway, although I am sure the money will eventually arrive . . . bong, bong, bong, the gong sounds. This is the first gong. By the time I have got up and got myself ready the second gong will sound. Then I will amble downstairs for breakfast.

Sitting up and putting on my drawers, I think how, instead of getting up at the hour of the tiger, I am getting up at the hour of the gong. I grin to myself. Then I get out of bed and stand before the dresser to wash my face. I commence my toilet. Unfortunately, in the West one cannot simply scrub one's face. I empty out the water from a bottle into the jar and wash basin and put my hands in, but then remember I have to drink my Carlsbad salts every morning before I wash my face. I take my hands out of the basin. Being too much bother to wipe my hands, I turn to the wall and shake them two or three times and then prepare my Carlsbad salts and drink them. Then I slightly wet my face, pick up my shaving brush and start liberally applying it to my face. The razor is a safety razor, so it is easy to use. I shave my beard as smoothly as a carpenter with a plane. It feels good. Then I comb my hair, dry my face, put on a white shirt, collar and tie and roll up the shutters. Outside the room the maid plops down my shoes with a thud. Shortly afterwards the second gong sounds. Everything is now ready.

I then descend two sets of stairs and go into the dining-room. As usual the first thing I have is oatmeal. This is the staple diet of Scottish people. But, whereas they eat it by adding salt, we eat it by adding sugar. It is a kind of oat gruel, and I like it a lot. In Johnson's Dictionary he says that oatmeal is something which in England is generally given to horses but in Scotland supports the people. However, it does not seem remotely unusual for the English of today to eat this for breakfast. The English must have become closer to horses. I have either one rasher of bacon and an egg or else two rashers of bacon. I also have two slices of toast and a cup of tea.

When I have finished eating four-fifths of my two rashers of bacon Tanaka descends from the first floor. He returned home late last night from his trip. But he is late every morning and has never once graced us by coming down from the first floor on time. 'Good morning.' The landlady's younger sister answers, 'Good morning.' I, too, say in English, 'Good morning.' Tanaka munches away. Then saying, 'Excuse me', I open a letter on the table. It is an invitation from Mrs Edgehill. She would like the pleasure of my company at 3 p.m. on the 17th. Well, well. I am someone who does not like socializing even when I am in Japan. Coming to the West and attempting to socialize awkwardly in broken English is something I positively loathe. Moreover, London is so vast that once one begins socializing it takes up all one's time. And one cannot exactly go out wearing a dirty shirt or having the knees of one's trousers sticking out. And when it is raining the little money I have would have to go towards paying for carriages. All of this is tiresome and a waste of time and money, and I try to avoid it. But, as there are eccentric ladies in the world, circumstances occasionally dictate that I am obliged to go. Dear oh dear. Just as I am thinking this to myself, Tanaka starts to talk about his trip. 'I've bought you a plaster model of Shakespeare and an album,' he says. 'Thanks,' I say, taking them from him. Then he shows me a photograph of a rubbing of Shakespeare's tombstone. 'What does this mean? Is it Latin? I can't read it.' He finally goes off to the office.

As usual I read the *Standard* newspaper. Western newspapers are truly voluminous. To read everything from beginning to end would probably take five or six hours. I first read about the China Incident. Today there is a Russian newspaper's editorial on Japan. If it should come to war, they say, it would not be a good idea to launch an attack on Japan, but better to fight it out in Korea. Fighting it out in Korea sounds bad enough to me. Then there is something about Tolstoy. Tolstoy has been excommunicated because he apparently recently belittled the Russian Church. Excommunicating the great Tolstoy has created an almighty fuss. A mountain of flowers was laid at a picture exhibition before Tolstoy's portrait, and everyone has been discussing what presents to send to him. The article says that Tolstoy's supporters are frantically attempting to spite the government. Interesting. Before I know it, it is 10.20.

Today I am going as usual to the professor's. I first go to the toilet, then dash up to my second-floor room, get myself ready and come down. There are still twenty minutes left before eleven o'clock. I look at the newspaper again. As yesterday was Easter Monday there were a variety of shows in town. There are various bits and pieces about this. At the Aquarium a bear trainer has performing bears, one column says. The bears apparently ride on horseback and race around the edge of the rink jumping over poles and through hoops. Sounds interesting. I then look at the adverts. It says that Irving is appearing in Shakespeare's *Coriolanus* at the Lyceum. Recently I saw Tree's *Twelfth Night* at Her Majesty's Theatre. It was infinitely more interesting than reading the play. I would also love to see the Irving production. It's 10.55. I pick up my books and leave the house.

If one was to describe my lodgings in terms of Tokyo, then Shinagawa first comes to mind. A suburb across the river from the centre of town. The rent is cheap, and, after all I will only be in this gloomy place for a little while . . . no, actually, I will probably be cooped up here for the whole of my time in England. I rarely go into town. Only once or twice a week. When I do go, it's bothersome. I first have to walk for about fifteen minutes to a place called Kennington and from there pass under the river Thames by the Underground and then change trains to get to the West End.

Arriving at the station, I pay twopence and get in the lift. There are three or four people inside. The station attendant closes the door and pulls the lift rope, causing the lift to go suddenly down. This is the means by which we pass underground. If going up, I would be like Nikki Danjo in a suit. The inside of the cave is brightly lit with electric lights. A train arrives every five minutes. Fortunately the train today is quiet and not too crowded. The people next to me and the people opposite me and the people in the next car have all taken out a newspaper or magazine to read. This is a kind of custom. I simply cannot read books or anything when I am in a cave. First, just the foulness of the air and the train's swaying makes me feel sick. It is truly unpleasant. After passing through four stations we arrive at the Bank. Here I must change trains and move from one cave to another. Just like being a mole, isn't it? I walk about a hundred yards inside the cave and arrive at the so-called Tuppenny Tube. This is a new underground line that starts at the Bank in the east and cuts across the whole of London heading west. It is so called because, no matter where one gets on or off, it costs two pence, or ten Japanese sen. I get on.

Making a rumbling noise, a train moving in the opposite direction to us emerges from another cave, and, taking this as a signal, our train also emits an equally loud rumbling noise and starts to move forward. The conductor says, 'Next station Post Office', and slams the car door shut. Telling us the name of the next station when we stop is a feature of this line. Across the way, a young woman and a woman of about forty sit facing one another. About one foot to my right an old woman and a young girl are chattering. The people opposite are nibbling on biscuits or something while reading their magazines. Ordinary passengers. Not at all the stuff of novels.

(I cannot face writing any more so hope you will not mind if I stop. Actually I would like to tell you about my tutor. He is intriguingly eccentric. But I have a bit of a headache so will break off here.)

The Cuckoo has arrived again so I will make a fresh start. As I wrote last time, the condition of my boarding-house is extremely pitiful, but you are doubtless asking how, like some modern sage, I manage to remain unruffled in such circumstances. Even if you are not asking, I will assume that you are since it is inconvenient to my purposes if you are not as I intend to answer you and answer you in all sincerity. So, with that as my intention, please listen.

I might sometimes try to come out with profound statements

like some Zen priest or occult philosopher, but, as you know, I am for the most part all too human and have absolutely no right to be praised with lines such as 'The wise man knows no greater pleasure' for living in such uncomfortable confinement. You will probably say, 'If that's the case, why don't you move to somewhere more pleasant?' Well, there is a very good reason, so do listen. The funding given to scholars overseas is so little as to be hardly worth talking about. When one is in London, it seems even less. Little it may be, but if I was to apportion all this allowance on food, clothing and accommodation, even I could have a slightly better lifestyle. It is doubtful whether I could maintain appearances at home with this (my rank at home may immediately be calculated by counting down five ranks from the first rank of the higher civil service. Of course, if you calculate from the bottom, you would only have to come up four ranks so even in Japan I have nothing to brag about . . .), but in any case I would be in a more pleasing house than this. Yet here I am practising every type of economy and living in such a wretched place. One reason is that I have a strong sense of not being the same person I was in Japan, but merely a student. Another thing is that, since I have gone to all the trouble of coming to the West, I want to buy as many books as possible relating to my speciality to take home. So I have forgotten about having my own house and employ-ing maids. Yet, even when I think about the time when I used to eat beefsteak as tough as the heels on leather shoes at the university dormitory ten years ago, was it not still a little better than this? I think it was. People will perhaps laugh and say here I am cooped up in a slum like Camberwell, but there is no need for me to be both-ered about such things. I may be in a dive, but I have never kept company with prostitutes or conversed with streetwalkers. I cannot vouchsafe my inner heart, but at least in my actions what I do is becoming of a virtuous man. Even if I say it myself, my conduct is exemplary.

But, when a whistling wind blows on a winter's evening and smoke backs up from the stove and turns the whole room completely black with soot, when the cold wind freely penetrates the gaps around the window and door and I am unbearably cold from legs to waist, when sitting on the hard, boarded chair feels as painful as having lumbago in my pelvis, then I have the pitiful feeling that, just as the clothes I am wearing have completely discoloured, so, too, I am gradually degrading myself and wonder why I am living in such reduced circumstances. Oh, I do not care. I decide it does not matter even if I cannot buy books, I will spend all my allowance on rent and live like a proper human being. Then, brandishing my stick, I walk around the neighbourhood.

Once outside, everyone I meet is depressingly tall. Worse, they all have unfriendly faces. If they imposed a tax on height in this country they might come up with a more economically small animal. But these are the words of one who cannot accept defeat gracefully, and, looked at impartially, one would have to say that it was they, not I, who look splendid. In any case, I feel small. An unusually small person approaches. Eureka! I think. But when we brush past one another I see he is about two inches taller than me. A strangely complexioned Tom Thumb approaches, but now I realize this is my own image reflected in a mirror. There is nothing for it but to laugh bitterly, and, naturally, when I do so, the image laughs bitterly, too. When I go to the park, herds of women walk around like horned lionesses with nets on their heads. Amongst them are some men. And some tradesmen. I am struck by the fact that they are for the most part better dressed than many a high-ranking official in Japan. In this country one cannot work out someone's status by their dress. A butcher's boy, when Sunday rolls around, will proudly put on his silk hat and frock-coat.

Yet, generally, people are of a pleasant disposition. Nobody would ever grab me and start insulting and abusing me. They do not take any notice of me. Being magnanimous and composed in all things is in these parts one qualification of being a gentleman. Overly fussing over trifles like some pickpocket or staring at a person's face with curiosity is considered vulgar. In particular, it is considered undignified for ladies to turn around and look behind them. Pointing at people is the height of rudeness. Such are the customs, but of course London is also the workshop of the world, so they do not laughingly regard foreigners as curiosities. Most people are extremely busy. Their heads seem to be so teeming with thoughts of money that they have no time to jeer at us Japanese as yellow people. ('Yellow people' is well chosen. We are indeed yellow. When I was in Japan I knew I was not particularly white but regarded myself as being close to a regular human colour, but in this country I have finally realized that I am three leagues away from a human colour – a yellow person who saunters amongst the crowds going to watch plays and shows.)

But sometimes there are people who surreptitiously comment on my country of origin. The other day I was standing looking around a shop somewhere when two women approached me from behind, remarking, 'least-poor Chinese'. 'Least-poor' is an extraordinary adjective. In one park I heard a couple arguing whether I was a Chinaman or a Japanese. Two or three days ago I was invited out somewhere and set off in my silk hat and frock-coat only for two men who seemed like workmen to pass by saying, 'A handsome Jap'. I do not know whether I should be flattered or offended. Recently I went to a play. As the house was full and I could not get in I stood and watched from the gallery. Some people beside me were remarking that the two men over there must be Portuguese.

– I did not intend to talk about these things. I have lost my thread. I will have a short break and start again.

Well, after going out for a walk, my mood changes and I feel refreshed. This lifestyle is only for two or three years anyway. When I go home, I will be able to wear ordinary clothes and eat ordinary food and sleep in the same way as everyone else. I go to bed telling myself that it is a matter of persevering, persevering, persevering. That's fine if I fall asleep, but when I cannot sleep I fall to thinking again. I seem to be telling myself to persevere because I have no peace of mind at present – gradually things start getting complicated – and the reason I sometimes become a little frantic is because my poverty is so hard to bear. What has become of the approach to life I have for the most part followed down the years? Be neither overly attached to the past nor pointlessly placing all one's hope in the future, but hang the consequences and exercise all one's energy in working for today is my philosophy. Indeed, it is futile to encourage myself to keep going by telling myself that I can look forward to living more comfortably when I get home. Nobody can guarantee that I will be allowed to take things easy when I do return. It is all up to me. That would be fine if, once I discovered I could not take things easy, I could immediately change tack and forget the delusions of the past; but putting all my trust in the future, as I am at present, and then seeing that future turn into the past without being in the least fulfilled leaves me incapable of easily forgetting the past. Moreover, working with reward as one's objective is the height of vulgarity. It is an even more ignoble thought than the kind of common wisdom that basely says, 'In this world let us do good works so that, when we die, we may go to heaven and pass the future with toads on lotus leaves.'

For five or six years before leaving Japan such lowly thoughts never occurred to me. I acted in the present, fulfilled my responsibilities in the present and felt joy and sorrow, pleasure and pain in the present. Worrying about the future, grumbling and complaining, was not only something that never passed my lips but something I hardly ever felt inside. I felt confident about myself and flattered myself that even if I went abroad, and even if I had little money, with a little something to eat and drink I would be able to live freely and easily in perfect serenity. Vanity, oh vanity! How by such things do we entirely lose our way in life. Well, from tomorrow I must reform myself and concentrate on my study. So resolving I go to sleep.

These are the circumstances in which I have been in this gloomy, squalid neighbourhood of the notorious slum Camberwell since the end of last year until today. Not only have I 'been' here but I will perhaps go on to have 'been' here from now until my study abroad ends. If, however, I say that there are certain goings-on here causing me to leave no matter how much I wish to stay, it will sound straight out of a novel but, when you hear the reason it is extremely mundane. Most of the goings-on in the world are unfortunately entirely mundane.

This house was originally not a boarding-house. Until last year it was a girls' school, but then the landlady and her younger sister began this strangely genteel, strangely lowly enterprise despite having neither experience nor money nor any firm objective for the future apart from a desire to demonstrate a means of self-employment. They are, of course, not dishonest people. They worked because they were capable of working while treading an honest path. Yet even a Christian God is more slipshod than commonly supposed and at such times does not do the slightest thing to help people. Thus the rent falls into arrears – London's rents are expensive – and loans are incurred. Fever breaks out amongst the boarders. One person leaves the school, two people leave the school and in the end the school closes . . . This is how it goes when fate spins against one and the pretty women – let's scratch 'pretty'. Neither of them have any claim to prettiness – er, the pitiful – the piteous women resolved to fight adversity unto the bitter end and finally opened a boarding-house. I barged in just after they had opened. Barging in and hearing their situation I devoted my prayers to hoping that the little women – no, I mean the women three inches taller than me – would be successful this time. If asked to whom did I devote my prayers I would be at a loss to say. Not being on speaking terms with any god worth praying to I just prayed aimlessly. And, sure enough, there are no signs of any miracle. Absolutely no guests come.

'Mr Natsume, do you know of anybody?'

'Well, I would like to find someone for you, but I'm sorry to say that I actually don't know anyone whom I would particularly call a friend in London . . .' Yet, until recently, there was one Japanese here. He is an extremely jovial person unsuited to this house. He is a man who, seeing me reading *The Cuckoo*, asked if I was also any good at Japanese poems. That Japanese fellow finally ran off. The only person left is me. When it gets like this, there would seem to be no alternative but to close down the house. An outskirt of London lying further south of here – I say outskirt, but London is so vast that it is hard to know how far it spreads – so that suburb must be a very out-of-the-way place. A reasonable, snug new house is available there, so the talk is of moving. One day the landlord and his wife went out and I and the younger sister were dining together when in a gloomy voice she said, 'Would you please move with us?' This 'please' is not the amorous 'please' found in novels. It is a dull, domestic 'please'. When I heard this word I had a feeling of extreme distaste and pity. I am fundamentally an Edokko. But, perhaps because it is unclear whether the place I was born in belonged to the city of Edo or the suburbs, I have, until now, never done any of the agreeable, charitable works Edokkos tend to do. I certainly do not now recall what reply I made. If I had the slightest trace of chivalry, I would have replied, 'Yes, so long as you are moving there, I will move anywhere.' It seems I did not reply like that. There is a reason why I could not reply like that.

It is true that this younger sister is extremely retiring and quiet, and indeed exceptionally devout in her religion, and I would not feel at all unhappy about living with this woman, but the elder sister is somewhat pert. I have also heard the life history of this elder sister, but will not go into it as it would be a long story, but, if I enumerate the things I do not like about her, they would be that, first, she is impudent, second, that she pretends to be knowledge-able and, third, that using trifling English she asks, 'Do you know this word?' If I counted these up one by one there would be no end of them. The other day she asked me if I knew the word 'tunnel'. Then she asked me if I knew the word 'straw'. There is no point in even a scholar specializing in English literature getting angry about this. Recently she seems to have taken the hint a little and does not say such rude things, and her general behaviour has become much

倫
敦
塔

more polite. This is because Soseki, without a word of strife, has subjugated this hussy without her realizing it . . . such self-flattering talk is all well and good, but when it comes to the women of this country, particularly the old women, perhaps because of what we may call 'the kindness of old women', they often add uncalled-for footnotes on the English they use and ask me whether I understand this or that word. The other day I was invited to a certain place and talked with the lady there. This person is a great believer in Christ and consequently unbearable. She held forth at great length about Divine Virtue. She is a truly refined, graceful old woman. But I was asked whether I knew the word 'evolution'.

'It may seem as if all is chaos and there are no laws in the world, but look closely and you will see that everything is governed by the principles of evolution . . . evolution . . . do you understand?' It is just like preaching to a baby. She means to be kind in speaking in this way, so there is nothing for it but for me to say, 'I see, I see.' After all, I cannot prattle on like this old woman. For my responses I merely use the words that rise into my throat and then pause for breath in relief, so it is only to be expected that I am looked down upon, but, speaking with regard to numerous different languages, then I feel like saying that it is I who know much more than they.

I often refer to old women, and there is another old woman. This old woman sent me a letter the other day with the word 'folk' inside. If it was just a case of using the word then there would be nothing peculiar, but a footnote is attached to this word. It said, 'This is an ancient English word.' Adding footnotes to one's own letters is in itself interesting, but the wording of these footnotes is even more interesting. When I was a passenger aboard ship with this old woman she told me that if I wrote something she would correct it for me, so I decided to give her a chapter of my diary and asked her to look at it. She handed it back saying she was extremely impressed, having corrected the odd word in two or three places. When I looked at it I saw that she had corrected things which in no way needed correction. And completely nonsensical things had, as usual, been written down as footnotes. This old woman is not at all a vulgar person. She is a middle-class person of respectable station in life.

As I am in England and able to meet people in this way, there is no particular need for me to have anything to do with the wife at my lodging-house and her impudent remarks, but, as I have come all the way to England, I would like to be in the house of someone capable of speaking with a little learning and would not even mind the house being dirty or cramped if I had the pleasure of their constant companionship. This being my desire, I did not answer, 'Yes, let's go', although whether there is a house accepting boarders with a landlord such as I am looking for is highly doubtful. In the wide world there surely is such a place. But coming upon it is extremely difficult. If there was a room free at my tutor's place, I could be put up there, but it seems I am unable to because there is no room.

At times like this Western newspapers come in useful. In a world where everything is advertisements, there are countless advertisements for lodgings. When I previously looked for lodgings, I looked at the advertisement column in the *Daily Telegraph*. I remember that to read it from beginning to end took three hours. Now I do not take the *Telegraph* but the *Standard*. This newspaper is a high-class newspaper, and, thinking that the advertisements that appeared there would be just the thing, I began reading the advertisement column for 17 April, but, contrary to expectation, discovered that commercial places were numerous while those saying they put people up in private houses were few. There are, however, a whole variety of them. 'Low rent, bath, excellent food', this type of thing is common. 'Facing Hyde Park, Central Line three minutes, Metropolitan Line five minutes, society with ladies,' one says. 'Free billiards, piano, gay society, late dinner', this, too, is not unusual. 'Late dinner' is the recent fashion. To people like me it is extremely inconvenient. Amongst them I spied the following one: 'A widow-lady living in her well-furnished house wishes a gentleman of homely taste to join her and sister as only boarder. Address XX stationer.' I thought that I might first try somewhere like this, so immediately wrote a letter

倫
敦
塔

asking for information about the rent and other details and took the liberty to tell them that my background is so-and-so, my occupation is so-and-so and that I would like to live somewhere as cheap as possible and as pleasant as possible.

That evening at around ten o'clock as I was reading in my room, there was a knock on the door. I said, 'Yes, come in', and the master of the house entered smiling. 'Now, you may have heard that we will soon be moving, but what do you think? It's even prettier over there than it is here and the furnishings and so forth will be excellent, so we were wondering whether you might come with us.' 'Well, if you insist on my coming along, then . . .' 'No, I don't mean you to come involuntarily, only if it suits you – actually we have grown fond of you, and my wife and her sister, too, are extremely desirous that you come along.' 'I realize that you wish to have a lodger in your new house, but I was thinking it need not necessarily be me', and telling him, you see, this and this, the master's face became a little gloomy. I, too, felt rather awkward. 'So let's do this. These people will probably send me a letter and, when it comes, I will first go and see the room, and if I don't like it I will go with you and stop looking for anywhere else. If I had understood before sending the letter how much you desired me to go with you, I would have never made enquiries but done as you desired, but it's too late for that now. We'll just have to wait for their response, won't we? In return I definitely won't go looking for anywhere else. If this place is no good, I will definitely go with you.' Saying, 'Excuse me for having disturbed you', the master went downstairs.

In the morning, when I went into the dining-room, there was no one there. Everyone had finished their meals. Thinking, Oh dear, I've slept in late again today, I looked on top of the table, and there was a letter, the four corners of its purple envelope tinged a deep violet colour. Undoubtedly the reply had come. From the appearance of the envelope they were using, I thought it must be a high-class boarding-house a little beyond my means and opened the envelope with a knife. 'With reference to your enquiry, this house belongs to a lady [the word 'lady' was underlined], the rooms are naturally well furnished, and each and every room uses electric light. We employ good servants and make all efforts to provide surroundings suitable for refined life. The rent is three pounds six shillings a week. This may not suit your requirements, but if you wish to call we will happily show you the rooms. Yours faithfully.' While eating my meal, I pressed the bell and called the landlady. 'I have decided to go with you. It's completely impossible for me to pay a rent of three pounds six shillings a week, so I shall go with you.' 'Oh, is that so? Thank you! We will do everything we can to make it enjoyable for you so do come with us.' After the wife had gone out, the husband's head half appeared in the doorway. 'Thank you, Mr Natsume, thank you,' he said smiling. I, too, felt a little happy. The wife and her sister are busy all day long with packing for the move. At seven o'clock, when I was drinking tea, I met them in the dining-room. 'Today I sold our parrot for a pound,' the younger sister said. Not to be outdone, the elder sister said, 'I sold our school noticeboard. I got a pound for it.'

The wheels of fate continue mercilessly to revolve. What events still lie in front of me and in front of both of them? Perhaps all three of us are doing a foolish thing. Perhaps foolish and perhaps wise. In any case it is a fact that my fate continues gradually to draw closer to the fate of these two. Looking back and imagining the purple lady and her sister and their splendid house, and looking forward and imagining this poor but honest pair of sisters and the humble abode they still expect to be a future paradise, I feel with keen interest the difference between the two. I also feel how prosaic a thing is the disparity between rich and poor. And I also feel like David Copperfield living with Micawber. (*20 April*)

Companion. I spoke a little last time about this companion and my companions, the sisters, with whom I am living, but apart from them there is another companion here whom I most admire and with whom I am most daunted. I somehow will not be satisfied until I have reported a little about this saintly person whose name is Penn and whose nickname is Bedge Pardon, so let me tell you a little about this person and present observations and appraisals of a different direction to last time.

First of all, the reason why I have given this nickname to Bedge Pardon, that is our maid Penn, is because the good woman, whether owing to her tongue being too short or too long, slurs her words and instead of saying 'I beg your pardon' always says 'Bedge pardon'. Like the name, Bedge Pardon is every inch to be bedged pardon. However, this is an enormously fluent speaker, a good person and an orator, who mercilessly sprays my face with the saliva from the end of her tongue when speaking, unreservedly wasting people's precious time with effusiveness without feeling the slightest regret. Despite being born in London, this good person and orator, Bedge Pardon, knows absolutely nothing about London. She, of course, knows nothing about the countryside either. Nor does it seem as if she wants to know. From morning until night, from morning until night, she works and works and then climbs to a third-floor attic room to sleep. The next day, when the sun appears, Penn descends from the third floor and starts working again. Breathing with difficulty – she is an asthmatic – she is a piteous sight to all. Yet she in no way harbours any feelings of self-pity. She who cannot distinguish A from B does not appear to feel even the slightest inconvenience. Since coming into contact with this female saint morning and night, I cannot help feeling reverence and affection for her, although whether being caught and spoken to by Penn is a blessing or a curse I must let others decide.

People in Japan will perhaps think that in English it really does not matter who is speaking, for they all sound the same, but there are of course, just as in Japan, regional accents and upper and lower classes and a thousand and one differences between them. Still, there is no problem with the speech of the educated upper classes, which is largely comprehensible, but when it comes to this London speech called Cockney then I am totally at a loss. This is the language used by the lower classes here, and it is not only pronounced in a manner not found in any dictionary but spoken at such speed that it is impossible to tell where one word stops and another begins. Cockney throws me out of sorts every time, but when it comes to Bedge Pardon's Cockney it goes beyond being thrown out of sorts and rather exhausts me by throwing me out of sorts all over again so that I feel I cannot stand it if I do not take a break from being thrown out of sorts. When I started lodging here, I had often to suffer Penn's assaults, and was forced to report this to the landlady, and poor Penn received an almighty scolding. How dare she act so rudely towards the guests, from now on she had better show some sense of decorum, Penn was told. Since then, meek Penn absolutely never says a word to me . . . that is, never a word is said when the mistress is in, but when her ladyship goes out it is the same old Penn as before. And the same old Penn, out of vexation at being forced into a vow of silence, spots a chance and comes intent on paying me back with interest. It is unbearable. It is rather as if someone who, after having managed to fast for a week, has, on the eighth day, to start furiously gorging herself.

When I come back from taking my usual walk around Denmark Hill, Penn opens the door for me and immediately starts chatting away. Sure enough, all the family have gone to the new house to sort out their belongings, and only I and Penn are left in the empty house. Rattling on and on, she tirelessly keeps on talking about something for about fifteen minutes, but I do not understand a thing. She is so eloquent and keeps spouting forth at such a speed that I am unable to insert a single word by way of question. There is nothing else for it but for me to give up on this talk as something incomprehensible, and so I begin scrutinizing Penn's facial features. The gentle double-set eyelids, the nose, whose tip goes slightly back in and approaches the base, the consistently ruddy, healthy complexion, and then the tongue exercising itself just as much as it likes with total freedom, and the white spittle pouring forth on both sides of the tongue . . . I lost myself gazing at this for a while, but finally I had a kind of sorrowful, kind of pitiful, kind of strange, mixed-up pot-pourri of a feeling. To express this emotion I bit my lip and let out a slight laugh. Harmless Penn is not likely to notice anything in

倫敦塔

that vicinity. Apparently having concluded that I was laughing because I was absorbed in the conversation, dimples appeared on the red cheeks and Penn laughed foolishly. Being at cross-purposes, I only feel more and more strange, while Penn becomes increasingly voluble, and the situation gets worse.

When I try to put together the little I have understood, a phrase here and a word there from what is being said, it appears to be something like this. Yesterday the owner's agent came over to discuss something. The women of the house were embarrassed and, pretending to be out, sent him home. The person who fulfilled the mission of turning him away at the front door was Penn. 'I dislike telling lies, but, God forgive me, I also cannot be indifferent to the master's orders, so I was forced to tell a lie.' As if looking at some distant fire, I guessed that this was roughly the gist of it and finally withdrew to my room.

My trunk and books were carried off to the new house by the landlord at about three o'clock this morning, so all that is left is my own person. I somehow have a desolate feeling. At eight o'clock in the evening there is a knock on the door and in comes – Penn as usual – to report that today the owner's agent came four times. Then something else is said that I cannot understand in the slightest. It is all too much bother, so I just send her away . . . at around ten o'clock Penn comes again. 'If the agent comes again, what should I do?' This time I am being consulted. I try to give reassurance by saying there is nothing to worry about and send her out. It is ten thirty, but the family have still not returned. If the master here is a swindler and has left me behind and gone off with my belongings, I realize that I will be laughed at as the most incredible simpleton. Finally I hear the sound of the front door opening. They seem to have returned. At least I have not ended up being made to look like a simpleton. Grateful, I go to bed.

The next day, 25 April, I got up around nine o'clock and, when I went downstairs, the husband and wife had just finished breakfast. Seeing me sit down at the table, the landlady asked me whether I had heard last night's disturbance. I sleep on the second floor. I have absolutely no idea what has happened downstairs. 'Disturbance?

What disturbance?' I ask. It was a quarrel with the owner's agent. As soon as the family had entered the house after coming back from the new house last night, the owner's agent, who had been waiting for them at the gate, flew in after them and, before the husband had time to close the door, said, 'What do you think you're doing moving out in the middle of the night and without permission? Is this what you call being a gentleman?' 'Whose permission do I need to move my own belongings? And what's it got to do with anyone else at what time I move them?' the husband retorted. After that the argument grew more colourful and apparently was the kind of disturbance to shake the whole neighbourhood.

Originally this house was rented in the wife's name. But the fact that seven years ago she ran into arrears with the rent has cursed them to this day and so they cannot leave. Moreover, their property will sooner or later end up being taken in the form of rent. The unfortunate sisters, however, do not have anything which would particularly be to their loss if confiscated. The owner's agent does not have his eyes fixed on that. The old agent's eye is on the husband's own belongings. The husband is also a person of the twentieth century and so has his wits about him in that respect. He goes to a lawyer and consults about it. He knows that if he carries out his furniture after sunset and before dawn then the agent will have to look on enviously. That is why he has hired a big cart at three o'clock in the morning and spent a sleepless night moving his belongings to the new house. He has an extremely enormous, stupid-looking face. To make up for it he has grown a little moustache below his nose, and yet he appears to be a shrewd man who will not give in to the agent.

I asked the husband when I might be able to move my own person, and he said today would be fine, so after lunch I decided to move with the wife to the new house.

While I was eating lunch with the wife, the husband came back from the lawyer's and said to his wife, 'Write a letter and post it to the agent, but make sure you send it by registered mail.' Then he went out again. The wife quickly began writing something. ' "Dear sir,

倫
敦
塔

I am shocked." Shall I read more slowly? "I am shocked. Yesterday you came not three but four times to our home while we were absent and addressed a variety of questions to our maid concerning our personal affairs. I would like to enquire where was your prudence in doing this and in searching people's homes without permission, and then even proclaiming to our maid such things as that I am not fit to be called a lady. In respect of your outrageous behaviour, I believe I have the right to seek an apology." That's it. This is a trap, you see,' she said. I, too, was a little shocked and asked, 'Trap? What kind of trap?' and she became as pleased as punch. 'Don't you see? I write this letter and make a copy, and should they one day take this matter to court, then this will be the proof for making the case that the agent acted outrageously. Until now they thought they were just dealing with two women and could do as they liked, but now we have a man by our side we won't be trampled on any more,' she said, indirectly making me look up at the pride she held in her husband. Then she said, 'Sorry to keep you waiting. Shall we be off?' and off we went.

I am holding an extremely heavy bag in which I have crammed a variety of things and also have two items in my left hand, an umbrella and a walking-stick. The lady is holding in her right hand a net bag in which she has placed four brown paper packages. In one of these brown paper packages are my pyjamas and waistband. She is also carrying in her left hand my bedsheets wrapped up in brown paper. Both of us have our hands full. It is an awful journey. We come to the corner and get on the tram. To Kennington it costs two sen each. The lady says that she will pay and takes from her black leather purse one penny and hands it to the ticket seller. Passengers are few. Opposite us are some brightly dressed young women. The lady accompanying me suddenly asks me in a loud voice whether I have read Marie Corelli's *The Master Christian*. This is a rather famous book which has recently sold 150,000 copies. I answered that I have the book but have not yet read it. 'That book is, well, extremely good, but I have absolutely no idea as to which denomination the writer belongs. All the people I know are talking about what Corelli's denomination

might be,' she says, making sure she is overheard by the ladies opposite. As this is something she has never read and we are in the middle
of a tram, I thought she would do better to desist, but there was no
choice but to make half-hearted replies and say, 'Oh, I see.'

Finally we arrive in Kennington. Here we change buses. This
time she says, 'Let's go upstairs,' so we climb the stairs and get on
the top deck. 'That on the left is a famous orphanage built in Spurgeon's memory. Spurgeon was a famous preacher.' Even without
being lectured, I do know who someone like Spurgeon is, and so, in
exasperation, I keep quiet. 'It's pleasant now that the trees are
gradually turning green. The scenery has completely changed in the
last two weeks, hasn't it?' 'Yes. By the way what are those row of
trees over there called?' 'Those? Those are poplars.' 'Really? Those
are poplars, are they? Well I never,' I say, letting out an expression of
wonder. The wife immediately becomes inflated. 'Poplars are often
cited in poetry. They come up in poets like Tennyson. The branches
sway even on completely windless days. They are also called aspens.
I'm sure that these are also mentioned in Tennyson,' she says, establishing a Tennyson monopoly. She does not say, however, in which
poems they are mentioned. Finding the conversation tiresome, I
merely say, 'Oh, I see.'

A splendid lady passes along the paving stones opposite, trailing a
long skirt. 'I am not in disagreement with trailing a skirt inside the
house but walking outside while trailing such a long skirt outside is
hardly seemly, is it?' the short-skirted lady informs me at one point.
Finally we arrive in a place called Tooting. Now we come by bus to the
street corner of our new house. 'Which is our house?' I ask. Opposite
us was a row of four or five rough, brick-built tenement houses. At the
front there is nothing at all. There is a large hole dug in the gravel. It is
a scene reminiscent of Tokyo's Koishigawa. Only one of the houses at
the end of the row is occupied; the rest are all displaying a 'To Let'
board. The one occupied is the landlord's house and the one next to it
is my new boarding-house, what they call our 'new paradise'.

Even before entering I think it a miserable house, inferior to what I have been told, and when I go inside it is even more distasteful. Not only that but luggage has been thrown into every room so that the house seems exactly like some place of refuge after a great fire. Only the room on the first floor where I am due to ensconce myself is in any kind of habitable order. It is prettier than my previous room. The furnishings, too, are tolerable. The husband appears and diligently puts up the curtains. 'I'm going to hang a framed picture over the fireplace. It's a mistletoe frame, is that all right? Some people might dislike it but just have a look,' he says, bringing it over and showing it to me. It is just a picture of a nude girl. 'Ho-ho, it's a nude, is it? Splendid,' I say half-jokingly. 'Tee-hee, I, too, don't mind it at all,' he says, diligently banging in a nail and hanging it up. 'How's that? The angle . . . down a little more . . . so that the nude girl is looking down in your direction – that's it.' Then he says he will make my bookshelves and takes the measurements of the wall and the measurements of the books and saying 'Good night' goes out.

Not a single carriage passes in front of this house. Not a single voice of a passer-by. It is an extremely desolate place. The husband and wife must go back to sleep at the old house every night until matters have settled down. Sleeping on the second floor of the new house are the younger sister and Carl and Jack and Ernest. Carl and Jack are the name of dogs, and Ernest is the name of the young person working in the husband's shop. Bedge Pardon, whom I both respect and am daunted by, has been dismissed. Hearing this after having moved, I gloomily imagine her future.

Russia and Japan keep on trying to make war. China is suffering the humiliation of incursions by foreign powers. Britain is trying to plug the gaps in its military expenditure by digging up diamonds in the Transvaal. While this busy world continues to revolve and reverberate by day and by night there are small revolutions and small reverberations in my small universe, too, as the hero of my boarding-house hazards his enormous body and continues to vie for supremacy with the little agent. Yet I, to console Shiki in his illness, continue to write this diary. (*26 April*)

Bicycle Diary (1903)

ON a certifiable day in a certifiable month in the autumn of 1902 I waved a white flag out of my bedroom window, begged the old woman at my boarding-house to accept my surrender and waited as she set about carrying her twelve-stone body up to the top of the second floor. I say *set about carrying up* rather than just *carrying up* in order to convey the effort it takes. There are about forty-two steps to climb, with around two pauses for breath on the way – time taken three minutes five seconds – after which this enormous woman's face, looking more pained than victorious, looms large in the doorway. My surroundings may be cramped and I may be in humbled circumstances, but I shouldered the glory of this meeting as the woman turned to me and, by way of decree and the first term of our peace treaty, commanded me as follows, 'Go and ride your bicycle!'

Oh, how terrible this bicycle business is! I eventually succumbed and, in compliance with the old woman's order, reluctantly went to Lavender Hill, where I was supposed to ride my bicycle or, rather, where I was supposed to fall off my bicycle. My coach and teacher is Mr X and, with me dejectedly in tow, he first flies into a bicycle shop and chooses something suitable for women cyclists. 'This will do fine,' he says. When asked the reason why, he assails me with all sorts of insults, looking down upon me as the surrendered party and saying that this is the only way possible for an absolute novice. Unworthy as I am, telling a man wearing an – albeit small – moustache under his nose to practise on a woman's bike is outrageous. 'Look, it doesn't matter if I fall off, but let me have a go with something decent,' I say, lodging my protest. If not responded to, I make silent preparations to spout forth grandiosely with some such nonsense as 'It becometh

倫敦塔

a man to die gloriously for the preservation of the self is shameful!'
But he says, 'All right, let's try this', and assigns me an extremely
ugly-looking man's bike. A great thinker reveals his greatness regard-
less of which pen he uses. If I am going to fall off anyway, am I likely
to be bothered about the aesthetics of the vehicle? The vehicle
assigned to me is, with difficulty, dragged out. My cause for complaint is that, when I try giving it a sharp downwards push it makes
a creaking sound. Crouching down and looking at it, it seems that I
have come all the way from the other side of the world to team up
with this decrepit, unoiled bicycle with loose joints. I wonder
whether the bicycle shop has any age limit for pensioners. Thinking
about it, this thing must have reached pensionable age a long time
ago and done nothing until today except rest in quiet convalescence
in a corner of the storeroom. Unable to bear the misfortune of being
dragged out unexpectedly by an Oriental customer and letting out a
shriek, the bike's fate was to be pitied. Yet, even before getting on it,
this customer is getting increasingly keen, thinking that since he has
been forced into surrender he may as well make this bag of old
bones really creak. However, the handlebars, being acutely sensitive, bump into my crotch when I pull them towards me, and when
I push them away they try to race off into the middle of the street.
Seeing that, even before getting on I am at my wit's end knowing
how to handle it, a sympathetic appraisal of what might happen to
me after getting on must be the occasion for tears.

'Where shall we go for a ride?'

'Where? Well, as I'm riding today for the first time I'd like somewhere with as little traffic as possible and where the road is not too
bad and where I won't be laughed at if I fall off,' I say, presenting, in
spite of my surrendered state, a host of conditions.

Taking pity on me, my benevolent coach whisks me away to a
horse-riding area next to an avenue on Clapham Common where
onlookers are fairly sparse. However, he then says, 'Right, here we are.
Get on.' It has finally come to the point where the surrendered party
must display the humility of a surrendered party. Oh, unhappy man!

For starters, 'Get on' are not friendly words. From the age long ago when I was at the height of fortune in my own country down to today when I am thousands of miles from home, dispirited and strapped for cash, I have seen people riding bicycles, but I have absolutely no recollection of ever trying to ride myself. 'Get on' are words that are too cruel and, infuriated by them, I decide to act out the role of the glorious warrior and begin promisingly by fiercely gripping the handlebar. But when it comes to the step of finally sitting in the saddle, turning around and glaring back in triumph, it does not quite go to plan. It's strange when at the last moment one falls down with a thud. The bicycle does not do any handstands but remains completely composed. It's only the rider who, completely unable to stay in the saddle, falls down with a crash and a bang. Trying to put something into practice in the real world in the manner once heard described in a lecture often goes contrary to expectation.

The coach says, 'Trying to steady yourself straight away is no good. Don't even try putting your feet on the pedals! If you can just cling on while the bicycle wheels turn you'll be doing well.' No end of discouragement! Oh, I give up. However much I cling on, the wheels will not even make a half-turn. 'I give up!' I incessantly repeat, surreptitiously petitioning for assistance. Whereupon the coach, having all along expected this, walks towards me. 'Look, I'm going to hold the bicycle firmly while you get on. Hey, if you get straight on like that you'll fall over. Now look what you've done. Did you hurt your knee? This time gently sit down and grasp here with both hands. Ready? I'm going to start pushing forward, so let yourself go and you'll start to race along,' he says, thrusting forward for his own amusement one who is obviously terrified. Yet just as I am starting to be thrust forward, all of these preparations, all of this effort, are turned into preparation and effort for throwing myself against the sandy ground. And who but a god could have known that? Verily I am in shock.

Here and there people stop and watch. Some grin as they pass. Beneath the oak tree opposite, a nanny sits with a child on a bench and for a while now has been greatly impressed watching me. What exactly she is impressed with I have no idea. Probably she is fascinated by the manly sight of me, dripping with sweat, fighting furiously with the bicycle. Now that my world has become enriched by having such an agreeable friend in it, I find I have no regrets about having grazed my shin in two or three places. 'Let's try again. Please push harder. What? Fall again? So what if I do! It's my body!' I grandly spout forth in sweaty big talk, forgetting all about my status as the surrendered party. Whereupon, all of a sudden, someone calls out from behind, 'Sir!' How odd, I think, turning around, I don't recall being acquainted with any Westerners. Unexpectedly, I find myself in the disconcerting presence of a large policeman. I myself might not be acquainted with him, but he obviously feels he has good reason to make the acquaintance of this clattering midget. The reason is that this is a place for riding horses, not a place for riding bicycles, so, if I wish to practise cycling, I must kindly go out on to the road. All right, certainly, sir, understood, I say, displaying in the jumbled-up nature of my response the great breadth of my knowledge. I then report this to my coach. Whereupon the coach, thinking that the surrendered party has suffered enough for today, says, 'Shall we go home then?' So, taking the unridable bicycle with me, we go home.

The old woman asks, 'How did it go?'

> The bicycle brays,
> the day closes, my ears
> ring as autumn approaches

expresses my sense of defeat.

A certifiable day in a certifiable month. Holding my bicycle, I wait at the top of a slope and slowly let my eyes roam around the far distance below. My intention is to wait for the coach's signal and then come galloping pell-mell down this slope. The length of the slope is over two hundred and forty yards, its angle of inclination about twenty degrees, the road width in excess of sixty feet with few passers-by and charmingly residential homes to left and right. Whether the British government, hearing that an Oriental celebrity would be practising falling from a bicycle, have specially ordered the Public Works office to build this road we will never know, but in any case, as a road for bicycles, it is a place beyond reproach. My coach, perhaps struck by terror after the policeman's scolding or else just to spare himself the bother of pushing my vehicle forward, yesterday hit upon this place as somewhere that man and vehicle would trundle down naturally, and brought me along.

The coach, timing it so that no one is passing by and there are no carriages around, says, 'Right, let's go! Quickly get on! Ride!' This word 'ride', however, requires a little explanation. This word is not being used between the two of us in its ordinary sense. When we say 'ride' it is not the same as when other people say 'ride'. It does not mean lowering my rear into the saddle or applying my feet to the pedals but, rather, entrusting myself to the principles of gravity without in any way sporting any technical prowess. It does not signify avoiding people or steering clear of horses but, rather, going through fire and water as I gamble precipitously onwards. My appearance, meanwhile, is rather as if someone with lumbago was performing ladder-top acrobatics in a fire-brigade review. Even I have misgivings about whether I might not be misrepresenting the word 'ride'. But, after all, riding is riding. It is not not riding. In any case a person is clinging to the bicycle. Moreover, he is clinging on for dear life. Having been ordered in this sense to 'ride', I start trundling down like the wind from the top of the slope. Whereupon – a strange thing – from inside one of the residences on the left some prankster, admiring my driving, applauded. I hardly had time to think how bizarre this was before my vehicle was already on the middle section of the slope. Now I encountered something extraordinary: about fifty schoolgirls coming in procession from the opposite direction. Even so, no matter how much I might be said to be in the presence of women, there is no question of my putting on airs or anything of that kind. Both my hands are occupied. My back is bent. My right leg is flung into the air. Even if asked to let me off, the bicycle would not listen. Desperate, and with no alternative, and in a bent posture all of my own creation, I narrowly manage to squeeze along the side of the female army. Whoosh! Yet no sooner have I caught my breath than the bicycle has already descended the slope and is on flat ground. However, there is absolutely no sign of it stopping. Rather it turns in the direction of a policeman standing at the crossroads opposite and rapidly gallops towards him. I anxiously wonder whether I am going to get another dressing-down from a policeman today, but of course there is no possibility of relieving myself from my bent riding position. The bicycle, intent on senseless double suicide, impetuously dashes towards the pavement. Eventually I run up on to the pavement from the road, yet still do not stop, crash into a fence, rebound three yards and narrowly stop a distance of three feet away from the policeman. 'You appear to be in a spot of bother, sir,' said the officer laughing. To which my reply is 'Yes.'

A certifiable day in a certifiable month. 'When you have something to research, do you go to the British Museum?' 'No, I don't go there much. You see, I like to scribble down notes and underline things in books.' 'Yes, it's better to have one's own books and use them as one pleases, isn't it? Yet I do go there when I want to write . . .'

'I hear that you study a good deal, Mr Natsume,' the wife suddenly interjects. 'No, I don't study that much. Recently everyone has been encouraging me to start riding a bicycle, so from morning until night I'm doing nothing but that.' 'Bicycles are interesting, aren't they? We all ride, you know. I suppose you also go on long rides?' The person considered by the wife to be an expert at long rides was actually a man incapable of even understanding what the word 'ride' meant according to its usual definition. Yet, in a kind of warped sense of the word, I was a man capable – just about – of riding from the top of a slope down to the bottom of a slope. Hearing the words 'long ride' I feel uneasy, but, in today's twentieth century, exaggerating matters has evolved to becoming second nature, and in this regard I can pass myself off just as well as anyone else, so I shrewdly answer as follows, 'Well, I haven't yet been on what I would call long rides, but racing down from the top of a slope to the bottom is most enjoyable, isn't it?'

Their daughter, who has until now kept silent, appears to have mistakenly concluded from this that I must be able to ride a little then, and with 'Why don't we all go with Mr Natsume to Wimbledon some time?' presents a motion to Father and Mother. Father and Mother simultaneously look at my face. I am here dropped into a somewhat embarrassing position. I cannot simply quash outright this challenge proposed by an attractive young lady. When a gentleman with any kind of civilized education fails to show respect to a lady it is an indelible disgrace and, besides, a three-inch-high collar is gripping my throat with a vengeance, so, purposefully adorning my face with calmness and pleasure in equal portion, I say, 'That sounds interesting, but . . .' 'I dare say you are busy with your study, but we can go this Saturday when you are free.' My defences are gradually being penetrated. 'But . . .' after which, as it is not certain that I will be particularly busy, I myself am unclear what the rest of this 'but' relates to and in the meantime lose the initiative and finally see the conclusion of 'but . . .' fail to appear. 'But somewhere with a great amount of traffic, er . . . you see, I'm not yet used to that,' I say, finally carving out a means of escape. 'No, actually the roads in that vicinity are really quiet,' comes the instant response, and suddenly my escape route is cut off. Being in a desperate plight is not restricted to being on top of a bicycle, I marvel to myself, but marvelling will not resolve the issue, so as a last resort I repeat 'but . . .' once more. 'But . . . I wonder whether the weather will be fine this Saturday.' Completely failing to make my position clear one way or the other, it was hardly likely that anyone would understand. Seeing that the male party has lost the contest, the husband in his capacity as referee acts as mediator and says, 'Let's leave deciding the day for now, but I will cycle over to your house some time soon. Then we can go for a walk or something together.' Saying to a cyclist, 'We can go for a walk or something together,' how strange was that? He eyed me as if having completely written me off as someone unfit to be a cyclist.

Whether not going with this beautiful young lady to Wimbledon was a blessing or my misfortune is something that I have thought about a hundred times but in the end am none the wiser. Haiku poets of the Japan School call this a condition of clouded consciousness.

A certifiable day in a certifiable month. After the hard-earned experience and exhaustive contemplation of some days ago, I have arrived at the following conclusion:

> The saddle and pedals of a bicycle are not there in some desultory way for keeping up appearances. The saddle is there for putting one's rear on to, and the pedals are for resting one's feet on, treading on and turning around. The handlebar is the most dangerous instrument for, once one takes hold of this, it works dazzling wonders.

Having emerged from my well of contemplation a little more enlightened on the art of cycling, consider that I am now with my coach and his friend, a certain young count, and that riding stirrup to stirrup together we have crossed Clapham Common and are about to turn into a wide road where horse-trams pass along. Consider that my vehicle is interposed between those of the other two so that its control is already out of my hands and that I can only emerge in a forward direction. Now consider that my only exit has become suddenly blocked. That is to say that, just as I start to cross, some unruly cart came out from the right and, without so much as a sorry or a by-your-leave, haughtily passed in front of me. Maintaining my present attitude, we can only collide. As a matter of principle I venture to collide with others only in circumstances when I am sure to emerge the winner. Otherwise in collisions where it is transparently obvious that I am going to emerge the loser my long-standing family motto has always been 'Absolutely Always Avoid Them'. A collision between this enormous cart and my bicycle, creaking in its senility, is accordingly something which, even if it was to be my father's dying wish, I would have to avoid. Saying that, if I try to dodge to left or right I will have to transfer the collision to one of the other two. Unworthy as I am, one is a young count and one my noble teacher. Such an insolent act would be a terrible thing for common people such as you and I. Furthermore, in my social standing as a prisoner of war, it will appear as rude behaviour. It seems that if one shows filial piety to one's teacher one show disrespect to one's lord; and if one shows respect to one's lord one fails to show filial piety to one's teacher. There is nothing for it but either to reverse or to fall from the bicycle. In an instant the matter was settled. Faced with events and showing no sign of panic and after deep consideration, I decide that although, if it were possible, reversing would not be wholly bad – and certainly a thousand times better than falling from the bicycle – sadly, in today's times, no facilities for reversing this vessel have yet been installed, so there's nothing for it but to cast caution aside and fall from the bicycle. And, with that, I fall crashingly between the two bicycles. At this juncture the policeman listlessly standing in a spot about twelve feet away from me – this bicycle's relationship with policemen appears to be something like the relationship of a main dish with garnishings, and for whatever reason they are excessively cited in proceedings – this policeman raised his voice and with 'ha, ha, ha' laughed three times. This manner of laughing was not a wry smile, nor a sneer, nor a burst of laughter, but a completely forced smile, a commissioned smile requested by others. Whether to perform this commissioned smile the policeman received sixpence or a shilling, I regrettably did not have the time to enquire into.

Huh! So what if the policeman and others laughed, I think, and with that immediately gallop off after the other two. Whether I would have galloped off quite so quickly had this not been a policeman but the young lady from the other day is something which no amount of interpretation will ultimately resolve, so better not to enquire and move on. Now, on the pretext that the other two are unfamiliar with the topography of this area, I, in all my undependability, am given strict orders that I should lead the way. Yet, although I might be knowledgeable about the area, I am completely unknowledgeable about bicycles and, whenever we come to a street corner, rather than going in the desired direction I just end up turning in whichever direction is easiest. And so we keep coming back to the same place. At first, I somehow bluffed my way out of this, but it was hardly likely that I would be able to keep that up for long. This time I meant to go in a different direction. Right, I said, but things not going to plan is the way of the world, and turning in the desired direction was not going to be easy.

I had already come two-thirds the way across the street when I finally managed to twist the handlebars sharply so that the bicycle turned ninety degrees at a stroke. Perhaps garnering unexpected glory with this sudden turn might be an appropriate place to break off and say, 'The story continues tomorrow', but then again maybe not, so I will tell you about it right away. Up until making this sudden change of direction, I had not realized that there was another cyclist right behind me heading in the same direction. However, taken unawares by my sudden attack and not having the time to dodge my bicycle, he promptly tumbled off at my side. I later learned that when one turns at a crossroads it is considered polite to give some type of warning such as ringing the bell or raising a hand, but as I prefer to fall back on my own inspiration, I do not hold with such trite conventions. Besides, under present circumstances there was absolutely no way I was going to have the leisure for such cumbersome operations as ringing a bell or raising a hand. Just as the act of performing a silent about-turn was the product of sheer necessity, so the man stuck behind me being surprised and falling from his bicycle was also not without reason. It was logical on both sides, so there was nothing strange about it. It was only natural, but it seems that the logic of these Westerners is not that far developed so this fallen person in an attitude of great imperial wrath hurled abuse at me: 'Chin Chin Chinaman!' As the victim of this abuse I might be expected to fire a salvo in return, but displaying my serenely heroic nature I left behind only the single word 'sorry' and turned the corner without looking back. Actually, I did attempt to look back, but the bicycle passed on by and apart from the 'sorry' no other word emerged. Being honest, I must say that I was only slightly heroic. I specify this for fear that I might be mistaken for some type of scoundrel, and yet, if by some chance you were to gain an exaggerated sense of my heroism, you might curse me for rude behaviour for lifetimes to come.

A certifiable day in a certifiable month. A bicycle is a whirligig of a social and Sosekian uncertainty, and, just when one thinks that one is about to fall off, one ends up knocking other people off. Still, I am not going to give up that easily, and assuming a posture of defiance I hurry towards Battersea Park. The park is very tranquil, but about three hundred yards this side of it is an extremely busy road, which, to a beginner such as myself, offers the most daunting of daunting barriers. My bicycle is now safely over Lavender Hill and is riding into the very centre of the maelstrom. Over there a horse-tram has stopped, facing towards me. On its right an extremely large wagon has stopped, facing the other direction. Between them about four foot. I am speeding along on my vehicle ready to squeeze through the four-foot gap. The front wheel of my vehicle has come alongside the front leg of the tram-horse, that is to say, my body has entered the gap between horse-tram and wagon, when a bicycle suddenly slips in from the other side. At such instants preserving one's life is the main thing and, without contemplating whether to retreat or fall off, my body has already let out an 'eek!' and fallen. My manner of falling is a little clumsy, and I only avoid the indignity of landing on all fours by giving the horse's thigh a nasty knock with my left hand. Yet hardly have I time to think, That was close!, before the horse-tram starts moving forward. The horse is startled and kicks away my bicycle. The other bicycle whizzes past as if nothing has happened. The cycle of events does not stop there. A gentleman riding in a flashy gig gallops up from behind and regards me, whip in hand, and, quietly shocked by my suicide attempt, says, 'It's all right! Don't worry! I won't kill you!' Come to think of it, perhaps they do sometimes end up putting people on bicycles and killing them in this country. If so, Britain is a dangerous place.

Since surrendering to my twelve-stone landlady and being subjected to bicycle torture, I have had five major falls and countless small falls, have crashed into stone walls, grazed my shins, collided with trees and had my nails torn off. I have fought a desperate war, but in the end it has all been for nothing. For starters, this twelve-stone old woman is someone who makes fun of people indiscriminately. While she is cynically making fun of people, her younger sister, a seven-stone old woman, fulfils the role of inspecting what changes appear in my features by keeping an unblinking eye on my yellow face. In this regard she is to be congratulated on her labours. Since being subjected to torment by these two old women, my sense of suspicion has only deepened and my sense of ill-treatment augmented day by day. In the end it's time to close the door and resign myself to having a face that is unavoidably yellow. The two old women plan their day according to fathoming the depths of my yellow face. To them I really have been a living barometer. Occasionally I ask myself what was gained by petitioning for surrender, and the answer is that I achieved nothing more than wasting precious study time and eating twice as much food at the boarding-house. My surrender was of no profit to me and costly to others, and in the end I can only think how regrettable it all has been.

From *Drifting in Space* (1906)

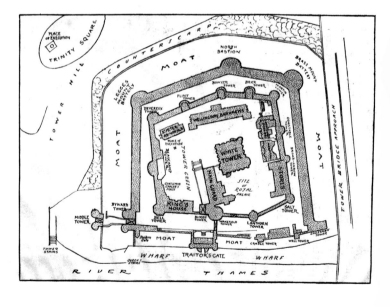

The Tower of London, 1885

The Tower of London

DURING two years of study abroad I visited the Tower of London only once. Afterwards, there were days when I thought I might go again, but I decided not to. I was even invited by other people, but I refused. Destroying memories of that single visit with a second visit would be a shame, and wiping them away completely with a third visit would be most regrettable of all. Visiting the Tower should, I think, be done only once.

I went there shortly after arriving. At that time I hardly knew one direction from another and, of course, knew nothing at all about geography. It felt just like being a Gotenba rabbit suddenly set loose in the heart of Nipponbashi. Thinking I might be swept away in a human wave when I went outside, and fearing that a steam train might come crashing into my room when I went home, I had peace of mind neither day nor night. If I have to live for two years amongst this noise and these crowds, I mused, the very fabric of my nerves will eventually become as sticky as a gluey plant in a cooking pot. I even had times when I thought Max Nordau's *Degeneration* all the more keenly to be the absolute truth.

Furthermore, not being in the position, like other Japanese, of holding an invitation from anyone to whom I could turn for help, nor of course having any old friends abroad, I had to walk about gingerly using a single map as my guide for my sightseeing and errands every day. I did not, of course, get on any trains, nor was I able to get in any carriages, and, when I did make a rare attempt to use a mode of transport, I had no idea where I was being taken. The steam trains, carriages, electric railways and cable railways that criss-cross like spider's legs the wide city of London were unable to provide me with any convenience whatsoever. When I emerged at a crossroads I had no choice but to open up the map and decide, while being pushed back by passers-by, in which direction to turn my feet. When I couldn't work something out on the map I asked someone. When I couldn't work something out by asking someone I looked for a policeman. If I couldn't get anywhere with the policeman I asked someone else. I accosted no end of people by calling out to them and kept on asking and asking until I found someone who knew the answer. In this way I finally arrived at where I wanted to go.

My visit to the Tower was, I think, of the time when I was able to venture outside only by relying on such methods. If I say, 'I came not knowing from whence I came, and left not knowing from whence I left', it will sound Zen-like, but, even now, I have no idea which roads I passed along to arrive at the Tower or what districts I crossed over to get back to my house. However much I reflect on it, I cannot recall them. The only thing certain is that I visited the Tower. Even now I can vividly visualize the spectacle of the Tower itself. Ask me about beforehand, and I am at a loss; question me about afterwards, and I cannot give you an answer. Only the middle part, which has forgotten beforehand and taken leave of afterwards, is unadorned and clear. It feels rather as if lightning were to tear through the darkness, fall on to my eyebrows and then disappear. The Tower of London appears as the centre of a dream of karmic destiny.

The history of the Tower of London is a distillation of the history of England. The curtain veiling the mysterious things called the past rending itself in two and reflecting ghostly light from out of the depths over the twentieth century is the Tower of London. The all-burying current of time flowing backwards and fragments of ancient times floating up into the present age, that is the Tower of London. Human blood, human flesh, human sins crystallized and left behind in the midst of horses, carriages and steam trains, that is the Tower of London.

When I gaze from Tower Bridge at this Tower of London, there before my eyes across the river Thames, I lose myself in an intensity of gazing, wondering whether I am a person of the present or a person of ancient times. Although one might say it is the beginning of winter, it is a calm day. The sky is the colour of a barrel of mixed-up lye, and the clouds hang low over the Tower. Looking as if plaster has been melted into it, the current of the Thames seems neither to raise any waves nor make any noise as it forcibly moves along. A single boat goes along with a sail hoisted beneath the Tower. As they are sailing on a windless river it seems like an irregular, triangular-shaped white wing constantly at rest in the same place. Two large lighters come upstream. A single boatman standing alone at the stern works an oar, and this, too, hardly moves. Around the balustrade of Tower Bridge a white shadow flickers, probably a gull. Everything I have surveyed is calm. They appear languid, sleeping; everything is the feeling of the past. Then, at their centre, standing coolly, as if pouring scorn on the twentieth century, is the Tower of London. As if to say, 'Steam trains may run along, and electric trains may run along, too, but as long as there is history I alone will be like this', there it stands. I am now all the more shocked at its grandness. This building is commonly called the Tower, but the Tower is only a name, and in fact it is a large castle comprising many turrets. Amongst the turrets soaring up side by side are round ones and square ones in a whole variety of shapes, but all of them are a gloomy grey colour, as if vowing to commemorate eternally previous centuries. If one was to build the Kudan Yushukan out of stone, line twenty or thirty of them together and then look at them through a magnifying glass, one might end up creating something that resembled this Tower, I reflect. I am still gazing at it. In the midst of air saturated with sepia-coloured moisture I vacantly stand and gaze at it. Twentieth-century London gradually disappears from the back of my mind and, at the same time, the image of the Tower before my eyes starts like a phantom to sketch the history of the past in my brain. I am made to feel as if the steam rising from tea sipped after getting up in the morning is pulling on the tail of a dream left behind through lack of sleep. After a while I begin to suspect that a long arm will come out from the opposite bank and pull me in. Having stood until now completely motionless, I suddenly start to want to cross the river and go towards the Tower. The long arm pulls me more and more strongly. I instantly move my feet and start crossing Tower Bridge. The long arm pulls and pulls. After crossing Tower Bridge I rush at full speed up to Tower Gate. A great magnet of the past, in excess of one hundred and twenty thousand square yards, has completely absorbed this small speck of iron floating in the present age. When I enter through the gate and look back:

> Through me you pass into the city of Woe:
> Through me you pass into eternal pain:
> Through me among the people lost for aye.
> Justice the founder of fabric moved:
> To rear me was the task of Power divine,
> Supremest Wisdom, and primeval Love.
> Before me things create were none, save things
> Eternal, and eternal I endure.
> All hope abandon, ye who enter here.

I wonder whether these lines are not inscribed somewhere. I have already lost a sense of normality.

When I cross the stone bridge spanning the empty moat there is a single tower on the other side. Its turrets are circular and stone built, in the shape of oil tanks, and, just like giant's gateposts, soar up on both sides. I enter below the building linking the central section and pass through to the other side. This is called the Middle Tower. When I proceed a little further, a bell tower rises up before me. When iron shields and steel helmets appear like autumn shadows covering the fields and tell that enemies approach from afar, they ring the bell at the top of this tower. When, on a star-black night, watching for a gap amongst the sentries walking along the ramparts, a prisoner attempts to escape and disappears into the darkness from shadows falling from downturned torches, they ring the bell at the top of this tower. And when proud citizens, finding fault with the king's government, surge like ants towards the tower and jostle and throng there, they ring the bell at the top of this tower. In an emergency they always ring the bell at the top of this tower. Sometimes they ring it fervently, sometimes they ring it intently. Even if a holy man came and was killed, they would have rung it; even if a Buddha came and was killed, they would have rung it. This bell which rang out countless times on frosty mornings, snowy evenings, rainy days, windy nights, now I wonder where it has gone. I raise my head and look up at the old ivied turret, but it is silent, having already stored up its sound for a hundred years.

When I again proceed a little further along, there, on my right-hand side, is the Traitor's Gate. Above the gate, soaring up, is St Thomas's Tower. Just by its name alone, the Traitor's Gate is already terrifying. From time immemorial thousands of criminals, buried from sight while living in the Tower, were all conveyed from boats to this gate. Once they had left the boat behind and passed through, the sun of the outside world did not shine on them again. The Thames was to them the river Styx, and this gate was the entrance leading to the Underworld. Swaying in waves of tears, they are rowed up to the bottom of this arch, cave-like in its gloominess. They have come to a place where a whale is waiting with an open mouth to suck up sardines, and as soon as they arrive, with a sharp grating noise, a thick oak door eternally separates them from the light of the everyday world. In such a way do they finally fall prey to the demon of fate. Will they be eaten up tomorrow? Or will they be eaten up the day after tomorrow? Or else will they be eaten up ten years hence? Only the demon knows. What, I wonder, were the thoughts of the criminals sitting inside the boat as it drew up alongside this gate? Every time the oars bend, every time droplets trickle on the side of the boat, every time the arms of the person rowing move, my life is being chipped away, is what they must have thought. A person with a white beard hanging down to his chest, loosely dressed in a black surplice, rises with tottering steps from the boat. This is Archbishop Cranmer. The fine-looking man wearing a blue hood low over his eyes and a coat of mail beneath sky-coloured silk must be Wyatt. He, without so much as a by-your-leave, leaps from the side of the boat. The person sporting a gay feather in his hat, with his left hand on the hilt of his gold-mounted sword, lightly tiptoeing over the stone steps in shoes adorned with silver buckles, is that Raleigh? I look below the dark arch and crane my head to see whether the light of waves washing the stone steps might be seen on the other side. There is no water. Since the completion of the embankment works, the Traitor's Gate and the river Thames have become completely disconnected one from the other. The Traitor's Gate, which swallowed so many criminals and spat out so many convoy boats, has lost contact with the sounds of wavelets washing its skirts in a relic of ancient times. The only thing left is a large iron ring hanging down from the wall of the Bloody Tower on the opposite side. In ancient times it is said that the boat's mooring line was tied to this ring.

I turn left and enter the gate of the Bloody Tower. In ancient times, the place that confined unspeakable numbers of people in the War of the Roses is this tower. The place that mowed down people like grass, that butchered people like chickens, that piled up corpses like dried salmon, is this tower. It is not for nothing that it was called the Bloody Tower. Beneath the arch there is a box like a police cabin, and to the side a soldier wearing a helmet-shaped hat is standing thrusting out a gun. He has an extremely serious face but looks as if he would like quickly to finish his watch, have a drink at his local pub, banter with a certain someone and make merry. The wall of the tower has been thickly built from irregular stones folded one on top of another so the surface is far from smooth. Here and there it is entwined with ivy. High up a window is visible, but, perhaps because the building is large, when one looks from below it is extremely small. It seems to be fitted with an iron grating. The sentry stands as bolt upright as a stone statue as he mentally frolics with his lady-love, while I screw up my brows, shade my eyes with my hand

96

Edward V and the Duke of York in the Tower by Paul Delaroche (1831)

and pause to look up at this high window. A faint light shines through the grating on to the ancient stained glass and reflects glitteringly back. Finally, like smoke clearing, the curtains open and the stage of imagination vividly appears. On the inside of the window a thick hanging drapes down so that even during the day everything is dimly lit. The wall facing the window is made up of completely bare stones not even covered with plaster, and it forms a partition, unmovable until the day of the world's extinction, with the room next to it. Only an area of about eighteen square yards in the very centre is covered with a dully coloured tapestry. The cloth is a greyish blue, with a pattern in light yellow of a picture of a nude goddess and, all around the picture, a dyed-in arabesque. Next to the stone wall lies a large bed. Permeating even to the core of the thick oak, deeply engraved grapes and grape vines and grape leaves shoot back the light where legs and frame meet. On the edge of the bed two children have appeared. One is thirteen or fourteen; one seems about ten years old. The younger one is seated on the bed, half leaning his body against the bedpost, with both legs meekly dangling down. Putting forward his right elbow and inclined face, he rests them on the elder person's shoulder. The elder one opens a large book, adorned in gold, on the knees of the younger person and puts his right hand on the opened page. Like rubbed ivory made smooth, it is a beautiful hand. Both of them are wearing tunics as black as ravens' wings, but their complexions are extremely white, making them stand out all the more. The fact that the colour of their hair, the colour of their eyes, their eyebrows and noses, even the details of their clothes appear almost the same in both of them is surely because they are brothers.

The elder brother, in a soft clear voice, reads the book upon his brother's knees: 'Happy are those who see before their own eyes the coming of their own death. Pray to die night and day. What is there to fear for one who finally goes before God . . .'

The younger brother says in a most pitiful voice, 'Amen.' Just then a cold winter wind blowing from afar shakes the tall tower, so that momentarily it seems that even the walls might fall down as it rings out. The younger brother gently draws his body over and nestles his face on his elder brother's shoulder. A part of the snow-white quilt swells up and down. The elder brother starts to read again: 'If morning, think that you will die before evening. If evening, do not pray for the morrow. Readiness is all. In an ignoble death lies the greatest shame . . .'

The younger brother says 'Amen' again. His voice is shaking. The elder brother quietly puts the book down, walks towards the small window and attempts to look outside. The window is high, and he is not tall enough. He brings over a stool and lifts himself on tiptoe. In the midst of black clouds enveloping the landscape for a hundred miles around, the winter sun dimly shines. It seems to have been soaked through with the blood of slaughtered dogs. The elder brother says, 'Will night also fall today in this way?' and looks back at his younger brother. The younger brother merely answers, 'I'm cold.' 'If our uncle would only spare us our lives, he could gladly have my crown,' the elder brother mumbles to himself. The younger brother says only, 'I want to see Mother.' At this moment, even though there is no wind the nude figure of the goddess embroidered in the tapestry hanging opposite slightly moves two or three times.

Suddenly the scene changes. I look over, and there, in front of the tower gate, a single woman dressed in black mourning-clothes stands dejectedly. Her face is pale and gaunt, but she seems somehow a dignified, noble lady. Finally, with the rasping noise of the lock, the door opens, and from inside a man comes out and respectfully bows before her.

'Am I allowed to see them?' the woman asks.

'No,' the man sadly replies. 'Know that I wish for you to see them but that, the public law being what it is, it is impossible. However, for a small consideration I can sometimes show mercy.' He suddenly closes his mouth and looks around. From inside the moat a dabchick floats to the surface.

The woman takes off the chain around her neck and, giving it to the man, says, 'I only wish to glimpse them for a moment. It would be heartless of you not to accede to a woman's petition.'

The man winds the chain around the end of his fingers as he thinks it over. The dabchick suddenly sinks below the surface. After a while he says, 'A gaoler cannot break the rules of the gaol. Know that your children are unharmed and pass their days in good health. Please put your mind at rest and go', and he pushes back the gold chain. The woman does not move. Only the chain falls on to the paving stones with a clinking sound.

'Is there no way for me to see them?' asks the woman.

'I'm sorry,' says the gaoler, turning away.

'The black shadow of the Tower! The hard wall of the Tower! The cold people of the Tower!' the woman says, weeping bitterly.

The scene changes again.

A tall figure in black attire appears in a corner of one of the courtyards. It seems as if he stole out from inside the moss-cold stone wall. Standing on the border of night and fog, he looks around his dim surroundings. After a while another identical figure in black floats up from the bottom of the shadows. In the corner of the turret, looking up at the figures of stars hanging high above them, the tall one says, 'Night has fallen.' 'In the daylight world we dare not show our faces,' the other answers. 'I have done many murders but I will ne'er have one which causes me as much remorse as that of this day,' the tall figure says turning towards the shorter one. 'When we stood listening to them talking on the other side of the tapestry, I thought for a moment about not doing it and taking my leave,' the short one confesses. 'When I strangled them their flower-like lips were all aquiver.' 'On their translucent foreheads purple veins appeared.' 'Those howling voices still ring in my ears.' As the black figures are again sucked into the black night, at the top of the turret, the sound of a clock chimes.

The vision disintegrates with the sound of the clock. The sentry, who had been standing like a stone statue, is now marching with his gun on his shoulder, clicking his heels over the paving stones. As he marches along he dreams of when he will be out strolling and holding hands with a certain someone.

Passing beneath the Bloody Tower and emerging on the opposite side there is a pretty courtyard. The centre of this is on slightly higher ground. On this higher ground is the White Tower. The White Tower is the very oldest thing within the Tower and was in ancient times the keep. One hundred and twenty feet in length, one hundred and eight feet in width, ninety feet in height, with walls fifteen feet thick, its corner turrets rise up on four sides and in places even the crevasses from the Norman period are visible. When in 1390 the people raised thirty-three articles of complaint and pressed Richard II to abdicate, the setting was inside this tower. When standing before priests, nobles, soldiers, lawyers, facing the whole world, he announced that he would abdicate, the setting was inside this tower. Henry, who then accepted the succession, stands, makes the sign of the cross on his forehead and chest and says at length, 'In the name of the Father, the Son and the Holy Spirit, and by the accession of my rightful blood, the grace of God and my dear friends, I, Henry, accept this crown and the throne of England.' Now, as for the fate of the former king, nobody knew. When his dead body was moved from Pontefract Castle and arrived at St Paul's Cathedral a crowd of twenty thousand were shocked by the emaciated countenance of his corpse. Some say that, when eight assassins surrounded Richard, he snatched an axe from one of their hands and cut down one of them and felled two more. Yet with one blow delivered by Exton from behind, he finally swallowed his mortification and died. Other people, looking up at the heavens, say, 'No, no. Richard starved himself and by his own will caused his life to be cut short.' Whichever is the case, neither is welcome. The history of the monarchs is a tragic history.

Tradition has it that the downstairs room is where Walter Raleigh wrote the manuscript of *The History of the World* while a prisoner here. I try imagining him in his Elizabethan breeches, his right leg with a silk stocking tied around the knee placed on top of his left, the end of his quill touching the paper, his head a little inclined in contemplation. However, I am unable to see the room.

I enter from the south side and ascend a spiral staircase, where there is a famous weaponry exhibition. Everything looks as if it is polished regularly and sparkles with light. It is extremely gratifying to be able to see, one after another, things which when I was in Japan I came across only in history books and novels and which had made not the slightest sense. However, my gratification was short-lived, for now it is just as if I have forgotten them all, and so I am back to square one. Yet, the things which, even now, remain in my memory are the suits of armour. Amongst them the one I definitely remember thinking really wonderful was that worn by Henry VI. The whole thing is made of steel and damascened in places. The most surprising thing is how enormous it is. The man who put on this suit of armour would have to be a giant at least seven feet tall. While I am gazing in wonder at this suit of armour, there is the click of footsteps as someone walks towards me. I turn around and see a Beefeater. When I say Beefeater, you might think that this is someone who is always eating beef, but he is not like that. He is a watchman of the Tower of London. Wearing something that looks like a squashed silk hat, his clothes are similar to those worn by pupils of the Art School. His wide sleeves are gathered at the end and a belt is tied around his waist. His clothing is also patterned. The pattern is the kind of thing found on the short coats worn by the Ainu people and is nothing more than an array of extremely simple straight lines arranged into square shapes. He even sometimes carries a spear. On the end of the short-headed shaft he has a spear with feathers hanging down like something out of *The Chronicle of the Three Kingdoms*. One of these Beefeaters stops behind me. He is not very tall and is a rather plump and white-whiskered Beefeater. 'You're Japanese, aren't you?' he asks smiling. It doesn't feel like I am talking to an Englishman of the present age. It feels as if he has just put in an appearance from some bygone era of three or four hundred years ago, or that I have suddenly looked upon the past of three or four hundred years ago. I silently give a slight nod. He says, 'Come with me', so I follow. He points with his finger to an old Japanese coat of armour and raises an eyebrow as if to say, 'Have you seen this?' 'This was presented to Charles II from Mongolia,' the Beefeater explains. I nod a third time.

I leave the White Tower and go over to the Beauchamp Tower. On the way, there is an array of captured cannons. A small space in front of them is enclosed with an iron railing, and on part of the chain a notice is hanging down. I look over and see that it says that this used to be the place of execution. Pushed into a dark underground room with no sunlight for two, or even three, or sometimes even ten years, the prisoner is one day suddenly pulled above ground only to be installed in this even more terrifying place. Seeing the clear sky after such a long time, he hardly has time to count his blessings, than, with dazed eyes and the colours of the world around him still imperfectly registered in his pupils, the blade of a white axe quickly cuts through three feet of air. The blood that flew out must have been cold even while he was still alive. A raven descends. Hunching its wings, its black beak protruding, it stares at people. I feel as if the rancour of a hundred years of blood have congealed and taken the form of a bird so as to guard this unhappy place for ever. In the blowing wind an elm tree rustles. I look over, and on the branches, too, there is a raven. After a while another one flies down. Where they have come from I do not know. Beside them a young woman with a boy of about seven is standing staring at the ravens. Her Greek nose and beautiful, polished gem-like eyes and the undulations of curves shaping her pure white neck move my heart more than a little. The child looks up at the woman and says with curiosity, 'Ravens, ravens.' Then, importuning her, 'The ravens seem to be cold. I'd like to give them some bread.' The woman says quietly, 'Those ravens do not want anything to eat.' The child asks, 'Why?' The woman, staring fixedly at the ravens with eyes that seem to be floating in the midst of her long lashes, says only, 'There are five ravens', and does not reply to the child's question. She looks lost in thought, as if reflecting alone over something. I wonder whether there is not some strange karma between this woman and these ravens. She speaks of the ravens' mood as if speaking of her own and declares that, although only three ravens are visible, there are five. Leaving behind the mysterious woman, I enter the Beauchamp Tower.

The history of the Tower of London is the history of the Beauchamp Tower, and the history of the Beauchamp Tower is a tragic history. The person entering the ground-floor room of this three-storey tower, built by Edward III in the second half of the fourteenth century, must surely notice, the instant that they enter, countless memorials congealed from a hundred generations of rancour on the surrounding walls. All the malice, all the indignation, all the grief and the sadness, together with the solace born of the extremity of this malice, this indignation, this grief and sorrow, are revealed in ninety-one varieties of epigraph, which even now cause the heart of the onlooker to freeze. Scratching unfeeling walls with a cold steel pen, the people who, in between heaven and earth, carved out their misfortune and fate, are buried in a bottomless pit called the past, and only their futile words continue to look upon the light of the world. One wonders whether they were not deliberately making fools of themselves. There is in the world a thing called irony. One says white and means black; one advocates small and suggests big. Amongst all ironies, there is none as fierce as the irony left unwittingly to posterity. Whether graves or monuments, whether medallions or cordons, these things are, so long as they exist, nothing more than a means of making one recall through a futile object bygone days. To think, I may be gone but the thing that speaks for me will remain, are the words of a person who has forgotten that it is the intermediate object lamenting the departing person that remains and that the person himself does not remain. Passing down the irony to a future world is, I think, a thing done by a person who ridicules the fleetingness of life. When I die I will not make a deathbed poem. After I am dead I will not have a tombstone erected for me. To think of having one's flesh burned, having one's bones ground and scattered on a day when a west wind strongly blows and such, is to do needless effort in vain.

The writing styles of the epigraphs are of course not uniform. Certain ones, having taken much time, employ a neat printed style, while others, either due to a flurried mind or out of vexation, are scratched on the wall and engraved in a scrawl. Again, some have engravings of their family crest with elegant antique letters inside or else are drawn in the shape of a shield with indecipherable words inside. In the same way that the writing styles differ, the inscriptions, too, are also definitely not the same. They are in English, of course, but also in Italian and Latin. On the left side, the carving 'MY HOPE IS IN CHRIST' is the inscription of a priest called Paslew. This Paslew was beheaded in 1537. At its side is the signature JOHAN DECKER. Who Decker is, I do not know. As I go up the stairs, by the entrance to the door, there is 'T.C.' This, too, is in capitals, and for whom it stands I have no idea. A short distance away there is an extremely elaborate one. First, on the right side there is a crucifix adorned with a heart and at the side an engraving of a skull and a crest. A little further along the following lines written inside a shield catch my eye. 'Since Fortune hath chosen that my hope should go to the wind to complain, I wish the time be destroyed, my planet being ever sad and unpropitious.' After that there is one with 'Honour all men. Love the brotherhood. Fear God. Honour the King.'

I try to imagine what was going on inside the minds of the people who wrote these things. There is probably nothing in the world as tormenting as the torment of boredom. There is no torment like having no change in the contents of one's consciousness. There is no torment like that of a serviceable body being bound with an invisible rope and being unable to move. Just as being alive means being active, being alive while having one's activity stifled is the same as having the meaning of life itself snatched away, and just being aware of it being snatched away is a greater agony even than death. The

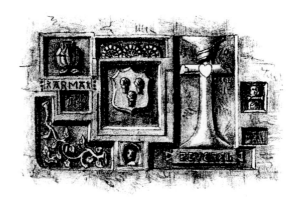

Sketches of inscriptions from the walls of the Beauchamp Tower

Sketches of inscriptions from the walls of the Beauchamp Tower

people who covered the surroundings of these walls to this extent had all tasted this agony more gruesome than death. After struggling with this agony to the limits of their endurance and tolerance, when it became completely unbearable, they began looking for work while they were still able, using a broken end of a nail and sharp fingernails, bewailing their complaints in silence, inscribing life's vicissitudes on flat surfaces. Each letter and stroke they carved must have been the inevitable result of the demands of their instinct, which, even after exhausting lamentation and wailing and all the other cathartic means that nature will allow, was still not satisfied.

Again I try to imagine it. Once having been born, one must live. One must be bold enough not to speak of one's fear of death and just live. Saying that one must live was true before Christ and Confucius and is true after Christ and Confucius. It needs no argument, only that since one wishes to be alive, therefore one must live. All people must live. The people bound in this hell were also in accordance with this great truth and had to live. At the same time they were confronted with a doomed fate. Every minute and every second the question that occurred in their hearts was: How may I continue to stay alive? Once a person entered this room he or she would certainly die. Those who lived to see the sun and sky again were only one in a thousand. Sooner or later they would die. But the great truth stretching across the ages instructs them, saying, 'Live!' and keeps on and on saying, 'Live!' They had no choice but to hone their nails. With the ends of their sharpened nails, they wrote '1' on top of the hard walls. Even after putting up '1', the truth as of old whispers, 'Live!', and keeps on and on whispering, 'Live!' They wait for the nails that have peeled away to heal and wrote once more '2'. They who expected their flesh to fly and their bones to be crushed by the blade of an axe on the morrow prayed to live just by means of a '1' or by a '2', or by lines or letters on the cold walls. The vertical and horizontal marks that remain on the walls are the ghosts of a tenacious desire for life. When I had reeled in the thread of imagination this far I felt as though the cold air inside the room had all at once blown inside my body from the pores of my back, and I involuntarily shuddered. Now that I think of it, the walls are for some reason damp. When I try touching them with my fingertips they are slippery with dew. When I look at my fingertips they are a deep red. From the corners of the room the drops of dew trickle down one by one. When I look at the floor the remains of those drops form an irregular bright-crimson pattern. The blood of the sixteenth century has, I think, oozed out. From inside the walls even the groans are audible. As the groans gradually approach they change into an unearthly song seeping out of the night. Here is a cellar running beneath the ground and inside there are two people. A wind blowing up from the land of demons passes through the cracks in the stone walls and kindles a small lantern so that even the ceiling and the four corners of the dark room appear to be swirling with smoky-coloured lamp soot. The sound of the faintly audible song is indeed the voice of one of the people inside the cellar. The singer has his sleeves rolled up high and holds a large axe against the grindstone of the lathe as he vigorously sharpens it. At his side an axe has been flung aside but, with the shifts in the wind, its white blade occasionally flashes. The other person stands with his arms folded, watching the grindstone spin. From inside a beard a face protrudes, and the lantern illuminates one side of it. The illuminated part appears the colour of a mud-covered carrot. 'With them being sent here every day from the boats like this, we executioners are having a busy time of it,' the beard says. 'That's right, just keeping the axes sharpened is difficult enough,' the singer answers. He is a short, sunken-eyed, smoky-coloured man. 'Yesterday I did a beautiful one,' the beard says sadly. 'No, she was a woman with a beautiful face but she had a stupidly hard neck bone. It was thanks to her that a bit of the blade chipped off,' the other says as he furiously turns the lathe, and, as it rings out with a whirr, whirr, whirr, sparks brightly appear. The one doing the sharpening starts to sing at the top of his voice:

It won't cut, you see.
A woman's neck
and the spite of love
will break the blade in two.

Apart from the whirr, whirr, whirr sound ringing out, nothing else is audible. The light of the lantern, kindled by the wind, shines on the right cheek of the one doing the sharpening. Over the soot he appears flushed. 'I wonder whose turn it is tomorrow?' the beard asks after a while. 'Tomorrow it's that old woman's turn,' the other nonchalantly answers.

Her hair's gone white with adultery stains
But cut off her head and the blood will stain.

He sings in a high pitch. Whirr, whirr, whirr, the lathe spins. Sparks brightly appear. 'Aha, that'll be about right,' he says, brandishing the axe and looking at the blade in the light. 'Only the old woman, nobody else?' the beard asks again. 'And then there's the other one to be done.' 'That's a shame. Is she being done, too? Bless her.' 'It's a shame, but it can't be helped,' the other declares looking at the jet-black ceiling.

Suddenly the cellar and the executioners and the lantern all disappear and I am standing vacantly in the middle of the Beauchamp Tower. When I come to my senses I realize that standing there at my side is the boy who said earlier that he wished to give some bread to the ravens. The mysterious woman is also with him as before. The boy looks at the wall and says in a surprised way, 'There are some dogs drawn over there.' The woman, as usual in her resolute manner, answers, 'They are not dogs. To the left is a bear, and to the right a lion, it is the crest of the Dudleys.' Actually I, too, have been thinking that they are dogs or pigs, so listening now to the explanation of this woman I am all the more struck by her strangeness. Saying that, when she said the word Dudley just now there was somehow a forcefulness contained within that word that made one feel that she had declared her own family name. With bated breath I closely observe them both. The woman continues with her explanation. 'The person who carved this crest is John Dudley.' Her tone is just as if John is her own brother. 'John has four brothers, and those brothers are denoted by the flowers and plants engraved around the bear and the lion.' I look and see that, like the frame of an oil painting, there are indeed four types of flowers or leaves carved around the bear and the lion. 'Here we have some acorns, these are for Ambrose. Here we have roses, which represent Robert. At the bottom, honeysuckle is portrayed. Honeysuckle relates to Henry. The one set at the top left is a geranium, and this is for G . . .' After this she is silent. I see that her coral lips are trembling as if having been electrified. They are like the tip of a pit viper's tongue when it faces a mouse. After a while the woman recites in a clear voice the epigraph attached beneath this crest.

> Yow that these beasts do wel behold and se,
> May deme with ease wherefore here made they be
> Withe borders wherein . . . .
> 4 brothers' names who list to serche the ground.

The woman, as if having spoken these lines every day from birth until today as part of a daily routine, finishes reciting them in a certain tone. Actually the words on the wall are extremely difficult to see. Even if racking my brains, somebody like me would be unlikely to read a single word. I find this woman more and more mysterious.

Feeling uneasy, I walk past them and pass on ahead. I emerge at a corner with crevasses, and there in the middle of a mass of confused writings, impossible to discern whether patterns or words, the small word 'Jane' is written in neat strokes. In spite of myself I stop and stand in front of it. Amongst those who have read the history of England, there is none who does not know the name Jane Grey. And there is none who has not shed tears of sympathy for her sad fate and cruel end. Because of the ambition of her father-in-law and husband, Jane was, at the tender age of eighteen, blamelessly and unsparingly handed over for execution. The fragrance from the pistil of a trampled rose does not easily disappear but distantly stands and, even reaching down to today, affects those who turn the pages of history. The anecdotes about her understanding Greek and reading Plato and garnering the admiration of the greatest scholar of the age, Ascham, serve as good materials for imagining this poetically minded person and are surely preserved in the hearts of many. Having stopped and stood in front of Jane's name I do not move. Actually, rather than saying I *do not* move, I should say I *cannot* move. The curtains of imagination have already opened.

At first, both my eyes become hazy and I am unable to see anything. Finally, at one point inside the darkness, a light is suddenly kindled. Little by little, the light grows larger, and I have the feeling of people moving inside. Next, it becomes by degrees brighter and, just as if adjusting the focus on some binoculars, starts to be clearly reflected in my eyes. Next, the scene gradually grows larger and starts to move forward from the background. I realize that a young woman is sitting in the centre and a man is standing on her right side. Thinking that I've seen them both somewhere before, in the blink of an eye they move closer and suddenly stop ten or twelve yards in front of me. The man is the sunken-eyed, smoky-coloured fellow who was singing inside the cellar. Holding the well-sharpened axe in his left hand, and with a ten-inch dagger hanging down from his waist, he stands ready. I am involuntarily struck with terror. The woman appears blindfolded with a white handkerchief and is fumbling with both hands for the block on which to place her head. It is about as large as a Japanese wood-chopping block and has an iron ring attached at the front. Hay has been scattered in front of the block, apparently as a precaution to prevent blood from streaming away. Leaning against the back wall two or three women have fallen down crying, ladies-in-waiting or some such? A priest trailing the long skirts of a fur-lined surplice bends down and helps to lead the woman's hand in the direction of the block. She is wearing snow-white clothes and occasionally sways, cloud-like, the golden tresses abundant on her shoulders. When I happen to look at her face, I am amazed. I cannot see her eyes, but the shape of her eyebrows, the slender face, even the delicate neck, is exactly the same as the woman I saw earlier. I instinctively try to rush over, but my feet shrink back and are unable to advance even one step. The woman finally gropes for and finds the executioner's block and puts both hands on it. The lips anxiously move. They are not the slightest bit different from when she explained the Dudley crest to the boy a little while ago. At last, slightly inclining her head, she asks, 'Is my husband Guildford Dudley already gone to the kingdom of God?' A handful of tresses that have swayed over her shoulder lightly undulate. The priest answers, 'I cannot say', and asks, 'Do you wish to enter into the true faith?' The woman sternly answers, 'The true one is that faith believed by me and my husband. Your faith is the deluded faith and the mistaken faith.' The priest says nothing. The woman in a rather composed manner concludes with, 'If my husband be first, I follow; if after, I beckon. I will tread the righteous path to the righteous kingdom of God', and then, as if falling, throws her head on top of the block. With a heave-ho, the sunken-eyed, smoky-coloured short executioner heavily takes up the axe again. Just as I think that two or three spots of blood have spurted on to the knees of my trousers, the whole spectacle vanishes into thin air.

When I look around there is not a trace, wherever she has gone, of the woman who was accompanying the boy. Bemused, I leave the Tower in a daze. When I again pass under the Bell Tower on the way back, from a high window Guy Fawkes quickly flashes his face. I could even hear his voice saying, 'If I'd just been an hour earlier . . . What a shame that these three matches were of no use.' Even I think that I am a little out of my senses and hastily leave the Tower. When I cross Tower Bridge and look back, perhaps it's usual in northern countries, but the sun has all of a sudden turned to rain. Droplets of drizzle so fine that they could pass through the eye of a needle are

The Execution of Lady Jane Grey by Paul Delaroche (1833)

melting the dust and smoke of the whole city, dimly closing up heaven and earth, while, looming over me like an image of hell, is the Tower of London.

Arriving at my lodging-house in a trance, I tell my landlord that I have visited the Tower today, but the landlord says, 'There were five ravens there, I suppose.' Well, I wonder with great surprise, is my landlord also a relative of that woman, but the landlord laughs, 'They're sacred ravens. They've been keeping them there since ancient times, and, even if they become one short, they immediately make up the numbers again. There are always five ravens there', and with this simple explanation half of my fantasy is, on the very same day as I saw the Tower of London, completely ruined. Again, when I tell the landlord about the epigraphs on the walls, he simply says with an indifferent air, 'What, those scribblings? Waste of time and completely spoil a perfectly pretty place. And, besides, the scribblings of criminals are not to be trusted. Lots of forgeries there, too, you know.' Finally, I start to tell him about meeting the beautiful lady and about how the lady fluently read things which were obscure and words which were absolutely indecipherable to us, but the landlord in a tone of great disdain says, 'So what if she did? Everyone reads the guidebook before setting off when they go. Knowing that much is nothing to be surprised at. What? A great beauty? There are lots of beautiful women in London. If you don't watch out, you'll be getting yourself into trouble.' The conversation was taking an unexpected turn. With this, the second half of my fantasy was again ruined. The landlord is a Londoner of the twentieth century.

After that I decided not to speak to anyone about the Tower of London. I also decided not to visit again.

★★★

This story has been dashed off as if it is a statement of fact, but actually most of it is fantasy, so I hope people perusing it will read it bearing this in mind. I now and then tried to choose what seemed like dramatically interesting things about the Tower of London and link them together, but, as it did not go so well, inevitably here and there traces of awkwardness remain. Amongst them, the scene where Elizabeth (Edward IV's queen) comes to see the two Princes imprisoned in the Tower and the scene where the assassins who killed the two Princes reminisce are both to be found in Shakespeare's history play *Richard III*. Shakespeare employs a direct style to represent the scene where the Duke of Clarence is murdered inside the Tower, but uses an allusive style to express how the two Princes were strangled to death, borrowing the words of the assassins to describe the scene indirectly. When I read the play, I felt that was very interesting, and so am now employing exactly the same concept. However, the contents of the conversation and the surrounding scenery have, of course, been worked out from my imagination and have no connection whatsoever with Shakespeare. And then, to say a word about the part where the headsman is singing as he sharpens his axe, this concept comes entirely from Ainsworth's novel *The Tower of London*, and I have no right to claim the slightest originality with respect to it. In Ainsworth the axe blade is described as being nicked as a consequence of having cut through the Countess of Salisbury. When I read this book, the spectacle of the executioner sharpening the blade of the axe used on the scaffold, owing to it having been nicked, occupies no more than one or two pages, but I felt them to be extremely interesting. Not only that but the business of nonchalantly singing an unruly song while doing the sharpening is the performance of the same fifteen or sixteen minutes, but I felt it to be deeply intriguing and a dramatic event sufficient to animate the whole book, and so have now followed suit with exactly the same concept. However, both the meaning and the words of the song and the conversation between the two headsmen and the scenery of the dark cellar are things completely additional to that concept and have been formed from my imagination. As I have the opportunity, let me introduce the song that Ainsworth has the gaoler sing.

The axe was sharp, and heavy as lead,
As it touched the neck off went the head!
> Whirr-whirr-whirr-whirr!

Queen Anne laid her white throat upon the block,
Quietly waiting the fatal shock;
The axe it severed it right in twain,
And so quick – so true – that she felt no pain.
> Whirr-whirr-whirr-whirr!

Salisbury's countess, she would not die
As a proud dame should – decorously.
Lifting my axe, I split her skull
And the axe since then has been notched and dull.
> Whirr-whirr-whirr-whirr!

Queen Catherine Howard gave me a fee, –
A chain of gold – to die easily:
And her costly present she did not rue,
For I touch her head, and away it flew!
> Whirr-whirr-whirr-whirr!

I thought about translating all this, but as it did not proceed in the slightest bit as I wished, and moreover in fear of it being too long, I decided not to.

About the scene of the two Princes in the Tower and the scene of the execution of Jane Grey, I should mention, as a token of thanks, that my imagination has been helped more than a little by the paintings of the famous Delaroche.

Amongst the prisoners rising from the boat, the one called Wyatt is the son of the famous poet, a person who raised an army on Jane's behalf, and I make a note of it because father and son have the same name and are easily confused.

I am aware that describing here in some detail all the Tower's features is a necessary condition – as far as introducing the Tower itself and giving an idea of what it is actually like to be there – but, anyhow, since it is not as if I went sightseeing with the objective of writing a certain type of story, and since, moreover, some years have now passed, it is inevitably quite difficult for me to visualize the scene clearly. Therefore it is probable that subjective comments abound, and there are points, too, where I sometimes wonder whether it does not give an unpleasant feeling to the reader, but then what's written is written and that's that. (*20 December 1904*)

The Carlyle Museum

IN a corner of the park someone is addressing a speech to the passers-by. From across the way an elderly man wearing a peaked, wide-brimmed hat and stooping in an old overcoat approaches and pauses to look at the speechmaker. The latter suddenly stops his speech, walks over and appears right in front of this provincial scholar. The two men's eyes directly meet. The speechmaker in a boorishly abrupt manner asks, 'Aren't you Carlyle?' 'Indeed I am Carlyle,' the scholar answers. 'Are you the one they laud as the Sage of Chelsea?' the other asks. 'Yes, people apparently do call me the Sage of Chelsea.' 'Sage is a bird's name; a human sage is rare indeed,' the speechmaker says with a high laugh. 'Yes, although we are all human, calling one person in particular a sage does seem to be the same thing as saying they are a bird. Humans are better off being left as ordinary humans,' the scholar answers laughing loudly, too.

Walking across the park before dinner, I sit down in a seat by the riverside and gaze at the opposite shore. The deep fog so characteristic of London is particularly evident by the river. I prop my chin on my cherrywood walking-stick and look straight ahead at the shadows of fog creeping along the road on the far distant bank as they become gradually darker until, from the bottom of the five-storey terraced buildings, everything disappears little by little into the trailing mist. In the end, like a distant, future world dragged in front of my eyes, rambling auburn shadows are all that remain in the deeply dark sky. Then, in the depth of this auburn colour, here and there droplets of dull light begin to appear. On second, third and fourth floors they've turned the gas lights on. Brandishing my walking-stick I head back to my boarding-house. On the way I invariably recall the story of Carlyle and the speechmaker. For this place of darkness and gas lights mixed in with fog is the Chelsea where the scholar once lived.

Carlyle is no longer with us. The speechmaker, too, is probably dead. But Chelsea still exists as it was then. No, even the house where Carlyle lived for many years has been carefully preserved. Since Cheyne Row was created in 1708, how many masters this house has welcomed and how many it has bade farewell, I do not know, but in any case it still remains just as it always did. After Carlyle's death some public-spirited men decided to bring together the furniture, personal effects and books Carlyle had used during his life and even arranged them in each room of the house so that anyone interested could inspect them at any time.

If one was to name the literary figures of the past connected to Chelsea, then Thomas More, and later Smollett, and later still, in the same age as Carlyle, such men as Leigh Hunt are the most distinguished. Hunt's home was in the immediate vicinity of Carlyle's, and Carlyle recorded how Hunt actually visited him on the evening that Carlyle moved into the house. It is also known that Hunt presented Carlyle's wife with a statue of Shelley. Apart from these, the houses in which Eliot stayed and Rossetti lived are immediately near by on a street facing the riverside. But, as times have changed, other people have now moved into all of these houses so that sightseeing is impossible. Carlyle's old haunt is the only one where, if you pay your sixpence, anyone at any time can freely look around.

Cheyne Row is a little street leading on to the riverside road to the south, and Carlyle's house is around the middle of the street on the right-hand side. The house is number twenty-four.

Having gazed at Chelsea in the fog from across the river almost every day, I finally crossed the bridge one morning and knocked on the door of this famous hermitage.

If I say hermitage it has an antiquated feel. At least it goes with a sense of elegance and taste. But Carlyle's hermitage is no such weak, lightly built thing. It is a four-storey, square house built on the roadside so that one can knock on the door directly from the street.

It has no protrusions or indentures but stands uniformly erect. It is just as if a large factory chimney had been cut off at the root and had a roof placed on it and windows inserted.

This is the place that Carlyle finally came upon after searching and searching for a home upon arriving in London from the north country. He had looked west and looked south and looked as far north as Hampstead and still was unable to find a suitable home,

but, when he finally came to Cheyne Row and saw this house, he did not have the courage to take it immediately. The man who had denounced the public as 'forty million fools' appeared to be flustered when it came to deciding on a place to live and turned to his wife, whom he presumably counted amongst the fools, to report the details of the house and ask her opinion. In his wife's response were the words, 'With respect to these two houses, I declare they both look attractive on paper so keep them both open, if you can, till I come to London; and if you are constrained to decide, do it with perfect assurance that I will approve your choice.'

In his writings Carlyle wrote of things that only he seemed to understand, but, when it came to choosing a house, he appears to have resigned himself to relying on his wife's help and sat back and waited for his wife to come up to the capital. Four or five days later she arrived. Now both of them chased around east, west, south and north, before they finally decided that Cheyne Row was, after all, the best choice. They both moved here on 10 June 1834, and it is even known that the canary the maid was carrying chirped in its cage while they were doing so. Mrs Carlyle may have chosen this house because she really liked it or by force of circumstance, there being no viable alternative, but in any case this chimney-shaped, square house with a rent of thirty-five pounds a year was the one that welcomed the couple into its household. With the vigour of another Cromwell or Frederick the Great, like a factory chimney churning out smoke, in this house Carlyle wrote his books *Cromwell* and *Frederick the Great*, turned down a pension recommended by Disraeli and lived a straight, upright and purposeful life.

I now stand on the stone step of this square house and tap-tap the devil-faced knocker. After a pause a plump woman of about fifty appears from inside and says, 'Come in.' From the beginning she appears to think of me as a sightseer. She eventually brings out what looks like a register and says, 'Write your name please.' I recall having entered this house four times and recording my name four times in this register during my sojourn in London. This occasion was in fact the first time I entered my name. I intended to write as neatly as possible but, as ever, produced extremely clumsy writing. Opening up the front of the register, I see there is not a single Japanese name. In that case, I must be the first Japanese to have come here is the desultory thought that amuses me. The woman says, 'This way', and, opening a door on the left-hand side, we enter a room facing the street. This apparently used to be the drawing-room. A variety of things are on display. On the wall are pictures and photographs. They mostly seem to be portraits of Carlyle and his wife. In the back room are the bookshelves Carlyle designed.

These are packed with many books. Difficult books. Trashy books. Antiquated books. Seemingly unreadable books. And also the silver and bronze medals minted to commemorate Carlyle's eightieth birthday. Apparently there were no gold medals. Contrasting all the medals and items with his name on, totally solid and blithely remaining until the end of time, to the smoke-like life of the man who received them, I felt rather strange. I climb to the first floor. Here, too, are large bookshelves crammed full, as ever, with books. Seemingly unreadable books, seemingly unheard-of books, seemingly impenetrable books in abundance. One may count one hundred and thirty-five. Apparently this room was also once a drawing-room. There is the letter and the Prussian decoration Bismarck sent to Carlyle. This seems to be thanks for his biography of Frederick the Great. There is the bed his wife used. It is an extremely clumsy, indecorous thing.

Guides appear to be the same whatever the country. For some time the old lady has been giving her explanation of each and every picture and piece of furniture in the room. She might not have trained herself for fifty years to become a full-time guide, but she is extremely proficient. On this day, in this month, in this year, this and that happened, she says, as if speaking whatever comes into her mind. Yet there is a sing-song and rhythm in her fluent speech. Her manner of speaking is so interesting that this is what I find myself listening to, and what she is actually speaking about I have no idea. In the beginning I tried to respond with questions and enquiries, but in the end this became too much bother, so I assumed an attitude of 'You carry on with the speech while I feel free to look around.' The woman showed no signs of being disheartened but, with an air of 'I'm going to say my piece whether anyone is listening or not', unflaggingly continues with 'On this day, in this month, in this year . . .'

I stick my head out of a window on the east side and survey the neighbourhood. Beneath my eyes is a garden of about forty square yards. To both right and left and at the back it is enclosed by a high stone wall so that its shape is also square. Squares seem to be in evidence all over this house. Carlyle's face definitely was not square. Rather he looked as if the middle of a cliff had collapsed and lay flat on a grassy plain. His wife could be taken for looking like a prime

shallot. The woman who is giving me the tour has a face that is round like a bean-jam bun. I look at the woman's face and think, Yes, very round, and the woman starts to recite again, 'On this day, in this month, in this year . . .' I stick my head out the window once more.

Carlyle says, 'From the back windows, nothing was visible but leafy clumps, green fields and red high-peaked roofs glimmering through them: a most clear, pleasant prospect in these fresh westerly airs.'

I have actually put my head out the back window thinking I would see dense leaves and view green fields. I have twice stuck my head out, but there is certainly no greenery or anything to be seen. To the right, one can see houses; to the left, one can see houses; at the back, one can see houses. Above them, like a patient with a sick stomach, hangs only a leaden sky stretched indolently as far as the eye can see. I draw in my head and pull away from the window. The guide is continuing to cheerfully chant, 'On this day, in this month, in this year . . .'

Carlyle also says that if one looks in the direction of London nothing is visible but Westminster Abbey and the topmost dome of St Paul's; other faint ghosts of spires disclose themselves as the smoke clouds shift.

'In the direction of London' is already an anachronism. To come to Chelsea today and look in the direction of London is equivalent to entering into the middle of a household and looking in the direction of the house, or pretty much the same as attempting to look in the direction of oneself with one's own eyes. But Carlyle did not himself think that he was living in London. He believed himself to be living quietly in the countryside and viewing the cathedrals of the city centre from a great distance. I stick out my head for a third time. I cast my eyes towards what he would have called 'the direction of London'. But neither Westminster nor St Paul's are visible. Tens of thousands of houses, hundreds of thousands of people, millions of noises are standing, floating and moving in the space between me and the cathedrals. The Chelsea of 1834 and the Chelsea of today seem to be completely different places. I draw my head in for a fourth time. The woman is silently standing still behind me.

We climb to the second floor. When I look at a corner of the room, Carlyle's bed is coldly lying there. Some green curtains silently hang over it and the lifeless centre of the bed is desolately gloomy. What kind of wood it is made of I do not know, but nothing distinguishes the craftsmanship apart from it being merely clumsy and plain. I am made to reflect upon the life of the man who laid in life upon it. The bath-tub he always used has been reverentially positioned by its side like some great treasure. Although I call it a bath-tub it is no bigger than a large bucket. Did he really wash off the soot of London in this big cooking-pot? I ask myself and increasingly find myself imagining what it must have been like to be him. When I suddenly raise my head, there on the wall is a plaster death-mask. So that's his face, I

The Knocker.

The Staircase.

The Bed.

The Study.

The Garden in winter.

think. This is the face of one who gets into a bath about the height of a foot-warmer frame, sleeps on such a plain bed and who, for forty years, continuously spewed out vociferous criticism. The woman's incessant speech sounds like listening on the phone to the greetings of someone from Yokohama.

'Shall we proceed upstairs?' the woman asks. Since I already feel I have left below the grime and noise of London and am sitting alone at the top of a five-storey pagoda, being quietly encouraged with 'Shall we go upstairs?' and realizing that there was still further to go seems curious indeed. 'Yes, let's go upstairs,' I respond approvingly. The higher we go, the more unearthly my feelings become.

When we reach the third floor I feel vaguely happy without knowing why. Or, rather than happy, I have a feeling of indescribable strangeness. This is the loft. When I look at the ceiling, it has the shape of a horse's mane, low on either side but high in the centre, and at the highest point of its spine a glass skylight has been installed. All the rays of light leaking into this attic enter from directly above one's head. And above one's head and separated by a single pane of glass is the great sky leading on to the whole world. Not a single particle obstructs the eye. It was Carlyle's own plan to build this room. He built it to turn it into his study. As a study, he shut himself away here. When he shut himself away he realized for the first time the drawbacks of his plan. This is an uncomfortable place to be in summer because of the heat and in winter because of the cold. The guide recites this much and looks back at me. Somewhere in that perfectly round face is a flicker of a smile. I nod without saying a word.

For what purpose did Carlyle trouble himself with this scheme of a room close to the sky? As his writing shows, he was somebody who had a touch of lightning about him. It seems his irritability did not allow him the luxury of serenely ignoring the noises that mercilessly surrounded him and absorbing himself in his books. The piano's voice, the dog's voice, the cocks' voices, the parrot's voice, every single voice affected his delicate nerves and inevitably caused him such extreme agony that in the end he was made to seek out a home in this third-floor attic as close to the sky and as far away from people as possible.

In a letter he sent to Mrs Aitken, he says:

All summer I have been annoyed with noises which get free access through my open windows: all the tinkering and repairing have done me no good in that respect. At length, after deep deliberation, I have fairly decided to have a top storey put upon the house, one big apartment, twenty feet square, with double walls, light from the top and artfully ventilated – and all the cocks in nature may crow around it, without my hearing a whisper of them!

The much anticipated study was completed at a cost of two hundred pounds, pretty much according to plan, and achieved the anticipated effect, but at the same time some unexpected difficulties once more occurred within earshot of our hero. Yes, the sound of the piano stopped, and the dog's voice stopped, and the cocks' voices and the parrot's voice became inaudible, but sounds not worth considering when on the lower levels, the church bells and the train's whistle, and unknown voices coming from the distant world below pursued him like a curse and tormented his nerves as of old.

Voices. The voices that tormented Carlyle in Britain are the voices that tormented Schopenhauer in Germany. Schopenhauer says:

Kant has written a treatise on *The Vital Powers*; but I should like to write a dirge on them, since their lavish use in the form of knocking, hammering and tumbling things about has made the whole of my life a daily torment. Certainly there are many people who will smile at this, because they are not sensitive to noise; it is precisely these people, however, who are not sensitive to argument, thought, poetry or art: a fact to be assigned to the coarse quality and strong texture of their brain tissues.

Carlyle and Schopenhauer are actually one of the nineteenth century's well-matched couples. While I am continuing to make these reflections, the woman prompts me with 'Well, shall we go downstairs?'

With each level we descend I have a feeling of approaching a lower world. It feels like a skin of meditation is peeling off. When I descend all the stairs and lean against the banister at the bottom and stare at the road, I have finally became an ordinary man as before. The guide looks indifferent but says, 'Please have a look at the kitchen.' The kitchen is beneath even the road. I must descend down another five or six steps from where I am now standing. This is the home of the woman who is guiding me. In a corner there is a large stove. The woman in her customary recitative style says, 'On 12 October 1844, when the famous poet Tennyson first visited Carlyle, they both sat facing one another in front of this stove and smoked tobacco together without exchanging a single word for two hours.' Did he who hated noise in the heavens love silence even when he went underground?

Finally I am guided from the back door into the garden. Looking around the customary square and flat ground, not even the slightest tree-like tree or plant-like plant is visible. According to the woman's account, in the past there were cherries and grapes. It seems there were also walnuts. Apparently Carlyle's wife one year obtained nearly sixpence worth of walnuts. The woman says, 'In the southeast corner of the garden, over five foot underground, Carlyle's pet dog Nero is buried. Nero died on 1 February 1860. A grave marker also existed at the time, but unfortunately it was subsequently removed.' She is certainly knowledgeable.

This is the garden where Carlyle, straw hat on the back of his head, still in his nightclothes and with a smoking pipe in his mouth, strolled around. This is the garden where, in the middle of summer, he pitched a small tent above the deeply shaded paving-stones and even brought his desk under it so that he could wholeheartedly occupy himself with his writings. This is the garden where on a starry night after taking one last puff of his pipe he looked up at the sky and cried out, 'Hah, in a little while I shall have seen you also for the last time. God Almighty's own Theatre of Immensity, the INFI-NITE made palpable and visible to me: that also will be closed, flung-to in my face, and I shall never behold that either any more. And I knew so little of it: real as was my effort and desire to know!'

To recompense the woman for her trouble I place a silver coin on the palm of her hand. Even the voice that says 'Thank you' is recita-tive. One hour later London's grime and soot and the sound of carriage horses and the river Thames divide me from Carlyle's home, which seems like a distinct world disappearing into the distance.

From *Short Pieces for Long Days* (1909)

Lodgings

THE first place I took lodgings was on high ground to the north of the city. A cosy two-storey, red-brick building took my fancy, so, paying a somewhat expensive two pounds a week, I rented a room at the back. Mr K, who was at that time the occupant of the front room, was presently touring Scotland and would not be back for a while, the landlady explained.

The landlady had sunken eyes, a turned-up nose, a sharp chin and cheeks; a face so severe and unfeminine it was impossible to judge her age. Perhaps some trait of peevishness, stubbornness or dull-wittedness, some prejudice or suspicion, or all such weaknesses combined had wreaked havoc with a gentle visage and turned it into such a perverse appearance, I reflected.

The landlady's black hair and black eyes were out of place in a northern country. Yet her speech was in no way different from any ordinary English person. On the day I moved in I was offered tea downstairs but upon descending discovered that none of the family was there. In the small north-facing dining-room the landlady and I sat alone facing one another. Surveying the gloomy, sunless room, I saw a forlorn daffodil arranged on the mantelpiece. The landlady offered me tea and toast and talked on a variety of subjects. Then, for some reason, she suddenly disclosed that she was not British but French. Turning her black eyes and looking at the daffodil placed in the glass bottle behind her, she told me that Britain was terribly cloudy and cold. She probably meant to imply that even the flowers here were not pretty.

I thought of the sadly drooping daffodil and the trickle of colourless blood pulsing across this woman's shrivelled cheeks and

倫敦塔

imagined what warm dreams they might have seen in distant France. Behind the landlady's black hair and black eyes was probably a sad history of a fragrant springtime that had vanished many years ago. She asked me if I spoke French, heading off any attempt to answer 'no' with a string of mellifluent southern words. It was such a beautiful accent that I wondered how it could have emerged from such a craggy throat.

That evening, at dinner time, a bald white-bearded old man appeared at the table. The landlady introduced him as her father, and so for the first time I became aware that the master of this house was an old man. The man had a strange way of speaking. One could immediately tell he was not English. Father and daughter must have crossed the Channel together and settled in London, I surmised. Then without my asking, the old man suddenly announced that he was German. 'Is that so?' I said, realizing I had misapprehended the situation somewhat.

When I returned to my room and opened my books, the father and daughter below strangely stayed in my thoughts. Comparing the old man with the bony-faced daughter, there was no resemblance whatsoever. His whole face was swollen with a pudgy, fleshy nose and two narrow eyes. There used to be a president in southern Africa called Kruger. The old man looked very like him. It is not a face that is pleasant to look at. Moreover, this man's way of speaking to his daughter was unpleasant. His teeth might no longer work, and he might mumble, but there was something rough in his manner. The daughter's stern face seemed only to intensify in the presence of her father. It was definitely no ordinary parent-and-child relationship. So thinking, I went to bed.

The next day, when I went down for breakfast, in addition to the father and daughter from last night there was another member of the family. The person present at the table was a fair-complexioned, attractive man of about forty. When I looked at this man's face from the entrance of the dining-room I felt for the first time that I was living amongst real human beings. The landlady introduced this man as 'my brother'. Unsurprisingly, it was not her husband. Yet their faces were so different that one would have never taken them for brother and sister.

That day I dined out for lunch and returned home at past three o'clock, but shortly after entering my room I was called down for tea. That day was also cloudy. When I opened the door of the gloomy dining-room the landlady was sitting on her own next to the stove with the tea things. She had lit the coal fire, so I felt somewhat cheered. I looked at her face lit up by the kindling flames and saw there was a little makeup lightly applied over her flushed cheeks. At the entrance to the room I fully appreciated the sadness of that makeup. She looked at me as if fully aware of the impression she gave. It was then I heard from her the family's history.

The landlady's mother had, some twenty-five years before, married a certain Frenchman and produced this daughter. After being together for a few years the husband died. Her mother now married a German, taking her daughter with her. This German was the old man from last night. He had opened a tailor's shop in the West End and commuted there every day. He had a son from a previous marriage working at the same shop, but relations between father and son were extremely poor. Even though they were living in the same household, they never spoke a word. The son always returned home late at night. At the front door he took off his shoes and crossed the corridor in his bare socks so that his father would not hear him entering his room and going to bed. The landlady had lost her mother a long time ago. At the time of her death her mother had repeatedly spoken concerning her daughter, but afterwards all the property passed into the hands of the father and she was left penniless. Her only option was to try to scrape together some money by taking in boarders. Agnes . . .

The landlady did not say any more. Agnes was the name of the girl of thirteen or fourteen who was working in the house. I then sensed there was a certain resemblance between the son's face I had seen that morning and Agnes. Just then Agnes appeared from the kitchen with the toast.

'Will you have some toast, Agnes?'

Agnes silently took a piece of toast and retreated to the kitchen. One month later I left this boarding-house.

The Smell of the Past

ABOUT two weeks before I left the boarding-house K returned from Scotland. The landlady then introduced me to him. Two Japanese accidentally bumping into one another in a small house in a London suburb is strange enough, but not having been introduced before and relying on the help of a foreign lady who knew nothing of our station, lineage and history in order to say 'Pleased to meet you' seems strange to me even now. At the time this old maid was wearing black clothes. Thrusting out her bony, emaciated hand, she said, 'Mr K, this is Mr N', and before she had even finished speaking stretched out her other hand and with 'Mr N, this is Mr K' impartially and equitably introduced us both.

The old maid's manner was so solemn and possessed of a formality so filled with a type of gravity that I was more than a little taken aback. Standing facing me, K wrinkled up the corners of his attractive double-set eyelids and smiled. Rather than smiling I felt a kind of sad incongruence. This is what it must feel like to have one's marriage ceremony brought about by the matchmaking of a ghost, I reflected, standing there. Everywhere the black shadow of this old maid moved seemed to lose its vitality and suddenly turn into a historical remnant. One could only imagine that if one was to inadvertently touch her flesh the blood of the person touching her would turn cold at that spot. I half turned my head to the woman's footsteps as they disappeared outside the door.

After she had gone, K and I suddenly became on friendly terms. His room was bedecked with a beautiful carpet, draped with white silk curtains and, as well as being furnished with an easy chair and a rocking-chair, also had a small separate bedroom. What was most pleasing was that he always kept his stove lit with an abundance of brightly burning coal.

From then on I made it a rule to drink tea with K in his room. At lunchtime we often went together to one of the local restaurants. K always paid the bill. He said he had come to investigate harbour construction or some such, and he had lots of money. In the house he looked extremely comfortable decked out in his maroon elegantly embroidered satin dressing-gown. I, in contrast, was still wearing the rather grimy clothes I had left Japan with and cut a shabby figure. K said enough is enough and lent me the money for some new clothes.

For two weeks, K and I chatted about a variety of things. He said, 'I'm going to form a Keio Cabinet!' The Cabinet would be apparently formed exclusively from people born in the Keio period and thus would be called the 'Keio Cabinet'. K asked me what year I was born in and, when I answered the third year of Keio, he laughed and said I qualified for the cabinet then. I seem to recall that he was born in the first or second year of Keio. If I had been born just a year later I would have lost the right to wield the reins of power with him.

While we were amusing ourselves with such conversations, gossip about the family below would occasionally arise. K would always frown and shake his head. He said he felt most sorry for the young girl Agnes. Agnes used to bring coal to K's room in the morning. In the afternoon she would bring tea, butter and toast. She silently brought them, put them down and left. Whenever you looked at her, her face was always pale and she greeted you only with large, moist eyes. She appeared like a shadow and disappeared like a shadow. Her footsteps never made a sound.

On one occasion I announced to K that the house was so unpleasant I was thinking of leaving. He agreed with me about the house, although adding that as he was flying hither and thither to do his research the house did not bother him, but cautioned that for someone like me it would be better to settle down in a more comfortable place and study. At that time he said he was going to cross to the other side of the Mediterranean and was busily making his arrangements for the trip.

When I came to leave the house, the old maid desperately implored me to stay. She said she would reduce the rent and even said that while K was away I could use his room, but I ended up moving south. At the same time K, too, went far away.

Two or three months later I suddenly received a letter from K. He had returned from his trip. He wrote that he would be around for a while, so I should come over and see him. I wanted to go straight away but for a variety of reasons did not have the time to travel that far north. About a week later I fortunately had reason to be in Islington and on the way back went around to K's.

Through the glass of the upstairs front windows I saw that the customary silk curtains had been drawn back. Looking forward to the warm stove, the maroon satin embroidery, the easy chair and K's lively account of his travels, I breezed through the gate and tapped the door knocker ready to race up the stairs. On the other side of the door I could not hear any footsteps, so, thinking I had perhaps not been heard, I was just about to put my hand to the knocker again when the door opened all on its own. I placed my foot over the threshold. Then my eyes met with those of Agnes, who was staring up at me apologetically. At that moment, in the middle of the narrow corridor the smell of my past boarding-house, which in the last three months or so I had forgotten, assailed my senses like a flash of lightning. Within that smell were encompassed all at once the black hair and the black eyes, the Kruger-like face, the son who resembled Agnes, Agnes like a shadow of the son, and the secrets lurking between them. When I caught this smell I clearly recognized in their emotions and behaviour, in their speech and complexions, a dark hell. I could not bear to go upstairs and meet K.

A Warm Dream

THE wind strikes the high buildings and, unable to pass directly through, turns in a flash and sweeps diagonally down towards the pavement. With my right hand I hold down my bowler-hat as I walk. In front of me a cabdriver is waiting for a fare. He seems to have watched this state of affairs from the driver's seat and, as I take my hand off my hat and correct my posture, he raises his index finger. It is the sign to say, 'Won't you get in?' I do not get in. The driver clenches his fist and strikes his chest ferociously. From five or six yards away I can still hear the beating sound. This is how London's cabbies warm themselves and their hands. I turn around and quickly look at the driver. Thick frosty hair bulges out from beneath his fraying hard hat. He draws back his right elbow inside a coarse brown coat that looks as if it has been patched together from blankets and, swinging his elbow around until it is parallel with his shoulders, he noisily beats his chest. It is like some kind of mechanical movement. I set off walking again.

Everyone going along the street overtakes me. Even the women do not fall behind. They lightly pick up their skirts behind the waist and hurry along, clattering the pavement so ferociously I wonder whether their high-heeled shoes will give way. If one looks closely, each and every face is pressed for time. The men look straight ahead; the women never look aside but intently run in one straight line in their desired direction. Their mouths are tightly shut. Their eyebrows are deeply set. Their noses are grimly raised up; their faces have repose only in profile. And their feet carry them in one sweep to their business. Their attitude seems to be that they cannot bear to walk the streets or endure being outside and must hide themselves away under a roof just as quickly as possible or suffer eternal shame.

As I slouch along, I feel somehow oppressed at being in this metropolis. When I look up, the great sky appears as though at some point in the past it has been partitioned by buildings soaring up like cliffs to right and left, with only a residual narrow band of sky left to traverse along from east to west. The colour of that band is from morning grey but little by little turns brown. The buildings are, of course, an ash colour. It is as though, having lost interest in warm sunlight, the buildings have simply blocked it out on both sides. The wide earth has been turned into shadows at the bottom of claustrophobic valleys, where second storeys have been piled on top of first storeys and third storeys on top of second storeys to prevent the high sun reaching down. Little people come and go along a section of the bottom, shivering in the blackness. I am the most inactive particle in the midst of those blackly moving objects. The wind, caught and trapped, scoops along the bottom of the valley as it passes through. Like small fish slipping out of the meshes of a net, the black objects scatter. Even a slowcoach such as myself is finally blown about by this wind, so I flee into one of the houses.

Winding around the long corridors and ascending two or three flights of stairs, there is a large door worked by springs. I slightly lean my body-weight against it and my body instantly, noiselessly, slides into the midst of a large gallery. Everything beneath my eyes is dazzlingly bright. When I turn around, the door has suddenly closed and I am in a place of spring-like warmth. To accustom my eyes to the light, I momentarily blink. Then I look around. There are lots of people everywhere. But everyone is quietly composed. Every single face appears relaxed. There are so many people here, yet there is absolutely no sense of discomfort despite their numbers. Everyone is at ease with one another. I look up. Above me is a large vaulted ceiling voluptuously coloured and appealing to the eye, brilliantly gleaming in awe-inspiring, resplendent gold leaf. I look ahead of me. The space ahead ends in a handrail. Beyond the handrail there is nothing at all, a big hole. I approach the handrail, slightly tilt my head over and peer inside the hole. Far below me is filled with little people seemingly painted into a picture. Notwithstanding their numbers, they stand out brilliantly. This is what they call a human sea: white, black, yellow, blue, purple, red, every bright colour imaginable, like ripples on a great ocean, crowded together on the bottom far below and, like an assemblage of multi-coloured scales, faintly, prettily, wriggling about.

Then this wriggling mass suddenly disappears, and, from the great ceiling down into the valley bottom far below, everything becomes dark. There are many thousands of people here, but now they are buried in darkness, not a single voice is heard. It is as though every single person's existence has been extinguished in this great darkness, and both shadow and form are no longer, and it is totally quiet. And yet, far below, a section to the front, cut out into a square, seems raised up in the midst of the darkness, and has suddenly started to faintly brighten. At first, I think it is just a different shade of darkness, but little by little it becomes increasingly less dark. By the time I have ascertained that it is indeed being softly lit, I have made out in the midst of the fog-like light some turbid colours, yellow, purple and indigo. The yellow and purple finally begin to move. I screw up both eyes, straining my senses, and unblinkingly stare at these moving objects. The haze suddenly clears beneath my eyes. Far below, beholding a sea glowing warmly in bright light, a handsome man wearing a yellow coat and a woman in long, purple sleeves are clearly visible on green grass. The woman sits down on a marble bench placed below an olive tree, while the man stands beside her and looks down at her from above. Enticed by a warm breeze blowing from the south, soft strains of music waft in from across distant waves.

The top of the hole and the bottom of the hole all at once begin to stir. The people have not disappeared into the midst of the darkness. They are watching in the darkness a dream of warm Greece.

Impression

WHEN I step outside, a wide street passes straight along in front of the house. Standing in the middle of the street and surveying everything around me, every house is four-storeyed and the same colour. The houses next door and the ones opposite are so similar in construction as to make them almost indistinguishable. If I was to proceed four or five yards and then turn back, it would be impossible to know out of which house I've just emerged. This is a strange street.

Last night I slept encircled by the noise of trains. Some time after ten o'clock I raced through the darkness as if in a dream, sped on by the sounds of horses' hoofs and bells. Hundreds of beautifully lit shadows grazed my eyes, but otherwise I saw nothing. This is the first time I have looked around.

I stand looking up and down this strange street two or three times and then turn left, walk about a hundred yards and emerge at a crossroads. I make a mental note and turn right into an even wider road than before. A lot of buses pass along this road. All of them are carrying people on the roof. The colours of these buses incessantly overtaking me are red, yellow, green, brown and blue. I peer into the distance but cannot discern how far the colours continue. When I look behind me, they are moving towards me like multi-coloured clouds. I stop to consider where it is they are taking people to and from but am overwhelmed by a tall person pushing me from behind. I try to get out of his way only to discover another tall person to my right. And to my left. The people pushing me from behind are in turn being pushed by the people behind them. And everyone is silent. And everyone moves spontaneously forward.

I am suddenly conscious of having drowned in a human sea.

How wide that sea as, I have no idea. But, despite its width, it is an extremely quiet sea. Yet it offers no escape. If I turn to the right, the way is blocked. If I look to the left, the way is closed. Even if I turn around, it is full of people. So I quietly move forward. As if governed by a single fate, tens of thousands of black heads have seemingly agreed to proceed forward in synchronicity one step at a time.

As I walk along, I recall the house I have just left. The strange street, with the same four storeys and the same colour everywhere, seems somehow distant. I feel like I would have no idea where I should turn and which way I should walk to get home. Even if I did get back I probably would not be able to pick out my own house. Last night the house had stood in the midst of utter darkness.

Feeling somewhat forlorn and pushed on by the tall crowds, I am forced to turn two or three times on to other wide streets. Every time I turn I have the feeling of moving in the opposite direction to the dark house from last night and feel an unspeakable loneliness amidst crowds of people so numerous as to strain my eyes. I emerge on to a gentle hill. This seems to be a square where six or seven large roads come together. The waves, having until now moved forward as one, converge at the bottom of the hill with those collected from many other directions, and quietly begin to rotate.

At the base of the hill, there are some large lions carved out of stone. Their whole bodies are ashen. They have slender tails, but their deep-set heads are enswirled in their manes, like twenty-gallon barrels. Front legs together, they are sleeping in the midst of crowds pulsing in waves around them. There are two lions. The ground beneath them is covered with paving stones, with a thick copper column in the centre. Standing amidst the quietly moving sea of humanity, I lift my eyes and look at the top of the column. The column stands tall and straight as far as my eyes can reach. Above it the great sky is completely visible. The tall column soars up as if piercing through the very centre of this sky. What is at the top of this column, I do not know. I am again pushed along by a human wave out of the square and, not knowing where, descend a road on the right-hand side. When, after a while, I look back, I see that, on top of the slender pole-like column, a small person is standing alone.

Fog

LAST night, throughout the night, I heard a pattering echo above my pillow. This is thanks to having the great station of Clapham Junction in the neighbourhood. In the course of a single day, over a thousand trains crowd into this junction. If one tries minutely dividing that, it means that about one train comes and goes here every minute. In times of deep fog, each train signals that it is on the brink of entering the station by contriving to raise a firecracker-like noise. It is so dark that the signal lights, whether showing green or red, are completely useless.

Getting out of bed and rolling up the blind on the north window, I look down outside and see everything is hazy. From the bottom of the lawn below to the tops of the brick walls over six feet high that surround it on three sides, nothing is visible. Only a total emptiness clogs the air. And that is silently frozen. Next door's garden is exactly the same. In this garden there is a pretty lawn, and in the warm days of early spring a white-bearded old man appears to bask in the sun. On those occasions the old man will always be carrying a parrot on his right hand. He will bring his eyes to within pecking range of its beak. The parrot will flap its wings and shriek continuously. When the old man is not there, his daughter, trailing a long skirt behind her, is always running a lawnmower over the grass. Now this garden, so rich in memories, is also buried in fog, and between it and the unkempt garden of my own boarding-house there is no boundary, as one seamlessly fuses into the other.

Across the way, on the far side of the back street, there is the spire of a Gothic church. From the grey of this spire, at the topmost point that pierces the sky, bells ring the hour. They are particularly noisy on a Sunday. Today, of course, not only can one not make out the sharply pointed peak but even the whereabouts of the main body of the church, made up of irregular sections of hewn stone, are obscure. Is that it? I wonder, looking at a place that seems a little black, but the sounds of the bells are completely silent. They are deeply sealed in the depths of a dense fog where the shapes of bells are invisible.

When I go outside only about four yards ahead is visible. When one proceeds four yards, another four yards ahead becomes visible. I walk along wondering whether the world has shrunk to four yards square, and the more I walk the more a new four yards square appears. In its place, the world I have walked through passes into the past and continuously disappears.

While I am waiting for the bus at the crossroads, the head of a horse suddenly cuts through the grey air and appears before my eyes. Yet the people on the top of the bus still fail to emerge from the fog. Braving the fog, I jump on and look down, but the horse's head has already become slightly hazed. When the bus comes across another vehicle, I think at that moment how pretty the scene is. But in an instant the coloured object disappears into the middle of the turbid emptiness. It is enveloped in the middle of a vast colourlessness. As I cross Westminster Bridge, a white object flaps fleetingly once or twice past my eyes. Straining my eyes and carefully looking out in that direction I dimly see in the middle of the stifling air a gull dreamily flying by. At that moment Big Ben starts solemnly striking ten o'clock. When I look up there is only sound in the emptiness.

Finishing my business at Victoria I come along the river by the side of the Tate Gallery as far as Battersea, and the world that has appeared grey until now suddenly turns dark on four sides. Like thick liquefied peat washing around my body, the heavy, black-stained fog has started to assail my eyes and mouth and nose. My coat is so damp I wonder whether something has been pressed down on it. As if inhaling light arrowroot gruel, my breathing is suffocated. My feet, of course, feel as if they are treading along the bottom of a pit.

I blankly pause for a while in the middle of this oppressive murkiness. I have the feeling that hordes of people are passing by my side. But so long as they do not rub shoulders with me I am actually unsure whether people are going past me or not. At that moment a pulse of yellow light the size of a pea dully appears at a single point in this ocean of haziness. With this as a target I move forward about four paces. When I do so, a face appears in front of a glass shop window. Inside the shop, gaslights are burning. The inside is comparatively bright. People are acting as normal. I finally breathe a sigh of relief.

Passing beyond Battersea, almost groping my way, I direct my feet towards a nearby hill, but at the top it is all private residences. Quite a few seemingly identical streets run parallel, and would be easy to confuse even on a clear day. I feel that I have crossed and turned into the second road on the left. After that I feel I have walked on for a couple of hundred yards. After that I have absolutely no idea. In the middle of the darkness I stand totally alone and tilt my head. From the right the sound of shoes approaches. Or so I think, but when they come to within eight or ten yards away they stop. Then they gradually move away. In the end they become completely inaudible; after that, everything is silent. I am again standing all alone thinking in the darkness. How can I get back to the boarding-house?

Long Ago

THE Vale of Pitlochry is deep into autumn. People go to bed and rise in the midst of fields and woods tinged everywhere a warm colour by the October sun. High in the sky, the sun envelopes the air of the quiet valley but does not directly descend to earth. Yet nor does it flee across the mountains. Above the windless village it is always calm and hazy and perfectly unmoving. And so the colours of the fields and woods gradually begin to change. Like something bitter suddenly turning into something sweet, the whole valley acquires a patina of age. The Vale of Pitlochry returns to the past of a hundred years ago, to the past of two hundred years ago, and gently mellows. Everyone turns world-ripened faces to look at the clouds passing over the backs of the mountains. Those clouds are sometimes white and sometimes grey. From their thin bottom one may occasionally see the earth of the mountains. Whenever one looks, one senses that these are old clouds.

My house stands on top of a small hill, well suited for gazing at the clouds and the valley. From the south the sun shines over all the walls of the house. Perhaps because of long years of exposure to the October sun, on the western side, where everything has a patina of grey, a single rose bush has begun to creep, inserting some flowers between the cold wall and the warm sun. The large petals undulate luxuriantly in yellow, fluttering from the calyxes with open mouths, everywhere perfectly silent. Their scent, absorbed by weak sunlight, disappears into the air four yards around. I stand within those four yards and look at the top of the rose bush creeping high up along the wall. Beyond where the rose tendrils have yet to reach, the grey wall soars directly upwards. Where the roof ends there is a tower. The sun descends from the midst of the haze still higher above.

At my feet the hill sinks into the Vale of Pitlochry, and everything I see far below is uniformly filled with colour. Rising up the opposite mountain, the yellow birch leaves overlap one on top of another, creating many shaded inclines. The whole bright valley reflects a sense of age, and, in its centre, a black line meanders along. The valley's peaty water, as if dissolved in dye, has turned an old colour. It is the first time I have seen this stream since coming into the midst of these mountains.

The master of the house approaches me from behind. His beard has been caught in the light of the October sun and seven-tenths of it has started to turn white. His dress, too, is unusual. Around his waist he is wearing something called a kilt. It is a cloth of large stripes like the rugs one puts over one's knees in a rickshaw. This is worn as a skirt, cut off at the kneecaps and with vertical pleats added so that the calves are covered only with stockings of thick wool. When walking the kilt's pleats sway and the area between knees and thighs fleetingly appears. It is a skirt belonging to a time long ago when no shame was attached to the colour of flesh.

A fur pouch about the size of a small drum dangles in front of him. Bringing his chair over to the side of the hearth of an evening and staring at the crackling red coal, he takes out his pipe and his tobacco from inside this drum. Then, puffing away, he smokes into the night. The drum's name is a sporran.

Descending the precipice with the master of the house, we come into a shaded path. Like clouds trailing over strands of kelp, it seems that the evergreen leaves of Scotch pine will not disappear even if brushed away. A squirrel waving its long thick tail flits about, racing up a black trunk. Meanwhile, on the old, thickened moss another squirrel quickly scampers out of sight. The moss is fulsome and unmoving. The squirrel's tale swishingly rubs the deeply green earth and enters the dark.

He turns to one side and points to Pitlochry's bright valley. The black river is as ever flowing across the centre. Four miles up river to the north, he tells me, there is the Pass of Killiecrankie.

When the Highlanders and Lowlanders fought at the Pass of Killiecrankie, the dead bodies were jammed amongst the rocks and blocked the water striking the rocks. Drinking the blood of Highlanders and Lowlanders, the river's stream changed colour for three days as it passed through the Vale of Pitlochry.

I resolve to visit the ancient battlefield of Killiecrankie early the next morning. And when I emerge from the precipice two or three beautiful rose petals are scattered beneath my feet.

Professor Craig

PROFESSOR Craig is nestled like a swallow on the third floor. Standing on the edge of the pavement and looking up, not even his windows are visible. Slowly climbing up, just as my thighs have become a little sore, I finally arrive at the professor's chambers. Although I say chambers, it is not as if there is a portico, just a black door, scarcely three feet wide with a brass knocker hanging down. After pausing to catch my breath, I knock on the door and it opens from the inside.

It is always a woman who opens the door. Perhaps because of short-sightedness she wears glasses and seems constantly startled. Her age is about fifty, so one may assume that she has been looking at and living in the world for quite some time, but she still seems startled. As if sorry for my having had to knock on the door, she makes big eyes and says, 'Come in.'

As soon as I enter, the woman disappears. The first room is a drawing-room . . . although at first I did not think it was a drawing-room. It is not especially decorous or anything. There are just two windows and rows upon rows of books. This is where Professor Craig is usually ensconced. When he sees me enter, he says hello and proffers his hand. This being the sign to shake hands, I go through the motions and grasp his hand, even though my own hand is never grasped in return. Since I, too, do not feel particularly comfortable about shaking hands, it would seem all the more reason for us both not to bother, but, nevertheless, after saying hello the professor offers his hairy, wrinkled and invariably retiring hand. Customs are a strange thing.

The owner of this hand is the tutor to whom I address my questions. When we first met, I asked about his fee, and he said, 'Hmm . . .', and, after briefly looking out the window, 'What about seven shillings a time?' If that was too much he did not mind giving me a reduction, he said. So I settled on paying a rate of seven shillings a time, the whole fee payable at the end of each month, but then unexpectedly found myself being occasionally pressed for payment by the professor. 'I am slightly short of money, so I was wondering whether you might be able to pay today?' he would say. 'Certainly,' I would respond, taking some coins out of my trouser pocket and unceremoniously handing them over. Saying, 'Many thanks', he accepted them by opening his as-ever-retiring hand and taking a brief look at them on his palm before finally putting them into his trouser pocket. To my discomfort, the professor never issues any change. Any hope that the surplus might be carried over to next month is dashed when the next week he importunes me with, 'Now, there are a few books I wish to buy so I was wondering . . .'

The professor is Irish, so his words are totally incomprehensible. When he becomes excited his words are as difficult to understand as a row between someone from Tokyo with someone from Satsuma. Moreover, he is an extremely absent-minded, easily excitable man, so, when things become too complicated, I simply resign myself to fate and watch the professor's face.

That face, too, is far from ordinary. Being a Westerner, he has a prominent nose, but it is indented and overly fleshy. In that respect it well resembles my own, but at first sight this nose does not give rise to any kind of pleasant feeling. Instead it is all out of sorts and somewhat rustic. His black-and-white beard is woefully overgrown. Once, when I bumped into the professor on Baker Street, I thought it was a cabman who had forgotten his whip.

I have never once seen the professor dressed in a white shirt and white cuffs. He always wears striped flannel, with fluffy slippers on his feet, and sticks out his feet, even inserting them into the middle of the stove, and sometimes taps his short knees – once when he did so I noticed for the first time that the professor wore a gold ring on his retiring hand – and sometimes, instead of tapping his knees, he rubs his thighs as he teaches me. Of course, what he is teaching me about I have no idea. As I listen, the subject is led remorselessly by the professor's fancy. And the professor's fancy is constantly changing like the changing of the seasons and the weather. It sometimes swings from one extreme to another from one day to the next. If I was to be cruel, I might say it is all nonsense, but, if I look on it positively, I might say he is providing literary conversation, and, when I think about it now, I realize that it is hardly possible to have comprehensive, methodical lectures for seven shillings a time. So in that respect the professor was right and it was I, who was inwardly grumbling about it, who was being stupid. Of course, the professor's mind, as illustrated by his beard, seems to incline somewhat towards disorder, so on the other hand, perhaps it is for the best that I did not raise his fee and ask him to provide grandiose lectures.

The professor's speciality is poetry. When reading poetry, the area from his face to his shoulders oscillates like a haze of heat . . . Yes, it actually oscillates. Instead of reading to me, he tends to forget my presence and reads to himself, so ultimately it is my loss. Once, when I brought along something by Swinburne called *Rosamund*, the professor said, 'Let me see', but after reading out two or three lines he suddenly placed the book down on his knee, deliberately removed his glasses and let out a sigh, saying, 'Ah, no, it's no good, Swinburne, too, has become too old to write this kind of poem.' It was at this time that I conceived of reading Swinburne's master-piece, *Atalanta*.

The professor thinks of me as a child. 'Have you heard of this?', 'Do you understand that?', he repeatedly asks me regarding trivial things. Yet, without any warning, he flits to treating me as an equal and suddenly presents me with a very difficult question. Once he read in front of me a poem by Watson and asked, 'There are some people who say this has points of similarity to Shelley and some people who say it is completely different, but what do you think?' What did I think? Unless I had first scrutinized a Western poem with my eyes before listening to it, it was completely incomprehensible to me, so I gave a perfunctory response. Whether I said there was a resemblance to Shelley or not, I have now forgotten. But, strangely, the professor then tapped his knee again and said, 'I think so, too', leaving me feeling greatly embarrassed.

Once he put his head out the window and, looking down at the people busily passing by in the world far below, said, 'So many people walk by, but sadly there is not one person in a hundred amongst them who appreciates poetry. Actually the English are a nation incapable of comprehending poetry. In that respect the Irish are remarkable. They are infinitely more cultured . . . In fact, we must say that you and I are blessed in being able to savour poetry.' I was extremely grateful for being included in the company of those who can appreciate poetry, but generally his treatment of me is extremely cold. From this professor I have never once observed any type of affection. He simply seems to be an old man talking entirely mechanically.

But then the following thing happened. The boarding-house I was in became extremely irksome to me, so, thinking I might be able to be put up at the professor's place, I waited until our lesson had finished one day and broached the matter with him. The professor immediately tapped his knee and said, 'I see. Come along and I will

倫
敦
塔

show you the rooms here', and I was shown around pretty much all the rooms from the dining-room to the maid's room and kitchen. Of course, as this place was on a corner of the third floor it was not spacious. After two or three minutes I had seen everything there was to be seen. The professor then returned to his original seat, and just as I thought he was about to say, 'You see, there is no way I could put you up anywhere', he immediately started talking about Walt Whitman. 'Many years ago Whitman came and stayed with me for a while' – he spoke extremely quickly, so I did not entirely understand him, but in any case it does seem that Whitman visited – 'At first, when I read his poems, I felt that they did not add up to much, but rereading them many times, they gradually grew on me, and in the end I became extremely fond of them. So . . .'

The business of putting up his student seemed to have been completely forgotten somewhere. I just went with the flow saying, 'Hmm, really', as I listened. He was now talking about how Shelley had apparently once had an argument with someone. 'Arguments are unfortunate, and I like both of them, and having two people I like arguing is extremely unfortunate,' he said, lodging his protest. However much he protested, since they had their argument many decades ago, there was not much he could do about it now.

The professor is careless, so he often misplaces his own books. And when he cannot find one, he gets into a great fluster and calls out in a tumultuous voice, as if a small fire or something has broken out, to the old lady in the kitchen. At which the old woman, with an equally tumultuous face, appears in the drawing-room.

'Where have you put my Wordsworth?'

The old woman makes saucers of her as-ever startled eyes and looks around the bookshelves, but, despite being startled, her eyes are acute and they immediately alight upon the Wordsworth. Saying, 'Here, sir', she then thrusts it in front of the professor as if slightly chiding him. He snatches it from her and, tapping the dirty cover with two fingers, launches into, 'Now, Wordsworth . . .' The woman makes increasingly startled eyes and retreats into the kitchen. The professor taps Wordsworth for two or three minutes. But, in the end, the Wordsworth he has gone to all the trouble of searching for remains unopened.

The professor sometimes sends me letters. The handwriting is totally illegible. Of course, they comprise only two or three lines, so I have the time to look repeatedly at them but never remotely come to any conclusion on them. If a letter comes from the professor, I decide from the outset to avoid the trouble of reading it and conclude that something must have cropped up and he cannot hold our lesson. Occasionally the startled old woman writes letters for him. On these occasions I have absolutely no problem understanding them. The professor, fortunately, possesses a handy secretary. He sighs to me that his handwriting is hopeless. He tells me that my handwriting is infinitely better.

I am concerned to know what manuscripts could be produced by such handwriting. The professor is an editor of the Arden Shakespeare. I think his handwriting can hardly qualify for being transformed into print. The professor, nevertheless, happily writes introductions and prides himself on the notes he appends. Moreover, after being told, 'Read this introduction', I was once made to read the introduction he had appended to *Hamlet*. When I next went to see him I said it was interesting, and he petitioned me to help introduce the book when I returned to Japan. The Arden Shakespeare's *Hamlet* is a book from which I would derive an enormous profit when giving university lectures after returning home. I think there is probably nothing as scrupulous and sensible as these notes on *Hamlet*. But, at the time, I was not so impressed. But I had even before then been amazed by the professor's research on Shakespeare.

Forming an L-shape with the drawing-room, there is a small study. The place high up where the professor has nestled himself is in fact a corner of a third floor, and in a corner of that corner there is to the professor an important treasure. Perhaps ten blue-covered notebooks around eighteen inches in length and a foot in width are on display. The professor constantly writes in the blue-covered books words he has written on scraps of paper and, like a miser storing away small coins, makes the incremental increase of their contents his lifetime's pleasure. I learned shortly after first coming here that these blue-covered books were the manuscript for a Shakespeare dictionary. In order to compile this dictionary, the professor has apparently given up a chair in literature at a certain university in Wales and made the time to go to the British Museum every day. Since he has even given up a university chair, it is hardly likely that he would pay much respect to a seven-shilling student. Morning and night this dictionary is the sole preoccupation of the professor's mind.

'Professor, why are you going ahead with such a work when there is already Schmidt's *Shakespeare Lexicon*?' I once asked him. At which the professor, seemingly unable to contain his contempt, said, 'Look at this', and showed me his own edition of Schmidt. I saw that each page of the two volumes had been turned completely black. I gasped and looked in surprise at the Schmidt. The professor looked exultant. 'If I was going to produce something of the same standard as Schmidt, would there be any need to go to all this trouble?' he said, and again began tapping two fingers, this time on the totally black Schmidt.

'When on earth did you begin all this?'

The professor stood up and went to the opposite bookshelf and started earnestly looking for something, but in his usual fretful voice shouted, 'Jane, Jane, what's happened to my Dowden?' He was asking the old woman about the whereabouts of the Dowden even before she appeared. Again startled, the woman did appear. She then chided him with her usual 'Here, sir' and went back, but the professor seemed completely indifferent to her words and, hungrily opening the book, said, 'Yes, here it is. Dowden has rightly included my name here. He writes of Mr Craig, a specialist in Shakespeare studies. This book was published in 187—, and my research is from much earlier than that.' I marvelled at the professor's perseverance. I took the opportunity to ask him when it would be finished. 'I have no idea,' he said, putting the Dowden back in its former place. 'I will just do as much as I can before I die.'

Shortly after that I stopped going to the professor's house. A little while before I stopped, the professor asked me whether they had any need for a Western professor at a Japanese university. 'If I was younger, I would go over,' he said, with a somewhat wistful expression. This was the only time any sentiment had crept into the professor's face. I consoled him by saying that he was still young, but he said, 'No, no, something might happen to me at any time. I am already fifty-six', and he became strangely downcast.

Two years after I returned to Japan an article appeared in a newly arrived literary magazine saying that Mr Craig had died. There were just two or three lines appended, saying that he was a specialist in Shakespeare studies. I put the magazine down and wondered whether that dictionary had ultimately been left unfinished and ended up as wastepaper.

Appendix
'The Yellow Lodger' by Yamada Futaro

Soseki's multifarious stories about Britain have had wide-ranging influences. In order to research the historical background to the stories, a stream of Japanese scholars have travelled to London and published a cornucopia of books enquiring into every aspect of Soseki's life there. The critic Hirakawa Sukehiro in particular has written extensively about the life of William Craig, a scholar now almost entirely unknown in the West but well known to lovers of Soseki's works in Japan. Thanks to such research, it is probably no exaggeration to say that many aspects of the London of 1900–2 are better known to Japanese scholars than to their British counterparts.

The Carlyle House in Chelsea, otherwise a largely forgotten shrine to a mostly unread British writer, receives to this day a disproportionate number of Japanese visitors lured to it by Soseki's mystical description. The visitors are intrigued to discover a house identical in every detail – from the comically small bath on the second floor to the eerie death mask in the soundproofed third-floor study – to how it is described in Soseki's story. By uncomfortable irony, a ghostly shrine to Soseki himself now exists across the river in the form of the Soseki Museum on the Chase, off Clapham Common, privately funded by the Soseki enthusiast Tsumematsu Ikuo. Comprising an upstairs flat directly opposite the house that was once Soseki's fourth and final boarding-house, it is kitted out with a variety of period memorabilia. Visitors are almost all Japanese.

Soseki's accounts of Britain have also had resonances beyond Japanese shores. The great modern Chinese writer Lu Xun was a student in the northern Japanese city of Sendai at the time when Soseki was first publishing his novels and stories in the *Asahi*

倫
敦
塔

newspaper. Although not impressed by other Japanese writers, Lu Xun was an avid reader of Soseki and specifically bought the *Asahi* to read his stories. Many years after returning to China, Lu Xun translated the story 'Professor Craig' into Chinese in the 1920s (one of only two Soseki pieces Lu Xun translated) and modelled his own memoir of his tutor in Sendai on Soseki's piece. Appropriately, Lu Xun's own memoir, 'Professor Fujino', was quickly translated into Japanese and from the 1930s has been widely read in both China and Japan.

In more recent years, Japanese author Yamada Futaro (1922–2001) has found inspiration from Soseki's British stories in an entirely different capacity. As one of Japan's most popular writers of detective stories and historical fiction, he regularly wove playful portraits of Japanese literary figures into his historical novels (even presenting Soseki as a small boy in one instance). Futaro was quick to notice that, at the same time as Soseki was attending classes with Professor Craig, not far away a certain detective by the name of Sherlock Holmes was said to be living at number 221b Baker Street. Cleverly drawing together aspects of Soseki's London memoirs and intertwining them with elements from the classic Sherlock Holmes stories, Futaro was able to spin an intriguing detective fantasy. Taking its place alongside modern pastiche novels which have, variously, sent Sherlock Holmes to Vienna to consult with Sigmund Freud or else involved him with the murders of Jack the Ripper or *The Strange Case of Dr Jekyll and Mr Hyde*, Futaro's fantasy centred on the question: what if Britain's master detective had run across a certain Japanese in London . . . ?

The Yellow Lodger

'WATSON, you haven't forgotten *The Macbeth Murder Case*, have you?'

'I remember it well. As you strictly forbade me from making it public, saying it's too commonplace, I have refrained from doing so, but I really don't understand your point of view. What on earth was there commonplace about that case?'

'Wasn't it commonplace? Carrying a corpse inside a large trunk; having a criminal disguise himself with a black beard and black glasses; having a scheme for five serial killings and the third one who received only a heavy wound, wasn't killed and was the only survivor turn out to be the criminal . . . Isn't it all quite nauseatingly obvious?'

'Yet I never imagined in that case that when the criminal prophesied, using those Shakespearian lines, "None of woman born has strength to kill" or "Until the wood moves you will never be vanquished", that the words held such a deep double meaning. Actually I didn't know that you were such a scholar of Shakespeare's plays and on that point alone reappraised you.'

'My dear fellow, you hold me too cheap. But then, according to the list of my peculiarities introduced by you in *A Study in Scarlet*, my literary knowledge is practically zero, so I suppose it's only to be expected. Yet I must confess that my knowledge was actually due to having received instruction from a certain obscure Shakespearian scholar. That is, Professor Craig, whom we are now on our way to visit.'

Looking at my notebook, I see this is a certain Tuesday evening in early May 1901.

倫
敦
塔

Having set out from my home on Queen Anne Street and called around to Baker Street after a long absence, I had found that Sherlock Holmes was just about to go out somewhere so immediately set off with him on to the streets of London. Gas lights, hazy like the moon, were already lit in the fog.

Holmes continued to talk along the way.

'You see, Professor Craig was originally a professor of literature at a certain university in Wales. Wanting the time to commute to the British Museum every day in order to compile a Shakespeare dictionary, he abandoned his chair and nestled himself like a swallow on a certain third floor of Homer Street. It seems he gets an income by giving personal tuition to foreign students, but, as far as Shakespeare is concerned, his scholarship is extremely profound. And yet . . .'

With a sigh Holmes looked at a letter held up to the street light. 'I am amazed at the clumsiness of his writing. I can never make out what he has written. It is a puzzle greater than the ciphers of "The Dancing Men" case of two or three years ago. After over an hour fiddling with this letter, what do you think I was able to decipher? Some anecdote related at great length about how Thomas Carlyle also had extremely bad handwriting.'

'Eh? That was all that was in the letter?'

'Naturally, there was a little something added at the end that seemed to be a request for assistance in a case. Apparently a rich man who lives next door disappeared about a fortnight ago and has gone missing, but it is not the type of case I would tend to get involved in. If the sender had not been Professor Craig I would, of course, have turned it down.'

Arriving at Homer Street, we entered a red brick building and climbed the stairs to the third floor. Tapping the brass knocker hanging on a black door scarcely three feet wide, an old lady with glasses perched over big, startled eyes peered out from inside.

'Jane. Good evening. Is Professor Craig at home? I wonder if you would tell him that Mr Holmes is here.'

Jane retired and then appeared again, and, escorted by her, we passed straight away into the drawing-room. Although I say drawing-room, it is not as if there was anything particularly decorous about it. Just two windows and row upon row of books.

A visitor was already there, and Professor Craig was speaking to the man in a loud voice. Professor Craig looked as if he cared little for personal appearance and was wearing terribly worn-out striped flannels and fluffy slippers. All around the pince-nez resting on his large fleshy nose was a shaggily unkempt black-and-white beard.

'You are amazed by how many people there are in London, but amongst them there is not one in a thousand who understands poetry. How pitiful they are. Actually there is no nation so incapable of understanding poetry as the English. In that respect the Irish are far more advanced. I, or an Oriental like you, are truly blessed in being able to savour poetry. And yet I wonder why you don't see that Wordsworth is more profound than Tennyson? Many years ago when I lived with Whitman for a while . . .'

Besides his inflections bearing a strong Irish accent, he spoke in a flustered manner and frighteningly quickly, and, into the bargain, his narrative was a little incoherent, so I had no idea what he was talking about.

The visitor did indeed appear Oriental, a small yellow-coloured man of thirty-four or thirty-five with a pointed moustache and slight pockmarks on the end of his nose. He stood frowning at the spittle flying furiously out of the professor's mouth.

Holmes whispered to me in a low voice.

'Looks like a Chinaman.'

'No, I am Japanese,' the yellow-coloured man suddenly said in a sharp voice as he turned towards us.

That his inadvertent *faux pas* should have been caught by such keen ears and that, most unusually, his observation should have been mistaken caused even Holmes to blush to the ears.

'Ah, my apologies, although one rarely tends to see a person from Japan, to mistake a person of the country which even tomorrow

倫敦塔

might conclude an offensive and defensive alliance with the British Empire. Well, on the recent birth of the first imperial grandchild, congratulations. According to this morning's newspaper, it seems he has been named Hirohito, I believe. To the only nation to have been able to cause Sherlock Holmes embarrassment from the outset, eternal prosperity!'

So concluding, Holmes wiped away the sweat with a handkerchief and a sigh of relief. I had never seen Holmes this flustered, so could hardly refrain from laughing. The yellow-coloured Japanese man also appeared to slightly wrinkle up the sides of his slightly pockmarked nose and smile.

Startled that his talk should have been interrupted and seeming to notice us for the first time, Professor Craig extended a ring-adorned hand and, shaking hands said, 'Ah, thank you for coming. This is a Japanese student, Mr Jujube . . .'

'Mister . . . ?'

'Jujube . . . or "Natsume" as they say in Japanese. Still a little unripe and yellow, though!'

Professor Craig appeared to be greatly amused by his own joke and burst into high peals of laughter, but the Japanese man, Mr Natsume, looked neither amused nor sad but stood with an expressionless countenance.

'This is Mr Sherlock Holmes, a private investigator famous throughout London.'

Mr Natsume started to extend his hand towards Holmes but then, as if taking offence at something, suddenly withdrew his hand and abruptly turned the other way. Holmes's pride looked hurt, but, after nonchalantly turning towards the professor and introducing me, he said, 'Right then, shall we proceed to hearing about the case in question?'

'The case?'

Professor Craig looked at us with a puzzled expression but then suddenly tapped his knee.

'Oh, that's right. That's why I called you. The fact is that about a fortnight ago Mr James Phillimore from next door went off some-where holding a black umbrella and completely vanished.'

'That's what we learned from your letter. This Mr Phillimore, what type of person is he?'

'That I don't really know. Though from the window there one may look down over Phillimore's large garden. He is an extremely rich man.

'I hear that when he was young and penniless he went over to work in Hong Kong and Taiwan and amassed a vast fortune and, after returning home, became involved in trade connected with the Orient but then, about five years ago, retired here to Homer Street. He seems to be highly eccentric. Despite being such a wealthy man, he is extraordinarily miserly and for domestic help makes use of only a single manservant. I have also sometimes seen Mr Phillimore strolling around the garden. He looks like a really old, thin man, with a crooked-back, large round glasses and a scruffy goatee, not at all like one whom one would think of as being so rich.'

As Professor Craig himself was more than a little eccentric, and as he was also an old man who was not exactly far from being scruffy, Holmes nodded with a flicker of a smile.

'Then, about a fortnight ago, he set off for the quayside with his manservant Klopman and has been missing ever since. It has of course been reported to the police, but so far there has been no promising news. Whereupon his manservant Klopman, being especially anxious about him, came to consult with me. You see, this Klopman fellow is always coming in and out of my place about some peculiar business. Indeed the history of Mr Phillimore I have just related is something I heard from him, and when I say that . . . ah, but here he is! It sounds like Klopman himself is here!' Professor Craig exclaimed, turning his ears in the direction of the door.

The sound of footsteps ascending the stairs and the wheezing sound of shortness of breath were indeed audible.

I, however, noticed that midway through Professor Craig's story Sherlock Holmes had been constantly glancing in the direction of the yellow-coloured Oriental. He for some reason looked extremely ill at ease and restless. His face had turned pale and on his forehead droplets of sweat had appeared, but, whenever he met Holmes's eyes, he recoiled towards the window as if taken aback and pretended to gaze at the garden opposite.

2

The door opened and an old man entered. He was a thin, unimposing man with a yellow-brown wart the size of a fingernail on his chin. Under his arm he was carrying a large flat board-like object wrapped up in a cloth.

'Ah, Klopman, heard any news about your master?' Professor Craig said.

Klopman shook his head as he wheezed and panted for breath and undid the cloth around the object he had brought.

'No, ain't heard anything at all. But, Professor, I got hold of one of these again, if you'd be so good as to have a little look at it for me.'

A picture appeared from under the cloth. It showed a pretty young girl wrapping a broken vase in her apron while looking sadly towards the sky. Holding it in both hands and scrutinizing it, Professor Craig eventually growled faintly, 'Klopman, where did you get hold of this?'

'At an antique shop in the West End.'

'What, again? How much?'

Klopman rubbed the palms of his hands together and laughed craftily.

'Thirty shillings.'

Peering over, I involuntarily burst out laughing.

The picture's signature certainly appeared to be that of Jean-Baptiste Greuze, but if it was a Greuze then it was hardly likely that one could get hold of it for thirty shillings. At even the cheapest estimate, it would surely be thirty pounds.

'The owner of the second-hand shop said that fakes are dirt cheap. Look.'

'It's genuine, Klopman,' said Professor Craig, drawing a deep breath. I silently uttered a cry and closely scrutinized it.

'Yes indeed, a former painter has an unerring eye for pictures,' Holmes said suddenly. Klopman had been gazing fondly at the picture and triumphantly raised his warty chin but then all at once became terribly confused and looked suspiciously at Holmes.

'And I see that you have also been to China.'

Holmes's godlike reasoning is something with which I am familiar, but it would certainly have dumbfounded one completely unused to it. Sure enough, Klopman looked bewildered and confused.

'Who might you be? And how do you know such things?'

'You have a large pen callous on the index finger of your right hand. Such a callous could only be formed if when growing up you were in the habit of drawing things with more than common frequency. Given that you have the ability to appraise paintings in excess of the owner of an antique shop, well, one may safely conclude that you were once a painter.

'Then, slightly peeping out from your rolled-up sleeves, is the figure of a fish tattooed above your right wrist and, from the deep staining of the red, one can see that it is something peculiar to China.'

'Well, I never, hearing that, I see there is nothing in it at all!' said Professor Craig tut-tutting and bursting into laughter.

Holmes smiled wryly as he turned to me and said, 'Watson, I begin to think that, by always explaining and carelessly blurting these things out, I do myself no profit. If I was just to inform them of my conclusions without telling them my reasons I might be much more appreciatively listened to.'

'Klopman, this gentleman is, and I'm sure that even you will have heard of him, England's pride and joy, that famous detective of Baker Street, Mr Sherlock Holmes. He has come especially to look into the disappearance of your master!'

The manservant, with eyes bulging out of his head in disbelief, stared at the figure of Holmes.

'What, you're the famous Mr Holmes? I didn't recognize you, sir.'

'So then, in what fashion did your master vanish?' asked Holmes impatiently. 'Pray tell us about the circumstances at the time.'

'Well, it was Wednesday, April 10th,' the manservant timidly began to say. 'Apparently some ship was supposed to be coming in from the Orient, so I set off with my master to the wharf. We went first to the office on Fenchurch Street – the office of the Anglo-Oriental Shipping Company that my master used to run before his retirement. I waited outside, for, according to what transpired later, it seems he had some business with Mr Martin, the manager there. Then he came out and we went to the wharf where a ship in St Catherine's Dock . . .'

'One moment. What was the name of the ship and where was it from?'

'It was Japanese, the *Hitachi-maru*. Yes, though what it was carrying, I have no idea . . .'

Holmes glanced in the direction of the window. It may be my imagination, but it seemed as if the ears of the man standing there with his back towards us twitched.

'Hmm. And then? Pray proceed.'

'The unloading of the ship had already started, but the master told me to wait there because there was someone whom he had to meet, so, leaving me at the wharfside and carrying his black umbrella, he boarded the deck of the *Hitachi-maru* and went down into the hold . . . and that's the last I saw of him.'

'Eh?'

'Yes, that was the last I saw of him. I waited for an hour and then waited two hours, but he never appeared. Eventually I realized that there was something amiss, so I, too, boarded the *Hitachi-maru* and looked around everywhere, but there was no one but those yellow Japanese monkeys, and neither sight nor sound of my master.'

'You presumably reported it to the police?'

'Of course. Then I rushed back to the office and urgently informed the manager Mr Martin. Mr Martin apparently contacted an acquaintance of his at the Metropolitan Police, an Inspector Lestrade or some such, and requested that they investigate, but it seems that since then they've been unable to glean any clues . . .'

Holmes was deep in thought as he stared at the face of the manservant narrating these mysterious things but finally said, 'Have you any idea about this person whom Mr Phillimore said he wanted to meet on the *Hitachi-maru*?'

'I'm afraid I haven't. When I was young I used to make all sorts of interesting voyages around the South China Sea with my master, but now I know absolutely nothing about such things, and, apart from looking after the garden and, well, looking for bargain pictures, I can't say I have any pleasures . . . Only . . .' Klopman elaborately tilted his head. 'I think that whoever summoned my master was definitely a yellow man.'

'A yellow man? Why's that? Because it was an Oriental ship?'

'No. From about two months before the master went missing, strange letters started arriving, and when he saw those letters my master would beat his forehead with both hands and roar "Damn that yellow rogue!" just like a madman or something and walk around the room in small circles, and even sometimes collapsed with his mouth quivering. And then there was always the mark of a red swastika printed on the letter's seal.'

'What was that? The letters were sealed with a red swastika?'

'Excuse me, but isn't that the mark of the Crimson Swastika Sect?' A voice was suddenly projected from the side of the window. It was Mr Natsume. He still looked pale, but his mouth was strangely quivering and he had a cynical smile on his face.

'The Crimson Swastika Sect?'

'It's a secret society in China derived from Taoism. The swastika . . .' he began, but then suddenly grasped the area below his heart, grimaced in pain and fell silent.

After glancing at this, Holmes again turned towards the man-servant.

'So you didn't see the contents of the letters?'

'That's what's so strange. There must have been more than ten letters in total. It looks like the master disposed of them all somewhere, but just once I happened to enter after the master had cut open the seal and so was able to glance at the letter. Yet the letter was completely blank . . .'

'Eh? Blank?'

'Yes, there were definitely no letters or pictures or symbols written down.'

The matter was getting more and more mysterious. Even Holmes, who had been largely unenthusiastic about it when he first visited this house, was now flushed in both cheeks with intense interest.

'The signature of the sender?'

'There didn't seem to be one.'

'You didn't see the postmark on the stamp?'

'That's the thing. The letters weren't delivered from the post office but were always left in the garden – that's right, they would be lying right under the window over there of this room. I never saw who threw them there, but anyhow the letters always arrived on Tuesday.'

Suddenly the Japanese man standing by that window seemed to issue a strange groan before walking up to Professor Craig and quietly taking his leave.

Holmes poked me in the side and whispered in a low voice.

'Watson, follow that Japanese fellow.'

He was certainly a suspicious-looking Oriental. I listened attentively to his footsteps on the stairs until they descended to about the first floor and then pursued him like a hound.

3

When I emerged outside, the fog was even deeper. Mr Natsume wore a strange discoloured coat and, brandishing a stick, set off from Homer Street in the direction of Baker Street. Possibly he might be going to ascertain Holmes's residence, I thought with a shudder.

Reaching Baker Street, he first entered a certain pharmacy. I wondered whether he was going to buy poison. I hid myself in the shade of a streetlight on the opposite side from the shop and observed his movements but then nearly made a huge blunder.

From out of the fog a loud voice suddenly addressed me.

'Dr Watson, what are you doing in a place like this?'

Turning around in amazement, I found Shinwell Johnson, Holmes's foremost young assistant since the beginning of last year, standing there with a bewildered look on his face.

'Shh . . . never mind, listen, find out what type of poison that Oriental bought at that pharmacy.'

Taking in everything in an instant, young Shinwell flew at a bound into the pharmacy just as the Oriental came out, and then immediately rushed back.

'Doctor, it's not poison. Only magnesium salts and a bottle of Carlsbad Spring.'

'Well, now . . . I wonder whether our friend has a bad stomach.'

'Doctor, I don't know anything about it, but may I be of assistance?'

'No, that's all right. It's better if there's one person rather than two when following someone.'

I am ashamed to say that it seems that I, who have for so long performed the role of being a shadow to Sherlock Holmes, appeared to feel a slight twinge of jealousy towards this quick-witted new assistant.

Coldly leaving him there, I began frantically pursuing the shadow of the Oriental that was already starting to disappear into the foggy distance.

From Baker Street he entered Oxford Street and there went into a bookshop and stared at books for nearly an hour before finally buying one and coming out again. I instantly went into the shop to investigate but found to my surprise that what he had bought was *Don Quixote.*

Leaving Bond Street at Piccadilly, he kept trudging on. Then, at a crossroads, a swarthy Italian was playing the violin while a young girl of about four years dressed in a red hood danced. He again looked at this with interest for a whole half-hour, but finally threw a single ha'penny coin into the Italian's outstretched hat and moved on.

At the entrance to the Underground a young boy was hawking the final edition of the evening paper. The Oriental asked for the *Daily Telegraph* and the *Standard* before finally descending to the platform. I deliberately got on to the carriage immediately behind his and continued watching him. In one corner of the evening edition there appeared to be a report on how the situation with Japan had become increasingly uncertain because the Russian army would not withdraw from Manchuria (a region in the north-west of China), but he seemed fervently to be reading the advertisements in the lodgings column.

Passing under the Thames and coming as far as Kennington, the Japanese man finally got off the Underground and changed to a train. I must say that the only reason I managed not to lose sight of his small figure, so liable to disappear in the crowds, was thanks to having on scores of occasions trailed with Holmes some pretty cunning rogues.

Mr Natsume got off at Tooting. A couple of ladies passing by at the time turned around and rudely cried out, 'Look at that little Chinaman!'

Seeming to have heard them, Mr Natsume slightly drew up his shoulders. This made me wonder if he really was Japanese? Perhaps he was a member of the Crimson Swastika Sect?

From all sides heavily bearded coachmen, looking rather like Professor Craig, raised their fingers and approached in landaus and hansom cabs, and the Oriental appeared to ponder whether he should get into one or not, but, finally making up his mind, got into the very dirtiest hansom. I grabbed another hansom and ordered the driver to 'Follow that cab!'

We were already in the outskirts of the outskirts, a district hardly able even to be called a suburb, with pools of water in dug-up holes everywhere, marsh glistening beneath the fog, houses that were nearly all squalid slums and a dark air of bleakness hanging over it all.

The cab passed through a dubious district of ill-repute not to my liking. Now and then I wondered whether he was not going to stop in front of one of the taverns resplendent in gaudily vulgar lights, but, passing right on through, his cab finally stopped at the fifth gateway of a row of houses thrown up in this new area. Other than that, there was only one other house lit up; all the others seemed to be empty and in pitch darkness. Around them there was nothing at all. Only an expanse of water, neither pond nor marsh, coldly glistening behind the row of tenement houses.

After getting out of the cab, the Oriental went into the fourth house along. I stealthily stopped my cab in a spot about three hundred yards away and immersed myself in thought. I had ascertained his destination, but there was not much sense in just going home now. I made up my mind to get out of the cab and inch my way over to the tenement houses.

Whereupon, to my surprise, the entrance door, having been once shut, opened again, and the same Mr Natsume as before suddenly came straight out. Too astonished even to think of escape, I cringed, unable to move as he made a beeline towards me. His furious face was visible even in the dark. He suddenly thrust out one of his hands and, startled, I made ready to defend myself.

'Hey, Mr Detective, thanks for coming out of your way! Did you think the ha'penny suspicious? I'll let you have it so you can take it home and study it at your leisure!'

And there, resting on the palm of his hand, was a ha'penny coin.

The look of blank amazement on my face as I accepted it is, my goodness, one thing I should not have liked Holmes above all people to have seen, but, foolishly, by the time I realized that the ha'penny mentioned appeared to relate to the coin he had given to the Italian he had already turned back and slammed the entrance door shut once more.

What on earth was all this about? Was this coin a forgery? Or else could it be that the Italian was also one of his gang?

I was confused and perplexed, but anyway the one thing that was clear was that my pursuit had ended in complete failure.

Crestfallen, I made to turn back, but at that moment another door, this time in the direction of the kitchen, opened, and a woman came out. In the light streaming from the kitchen window I momentarily glimpsed the face of a red-cheeked, seemingly good-natured young woman. It was, moreover, unmistakably the face of a young girl of one of my fellow countrymen. Surely she could not be the wife of that Oriental.

She walked towards me with buckets hanging down from both hands. It looked as if she was going somewhere to fetch water. After hesitating slightly, I quietly approached her. Since I had already been discovered by that man, my feeling now might be best described as one of desperation.

'Good evening, miss.'

'Ooh, you surprised me. Who's there?'

She dropped one of the empty buckets in alarm.

'Oh, I'm sorry. You see I've been walking around looking to see if there wasn't a good boarding-house in the area. You wouldn't happen to know of anywhere, would you?'

Peering into my face, her voice suddenly brightened, 'Ah, if that's what you're after, then Mrs Brett's might be just the place for you.'

'Mrs Brett, miss?'

'Stop that with your "miss". I'm the maid after all. That is, Mrs Brett's maid. And this is her house I've just come out of. As you see, it's not much to look at, but the rent is cheap. Only twenty-five shillings a week.'

She spoke with great speed, like a waterwheel spraying droplets of spittle, and on top of that had such a strong cockney accent that if one did not pay close attention one would not grasp what she said. Chuckling to myself that this was no mean chatterbox, I nimbly pressed a sovereign into her apron pocket.

'That's just what I'm looking for, but, you see, I'm slightly wary of strangers. Of course, it would be all right if they were all nice people at your place.'

'But they are all nice people. Mrs Brett used to run a girls' school in Camberwell, you know. When that didn't go too well she opened a boarding-house, but that, too, didn't go to plan, and about a fortnight ago we moved further out to this place. As she used to run a girls' school, she's forever scolding me that I shouldn't talk too much, although I'm never impolite to the guests, you know.

'There's a younger sister, but she's always praying to God. The other day, she latched on to this Oriental person who is boarding with us and cried and cried about how shameful it was that he didn't believe in Jesus . . .'

'Oh, so there are already people lodging with you then?'

I gulped.

'Yes. Two of them. But we have three rooms on the first floor, and one is free. Living in the middle room is the Oriental I just mentioned – a person from some country called Japan or some such. Apparently this Japan is in India somewhere. He has been lodging with us since we were in Camberwell at the end of last year and moved here with us.

'Well, he's a really strange man. He scarcely eats anything at all, reads nothing but fusty books, like one of those clever magicians of days gone by. The other day, wondering what on earth he was up to, I tried sneaking a peek from the keyhole to his door. Whereupon, oh my dear, what should a grown man like him be doing but crying!'

'Eh? Crying?'

'That's right. But the really terrifying thing happened after that. Well now, I don't know how he knew that I was snooping on him, for he had his back turned towards me, but all of a sudden he gets up, comes flying out and roared at me with a truly frightening look on his face, "Penn, have you turned detective now? Hussy!" Yet, seeing me burst into tears, he suddenly looked perplexed and apologized, saying, "I've been under a lot of strain recently so forgive me snapping at you like that." He definitely isn't quite right in the head, that man . . .'

'Does anyone visit him?'

'Very rarely. In the last six months, the only ones to come have been two or three of those yellow-coloured people. Provided it isn't snowing or raining, he seems to go off somewhere every day. And then he always comes back carrying a mountain of books . . . but perhaps even he is not as strange as the other one, Mr Gibson.

'Mr Gibson is in the north-facing room, and he recently joined us when we moved here from Camberwell. He's an old man with round glasses and a goatee beard. He's here on strange terms, you see. He said he wished to be given a key to the front door so that he could go in or out any time of the day or night, and that, since he'd take his meals in his room, he wished to always have them left outside his door. Not having anyone else likely to board with us, and since he said he would pay thirty shillings a week, Mrs Brett accepted. He's rarely in during the day. He only returns at night and strangely paces around his room. Then he's sometimes in the habit of raising a terrifying scream and throwing chairs or vases into the back pond . . .'

Having heard about the strange Oriental, I was not paying much attention to the maid's loquacity and was deep in thought. At which point this frighteningly talkative maid appeared to notice my demeanour with a start and became intensely flustered.

'Even so, such things rarely happen, you know. Neither of them are the type to do anyone any harm and they are more reserved and quiet than most.'

'Penn! Penn!'

A piercing voice cried out from the direction of the kitchen. Undoubtedly it was Mrs Brett. Almost taking me by the hand, Penn said, 'Listen, please come and stay with us. I'll introduce you to Mrs Brett.'

'Thanks. But it's already late tonight, so I'll come again tomorrow. Goodnight, Penn.'

That would do for the time being, I thought, and turned back down the road I had come.

4

When I returned to Baker Street, Holmes had his black pipe in his mouth as usual and was pacing around the room but, upon seeing me, broke into laughter with an animated look on his face, 'Watson, this case is perhaps more intriguing than I supposed. Interesting, very interesting. After you left I asked Klopman a variety of things. It seems that when Mr Phillimore was young he employed Chinese and Japanese fellows to smuggle opium from Shanghai to Taiwan on board a schooner. He even once shot a group of them with a rifle when they tried to protest.'

'Good gracious, are you saying that they are part of the Crimson Swastika Sect and that they threw in those mysterious blank letters out of revenge?'

'No, I don't yet know about that. At the time Klopman was just a menial and maintains that he doesn't know much about the matter, but, given the way he turned up that picture, it seems he, too, is something of an impostor. In any case, unbeknown to his master Mr Phillimore, he has been buying up hidden masterpieces dirt cheap and bringing them to Professor Craig for his appraisal for a good while now.'

'And the connection with the Japanese ship the *Hitachi-maru*?'

'On my way home I went to the police station and saw Lestrade about that, but it seems that, despite extensive enquiries, no connection has been established with Mr Phillimore. The manager Mr Martin also says that he talked with Mr Phillimore regarding a completely different matter that day and that he has absolutely no idea why Mr Phillimore should have afterwards gone to St Catherine's Dock. Apparently, though, there was something a little strange about Mr Phillimore that day, for he was not his usual self.'

'Don't you think that Klopman might have had something to do with it?'

'I did give that some thought, but it would surely be impossible to kidnap or kill someone at a wharfside with so many onlookers about. Though we certainly do need to go to the wharfside and investigate once more. I do, however, think that the actions of that Japanese fellow who was at Professor Craig's place are highly suspicious. I assume you remember the account of how every Tuesday a letter with a red swastika seal was found lying in the garden outside the window where that man was standing. It seems that since December of last year he has been receiving personal tuition for a fee of seven shillings a time. And what day of the week do you think he comes?'

'The same as today . . . Tuesday?'

'That's right. So, come, let me hear your account.'

I reported in detail the outcome of my pursuit that evening. Holmes listened with interest and occasionally questioned me about small details but then suddenly raised his head with glaring eyes. 'Watson, you didn't happen to see this old man, Mr Gibson, did you?'

Hearing but not grasping the meaning of Holmes's words, I looked blank.

'You said that the old man took up lodging there from about a fortnight ago? And that he has a goatee beard?'

I jumped up and screamed.

'Holmes! You mean that the old man is Mr Phillimore?'

The more mysterious the case became, the more sparkling was the sprightly smile that flickered in Holmes's eyes.

'Whether that's the case or not, let's take a little trip down to Tooting again early tomorrow morning!'

The next day I had an emergency case early on and, after impatiently treating this, the morning was already well advanced. By the time I rushed over to Baker Street Holmes was already dressed to go out, but I found to my surprise that he was walking around the room with a scowl on his face.

'Watson, it's too late.'

'What's happened?'

'Inspector Lestrade was just here and told me that Mr Gibson was murdered last night at the boarding-house in Tooting.'

'Eh? When? It must of course have been after I left. Have they already arrested the criminal, that yellow lodger?'

'It seems that Mr Gibson's corpse was found floating in the pond behind the boarding-house this morning, and that the Japanese fellow completely vanished before the discovery without informing anyone of his whereabouts.'

Recalling the yellow face which, the night before, had almost seized me by the collar as it showered me in a torrent of abuse, I could not help shivering as a watery substance ran down my back.

When we visited the Brett house in Tooting, Inspector Lestrade, who had arrived just before us, was informed by a policeman and came out.

'Mr Holmes, when I saw you yesterday at the police station you said that the disappearance of Mr Phillimore was an unusually complex case – regrettably Mr Phillimore has since then been murdered – but, as far as the culprit is concerned, no case could be more clear. There are two or three strange things about it, but if we just look for the yellow man who lived in the next room all will be well. It's just a question of time. Oh, you haven't heard about this yellow fellow yet, have you?'

'I know all about him. A scholar from Japan, isn't he?'

Lestrade looked pained but collected himself and showed us around the boarding-house.

'Mr Gibson's corpse has been left on the side of the pond where it was dragged out. A box of wax matches, a gold watch and seven gold sovereigns were all that was in his pockets – but that Mr Gibson is Mr Phillimore is certain from the photographs. I've sent someone to call the manservant Klopman, but it seems that he has been out since morning so we're looking for him. Anyway, have a look at the room where the murder was committed.'

'Lestrade, you said that Mr Gibson's corpse was floating in the pond. So how do you know that the murder was committed in the room?'

Lestrade's gaunt face grinned.

'Well, you see, a big red swastika was left on the wall of Mr Gibson's room. And . . .'

At that moment I heard a gasp of surprise. Turning around, two women with pale faces were sitting vacantly in the dining-room downstairs – presumably Mrs Brett and her younger sister Miss Sparrow – and, behind them, the maid Penn stood up with eyes starting out of their sockets as she closely watched me. She doubtless thought that I was one of the police officers. I would have to apologize properly later.

'And – at about twelve o'clock last night the maid says she heard a splashing sound when Mr Gibson was thrown into the pond from the window of his room. Of course, at the time she didn't dream that it was a body. Mr Gibson was apparently always in the strange habit of throwing things into the pool, so, thinking that he had probably thrown out a vase or something again, she didn't give it much thought. Even so, it's odd that she didn't become suspicious given the noise, but then it seems that she had just fallen asleep and was half-dreaming.'

'I see.'

'There were scratches here and there on the body, but as we cannot see a fatal wound, and there being also no sign of poison, it is definitely death by drowning. And from the rigor mortis it seems that the murder was committed between about ten o'clock last night and one o'clock this morning.'

'And, before that, were there any raised voices or sounds of fighting?'

'They say that nothing unusual was heard. Only that at about eleven o'clock the sound of footsteps were heard when Mr Gibson returned home from somewhere.'

'It was definitely Mr Gibson?'

'From the manner and sound of the footsteps, the maid Penn testifies that it was definitely him. The criminal perhaps made the victim suddenly inhale opium . . .'

'One moment!'

When we had climbed the stairs Holmes peered inside a door left open right in front of us.

'This is the room of the Oriental in question, isn't it?'

'Yes, there appears to be nothing suspicious in it as far as I can see, but, when we presently do a more thorough-going search I'm sure that pieces of evidence will turn up.'

It was a meagre room with some dirty nondescript calico or hemp curtains hanging down over the window shutters, with cracks in the ceiling, and was adorned with just a small plaster bust of Shakespeare on a shelf and a bottle of Carlsbad Spring and a tin of cheap biscuits on the desk.

However, what really caught our eye was the huge collection of books piled up on the desk, on the shelves and even on the floor. I could see Warton's *History of English Poetry* and the names Spencer, Hazlitt and Swinburne. There could not be many English people who had read so much of our nation's literature. There did not seem any sense of Oriental mysticism about the place at all.

'Now look at this!' said Lestrade as he fidgeted and opened the door of the adjoining north-facing room.

This room was the same in layout but far superior in its furnishings, with a genuine portrait of a lady by Gainsborough hanging on the wall. But under the frame was smeared the ghastly blood-like – on closer inspection it seemed to have been written by a finger dipped in red ink – mark of a crimson swastika.

Holmes investigated the area with a magnifying glass but eventually picked something up between his fingers and grinned.

'Oh, a hair, is it? Given its whiteness, it must be one of Mr Phillimore's that fell out,' said Lestrade, looking quizzically at it with an air of surprise.

But Holmes, taking no heed of him, said, 'So Mr Gibson's drowned body was found floating beneath that window?'

'That's right.'

'The depth of the pool?'

'Let's see, at its deepest it would come up to an adult's chest. All the junk he threw in previously was submerged beneath the corpse.'

Holmes again silently smiled and chanced to look towards the window. 'Well, well, the officers crouching down and examining Mr Gibson's corpse have suddenly stood up. It looks, Lestrade, like something unexpected has come to light.'

'Eh? I wonder what?'

'I fancy that they've discovered that the corpse is not Mr Phillimore. While fiddling with the chin, the false beard will have dropped off . . .'

Holmes rubbed his hands in glee as he watched Lestrade and I stand like idiots in complete amazement.

'You see, the hair that dropped here was clearly a hair belonging to a false beard.'

Lestrade said with a gasp, 'Who is it then . . . ?'

'The first person that comes to mind, given his age, is the manservant Klopman. Shall we go down and check?'

The three of us hurried out to the back garden, but we were met by an officer breathlessly racing towards us.

'Inspector, something really unexpected –'

'I know, I know. The corpse isn't Mr Phillimore, right?' Lestrade snarled with a sullen look.

Scum floated on the weirdly coloured pond foaming in places with black bubbles. At the edge stood a forlornly malnourished laurel tree and, apart from that, there was nothing but wretched weeds on the ground where the drowned body had been lifted out and laid down. As soon as I saw the big wart on the chin I, of course, instantly realized that it was the terrifying visage of Klopman's lifeless corpse.

I have, on many dozens of occasions, both as a doctor and as Holmes's assistant, experienced seeing people who were until yesterday full of life become the next day a silent corpse, but in the latter case I cannot help but always feel an indescribable terror. Rather than calling it a fear concerning life, it is perhaps better described as a fear of fate.

However, it was the totally inexplicable reality rather than such a fear that now had me completely confused.

'Holmes! What on earth has happened here? Are you saying that Klopman was his master's double and that he fell victim to adherents of the Crimson Swastika?'

'A faithful servant indeed.' Holmes laughed his peculiar silent laugh. 'An extremely faithful servant. And how spiteful of the god of vengeance to inflict divine punishment on such a faithful servant.'

'What do you mean?'

'The Mr Gibson who lodged here was Klopman from the beginning.'

'Eh? Did you first realize that when you discovered that Mr Gibson's beard was false?'

'That's when I knew for sure. However, from the first time I heard about Mr Gibson's strange behaviour I suspected that it was somebody in disguise. Having the key to the front door and coming back for the most part only at night, and having one's meals left outside the door of the room, are things done by someone wishing to conceal his face from other people.'

'With what objective would Klopman disguise himself as Mr Phillimore?'

'In order to make it look like Mr Phillimore was murdered by the yellow lodger. In the first place, the story about Mr Phillimore disappearing at St Catherine's Dock is extremely odd. Probably

Klopman was playing both roles himself there, too. He first disguises himself as Mr Phillimore and meets the agent and then, hiding behind the cargo or some barrels, returns to being Klopman and races back to report the incident. If his master had vanished at his own residence, Klopman himself would have been suspected, so he deliberately chose a congested place but then faced the problem that because it was a busy place people would be suspicious that his master's corpse had not been discovered afterwards. So he now made up the story of those red swastika letters and Mr Phillimore's fear of receiving them to lay the blame on the Oriental student visiting Mr Craig's place next door.'

'So you're saying that the Japanese fellow is innocent of any crime? If so, how do you explain his strange behaviour?'

'It may be strange, but if you discount Klopman's story of the red swastika letters being left outside the window of Mr Craig's room every Tuesday as a fabrication, then there's nothing else inextricably linking him with this case, is there? And if it comes to acting in what seems to others to be a peculiar fashion, then I am far from being above censure myself. First and foremost, if Klopman's story was true, and the person living here in Tooting was really Mr Phillimore, wouldn't that in itself be strange? Going out of his way to live in a room next to the yellow lodger he so feared, and, despite having the chance to run away at any time, why didn't he do so?'

'So, am I right in thinking that Mr Gibson – well, Klopman, wasn't pushed out by that yellow fellow?'

'That's right. Klopman hurling things and acting eccentrically was perhaps his means of creating a pattern of behaviour to make it seem as if Mr Phillimore was terrified of the resident in the next room. However, being an old man, the momentum of throwing something like a heavy vase caused him to fall out.

'The maid says she heard footsteps when Klopman returned home at about eleven o'clock last night and that she heard the sound of something falling into the water at about twelve o'clock. However half-asleep she may have been, if a third person had committed the murder it would be strange if no noise was heard during this time. This proves that Klopman was acting it all out on his own, and that's why I said that it was divine punishment.'

'My goodness. Now I understand. Yet why did Klopman murder Mr Phillimore?'

'If you just think back to that episode of the Greuze picture, you will have surely seen that he was an impostor. Perhaps as a reaction to having been discovered by Mr Phillimore to be doing something illegal or else, more likely, that he conceived the audacious ambition of wanting to collect more masterpieces – we'll probably find out more when we ask Mr Phillimore.'

'Eh? Mr Phillimore is alive?' Inspector Lestrade jumped up.

Holmes smiled. 'Of course, according to Klopman's plan, it was supposed to be Mr Phillimore who would be undergoing this kind of tragedy today. If, however, Mr Phillimore had already died a fortnight ago, then there would be no point in going to all the trouble of impersonating Mr Phillimore thereafter. Therefore, I think we may safely say that the rich old man is still alive.'

'Where? Where could he be?'

'Naturally, the easiest place for Klopman to imprison him would be Mr Phillimore's own residence.'

After standing for a while open-mouthed with surprise, we came to ourselves and rushed off to Homer Street.

5

Holmes's godlike insight was on the mark. Sure enough, Mr James Phillimore was rescued from the basement of his own mansion.

The old magnate was in a pitiful state when we found him. Even after we came in, far from any expression of joy filling his face, his right cheek slackened, the corner of his mouth drooped and a

倫
敦
塔

stream of saliva oozed out. I immediately examined him and found that both his right arm and right leg were paralysed.

'Holmes, let me assure you as a doctor that this poor old man has had a stroke.'

'Ha, I see.' Holmes, too, nodded gloomily. 'That must have been what tempted Klopman! Mr Phillimore, can you hear me? We're from the police. About a fortnight ago, after you had your stroke, Klopman shut you up in here, didn't he?'

A flicker of light appeared in Mr Phillimore's glazed eyes and he seemed to nod listlessly.

Lestrade said sullenly, 'Anyway as far as the case is concerned, we've been completely outdone by Mr Holmes.'

That was certainly the truth. However much of a tragedy it may have been to Mr Phillimore, another star had here been added to the brilliant casebook of Sherlock Holmes, and the final curtain was beginning to fall.

It was immediately after this that a person intruded with words amazing enough to raise that curtain again and astonish us all. For who should come in with one of the officers left behind in Tooting but that inscrutable, slightly pockmarked yellow-coloured Japanese fellow.

'Where have you been hiding yourself since this morning without informing anyone of your whereabouts?' Lestrade cried out ferociously with eyes starting out of their sockets.

The Japanese fellow stared at him with the most scandalized face imaginable but said calmly, 'I was looking for lodgings around Clapham Common. I'm not too happy where I am now, as I'm unable to read my books in peace. I've been thinking about moving for a long time but couldn't come straight out and say so to Mrs Brett, so set off without saying a word to anyone. Does one now have to report looking for lodgings and every other little thing to the police in England?'

'No, that . . .' Lestrade was flustered. 'But after you went out a murder was discovered!'

'If it had been discovered before I went out, I would of course not have gone. I first heard about it from the officers and Penn when I got back and was amazed. It seems, Mr Sherlock Holmes, that during my absence it was assumed, preposterously, that I was the murderer of the drowned man. In Japan we speak of being framed as being dressed in "wet clothes", and now I see just how extraordinarily apposite that saying is.' He grinned at his own joke. 'It seems that you dried my wet clothes for me, and for that I thank you.'

'No, no,' said Holmes, blushing like a young girl, as was his custom when praised or thanked. 'If one has the slightest ability in reasoning then one may easily disprove such misapprehensions.'

'But, if you don't mind me asking, I have a slight quibble with some of your reasoning. In fact, that's why I came to see you,' the Oriental said quietly with a serious look on his face.

Even Holmes appeared startled at this unexpected request. But his countenance suddenly became stern, sardonic and proud as he turned up his nose and said, 'Go ahead then, please, my Oriental friend.'

'The art of detection is something with which I am not very familiar, but, in that its objective lies in "how", I suppose it to be something akin to science. I should say that I am pursuing literary research, where the emphasis lies in "why", so the two things are conceived completely differently which may cause you some amusement but . . .'

'Come, come, pray tell us what is your opinion regarding this case,' Holmes said, getting agitated at the lack of progress.

'Well then, if you will hear me out, at about twelve o'clock last night I, too, like Penn, heard the sound of water when something fell into the pond from the window of Mr Gibson's room. And again, like Penn, it didn't sound to me as though it was a person who had fallen in. That's one point to consider when I say that even this morning I didn't dream that Mr Gibson was floating in that pond.'

'But he was actually found drowned, wasn't he?'

'That's probably because someone pushed him in.'

倫
敦
塔

'I don't follow you.' Holmes scowled with an irritated look at his opponent. 'Was the person who fell from the window Mr Gibson or not . . . ?'

'It was probably, as usual, a vase or something that was flung out from the window. If one was to search the bottom of the pond one would probably find it down there with all the other junk. After throwing it in, Mr Gibson then went out again on tiptoe and this time pushed Klopman into the water from the other side of the garden pond.'

'What? You're saying that Mr Gibson wasn't Klopman?' Holmes shouted in a loud voice the like of which I have never heard. The ends of his fingers shook and the colour drained from his cheeks. 'The drowned body was underneath the window. The marsh water is stagnant. So how do you know that he was thrown in from the other side of the pond?'

'He probably made use of the fact that the marsh water is stagnant. I had a look earlier at the other side of the pond, and there are definitely traces on the grass where a heavy object has been pulled along. If the corpse was definitely drowned, then he was probably made to inhale opium before being thrown into the water. After the murderer dressed the body in his own clothes, put some black, round glasses on his face, stuck on a goatee beard and dragged him to the pond, the rest was easy. As the water only comes up to the waist, the body could be easily pushed through the water and brought beneath the window.'

'What grounds have you for saying that Mr Gibson was not Klopman?'

'Well, I hesitate over the boldness of my conjectures, but when Mr Gibson moved in I happened to glimpse amongst his luggage that portrait of a lady by Gainsborough. But the frame wasn't at all in keeping with the picture. Of course, I am no specialist in paintings, but, even so, I can still recall thinking that this Gibson person must be completely uninterested in paintings. So when I later heard that you had said that he was Klopman, I immediately thought that, no, that cannot be. You surely haven't forgotten the way the man-servant's eyes lovingly doted on the Greuze picture when he gazed at it yesterday.'

'That's enough. So who killed Klopman?' Lestrade bellowed.

'The one for whom it was easiest to call Klopman out to Tooting last night.'

'The Crimson Swastika Sect.'

'Are you still going on about that? My graduation thesis at university was on Lao-tzu, and while studying Taoism I also learned a little about the Crimson Swastika Sect. It is not some terrifying secret society of killers like the Ku Klux Klan in America . . . That man over there looks the spitting image of Mr Gibson, however.'

'Mr James Phillimore?' The three of us cried out in unison. Ah, how simple and clear, and yet how infinitely unexpected an observation.

We had good reasons, however, for being surprised. With a caustic smile, Holmes finally said in a hoarse voice, 'He might look like him. But saying that Mr Phillimore disguised himself as Mr Phillimore, how utterly ridiculous . . . I even found in his room a hair from the false beard that Mr Gibson used to wear!'

'Mine is simply the opinion of a layman, so please forgive me if I'm mistaken. But could it be that Mr Phillimore didn't simply dis-guise himself as Mr Phillimore but, rather, that he wanted to pretend he was Klopman living in disguise as Mr Phillimore? Would it be invalid to see his disappearance at the wharfside, or the Crimson Swastika letters, as all things dreamed up by Mr Phillimore as preparatory actions designed to lead Mr Holmes and the police into the trap of deduction that they presently find them-selves? He set it up to look as if the crime was done by some Oriental cur like myself, or, if the police were smart enough to see through that, he arranged it so that one could only think of it in terms of Klopman's suicide or accidental death . . .'

For a while a profound silence ruled over the cellar. Holmes, seated in a half-broken chair in the corner, buried his head in both

倫
敦
塔

hands. Lestrade said, 'What was the point of it all? What on earth could a millionaire like Mr Phillimore have to gain by murdering a small, miserable manservant?'

'If we put aside the fanciful story about the Crimson Swastika Sect, and assuming that Mr Phillimore had no other important secrets' – the yellow man looked up with eyes overflowing with incisive human insight – 'surely the motive must have been that Mr Phillimore knew that the pictures which Klopman had acquired for next to nothing were all superb masterpieces. Amazed, displeased and displaying mounting hatred, the flame of his desire was lit. To assume that covetousness of another's money and wealth is solely the preserve of the poor is a superficial opinion. Rather, it is the self-made millionaire who will stop at nothing as he becomes eaten up with envy over the poor man's little luxuries and who will show a rapacious craving even for one shilling. Speaking in terms of countries, it is rather like this British Empire of yours.'

With that, this fearsome Oriental grinned a sarcastic but elegant and somehow magnanimous smile.

'But on this point I fear I may have over-indulged my literary imagination. Should by any chance what I have said so far be correct, you may confirm this point with Mr Phillimore there.'

'Mr Phillimore is paralysed. The poor man has been incapable of any of the strenuous activity of which you speak!' I shouted in rage, my body shaking all over.

From the instant I had again caught sight of the dejected figure of Holmes out of the corner of my eye my whole body had started to burn in indignation.

There had been, even before now, cases such as that of the cutter *Alicia*, which entered a patch of mist one beautiful spring morning and was never heard of again, or the case of Isadora Persano, who was discovered mad after staring at a match box containing a remarkable insect, where the case had been left unsolved. But these were cases which would have been completely insolvable to absolutely anybody. Not once had the peerless master detective Sherlock Holmes met with defeat at the hands of someone else.

The impudent Japanese fellow peered sympathetically at the prostrate form of Mr Phillimore.

'Oh, I see. Perhaps I was mistaken then,' he said with a smile.

Despite his theory having being fundamentally overthrown, he seemed neither overly surprised nor disappointed, and it was rather I who felt discouraged.

At this point, Holmes quietly raised himself from his chair. The instant I saw his face I froze. It was a grave, terrifying moment.

'Watson, I am defeated. What this man says is correct. Just look at that!'

His fingers led to the pale face of Mr Phillimore staring towards us. The facial muscles were as slack as ever, and saliva was drooping down from the mouth. But tears had welled up in those blurry eyes, and in the depths of those tears was clearly a tinge of conscience speaking of the greatest fear and contrition.

'Holmes! But how did a half-paralysed man . . . ?'

'He did not necessarily become paralysed a fortnight ago. It was probably this morning, after he had committed the murder and returned home, that God wreaked His vengeance inside this fearsome brain.'

At that moment Mr Phillimore raised a weird cry and his whole body went into convulsions. I ran over and lifted him up, but he had already stopped breathing and his pulse had stopped.

'My God! He's had another stroke.' Shaking my head, I looked around. 'There's nothing to be done. It looks like he's had a haemorrhage in the afterbrain.'

For a while we were all downcast as we regarded the corpse of this murderer summoned to eternal judgement, but finally Holmes turned to the yellow Oriental with a look of deep admiration.

'The case has been entrusted to the judgement of God, but I have been gratified to learn that, even in the Orient, there are prodigious geniuses like yourself with such a wonderful ability in

倫
敦
塔

detection. When you go back to your own country I'm sure you will meet with great success if you go into that line of business.'

'Don't be absurd. I absolutely loathe detective work. To be frank, I think there is no trade in the world as hateful and vulgar,' he said brusquely with the most disgusted look on his face. I was slightly nettled.

'There were, however, some rather strange aspects to your own behaviour. At Professor Craig's place, why did you turn so pale and suddenly fly out of the room?'

'Eh? Ah, that's because my stomach was starting to hurt. It's always been bad. It had become unbearable. Naturally, while I was out walking, the pain started to ease off somewhat, though,' he said with a gloomy expression. 'Of course, it's not only my stomach, lately my mental state, too, has not been very good, so I may have done things which might be construed as strange. I'm here to study only for a short period, and my expenses are tiny, and perhaps I've been suffering recently from the strain of trying to do the maximum amount of study. I have even taken sudden fits of wanting to break into gales of tears or burst out laughing. Perhaps moreover it's because of the terrible sense of inferiority which anyone from an undeveloped country tends to experience when they come to a civilized country, but I have become obsessed with the idea that everyone in England is incessantly making fun of me, watching me, following me and speaking ill of me.'

'Not at all. Why should we despise a country that has produced someone like yourself? It's obvious that Japan is soon to become our fearsome enemy – I mean, our staunch ally.'

Plucking the words from the bottom of his heart, Holmes said in an unusually sincere tone, 'Well, even if you don't become a detective I pray that your wonderful ability to analyse and synthesize ideas, together with your imagination, is put to good use in people's hearts in the world of literature, and that it meets with great success. Pray tell me your name again.'

The yellow Japanese fellow wrinkled up the top of his slightly pockmarked nose, laughed and quietly answered in a sincere manner, 'I'm hardly likely to amount to much, but, anyway, please remember the name Kinnosuke Natsume. Of course it doesn't matter if you forget it.'

The two years I spent living in London were a most unhappy two years. Amongst the English gentlemen I was like a poodle amongst a pack of wolves and led a pitiful life . . . The English looked at me and said I was having a nervous breakdown. One Japanese fellow wrote home saying that I had gone mad. The words of the wise should really speak the truth.

Natsume Soseki, Introduction, *The Theory of Literature*

Notes

Introduction

p. 9 *an institute of higher education in Kumamoto*: Between 1896 and 1900 Soseki was teaching English at the Fifth Higher School in Kumamoto in the far south of Japan. Although referred to as a 'higher school', this institution is best thought of as an élite proto-university.

When Soseki graduated from the Imperial University in Tokyo in 1893, it was the only officially recognized university in Japan, and to be a graduate of such an institution meant one was part of an intellectual super-élite. Throughout his life Soseki maintained close ties with his fellow Imperial University graduates. In 1896, when Kyoto Imperial University became the second university in the country, the Imperial University in Tokyo changed its name to Tokyo Imperial University. The higher schools, one in Tokyo (the First Higher School) and others spread out throughout Japan, prepared outstanding students for entry into the Imperial Universities, where the teaching was mostly conducted in English by Western professors. Students would, however, usually be in their late teens when they entered a higher school and in their early twenties by the time they transferred to one of the universities. It was at one of these higher schools that Soseki was teaching before his departure for England.

Although the Fifth Higher School was a highly regarded institution, it was a long way from Tokyo, and after four years in Kumamoto Soseki was keen to return to the capital. Part of his reason for agreeing to the government's request to go and study in Britain was his hope that by doing so he would in due course be offered a prominent academic post in Tokyo. This is indeed what happened, and, after his return to Japan, Soseki assumed lectureships at both Tokyo Imperial University and the First Higher School.

After the Second World War Tokyo Imperial University amalgamated with the First Higher School to become today's Tokyo University.

p. 12 *rumours . . . that Soseki had gone insane*: The claim that another Japanese scholar in London reported Soseki's madness to the Japanese Ministry of Education was made in *Memoirs of Soseki* (*Soseki no Omoide*) by Soseki's wife, Kyoko. The finger of blame was pointed at Tsuchii Bansui, a privately funded scholar who lodged with Soseki for ten days in August 1902, although Tsuchii himself rejected the suggestion. Whatever the identity of the reporter, rumours of Soseki's nervous breakdown were certainly circulating amongst the Japanese in Europe and in academic circles in Japan, particularly after Soseki famously submitted a blank sheet of paper as his annual report on the progress of his literary research.

So concerned was the Japanese Ministry of Education about Soseki towards the end of his stay in London that one of the other government-sponsored scholars in Europe, Fujishiro Teisuke, was asked to keep an eye on Soseki on their way back to Japan. However, when Fujishiro arrived in London in November 1902 Soseki surprised him by declaring that he would not be returning home on the same ship. Having spent time in the Scottish Highlands in October, Soseki announced that he needed more time to arrange for the transportation to Japan of the hundreds of books he had bought in London, and Fujishiro was forced to return to Japan before him.

p. 12 *British liberalism under the threat of German militarism*: Initially, Britain was the only major combatant in the First World War that relied on an entirely volunteer army. However, in January 1916 the British House of Commons passed the Military Service Bill, providing for the conscription of single men, extended to universal male conscription in May. This was the first time in British history that conscription had been used. In an essay called 'Tentoroku' (1916) Soseki analysed the relationship between recent intellectual trends and historical developments in Germany, and then turned his attention to what effect involvement in the war was having on Britain. In Western Europe the conflict had started off as being seen as a struggle between a militaristic regime (Germany) against liberal democracies (Britain and France). Yet with the introduction of conscription, Soseki observed, Britain, too, was turning to increasingly militaristic and authoritarian measures. In this sense, it was militarism that was emerging triumphant, and Soseki wondered what the implication for Britain's liberal traditions would be. Soseki died in December 1916, while the war still raged across Europe and before the revolutions of 1917 that swept away the old world order for ever.

p. 14 *Mrs Nott and her consorts*: Mary Nott was a 64-year-old widow who travelled on the same ship as Soseki to Britain from Japan and played a key role in his time abroad. Mrs Nott's husband had been a commander in the Royal Navy and had seen action in a skirmish between a British squadron and the Choshu domain in Western Japan in 1864. He had died in 1874, but Mrs Nott's daughter Grace had come to Japan in 1890 and was active as a missionary in Kumamoto when Soseki was teaching there. When Mrs Nott visited her daughter in Japan in 1900 Soseki, knowing that he was shortly to be sent to Britain, was introduced to her. It was by chance that they met one another on board the ship to London.

On 4 October 1900 Mrs Nott invited Soseki to her first-class cabin and on 10 October presented him with a Bible. Hoping to convert Soseki to Christianity, she enticed him with the offer of daily half-hour lessons in English conversation. Appreciative of her kindness and glad of the chance to improve his English, Soseki went along with this and even sought from her an introduction to an English university. However, he soon found himself the target of an incessant proselytizing campaign.

When the *Preussen* stopped at Shanghai and Hong Kong, it had collected large numbers of Christian missionaries returning home after the turmoil of the Boxer Rebellion. As the ship passed

倫
敦
塔

up the Red Sea, Soseki was increasingly drawn into debates with them about Christianity. Soseki's criticism was that, although the missionaries claimed to be replacing icon-worship with a higher religion, this religion was itself a form of icon-worship, God being only comprehensible to Christians through the icon of Christ himself.

Meanwhile, Soseki noted in his diary that Mrs Nott was going to write a letter of introduction for him to 'Mr Andrews, Dean of Pembroke College, Cambridge'. What Soseki might not have realized was that the word 'Dean' actually meant 'Dean of the Chapel' and not the head of the college. Furthermore, Charles Freer Andrews (see note below), although having links to Pembroke College, was actually the vice-principal of a seminary college in Cambridge.

When Soseki opted to remain in London rather than studying in Cambridge, Mrs Nott began to redouble her missionary efforts. On 16 February 1901, probably through Mrs Nott's introduction, Soseki received an invitation to have tea with a Mrs Edgehill at her home in Dulwich, south London. The wife of a distinguished army chaplain, Mrs Edgehill was an even more determined proselytizer than Mrs Nott. Soseki trudged through the snow to her home on 21 February, Ash Wednesday of that year – the beginning of Lent was clearly seen by Mrs Nott and Mrs Edgehill as a suitable time to renew their attempts at conversion.

Soseki loitered outside in the cold for half an hour, but when he finally entered Mrs Edgehill's drawing-room he discovered that six ladies, none of whom he had met before, were waiting to greet him. Flustered by this, Soseki managed to say a few words before tea was served and the master of the house, a white-haired priest, appeared. Soseki immediately formed an unfavourable impression of John Edgehill and quickly returned home, recording in his diary how foolish and constricted Western society was.

Mrs Nott was not about to give up, however. On 9 April 1901 her son Percy, a vicar, suddenly appeared at Soseki's boarding-house and invited him for tea the following day at the home of a Mr and Mrs Walker. On 17 April Soseki was again taking tea at the Edge-hills. This time Mrs Nott's missionary daughter Grace, who had just returned to England, was also in attendance. It is this event that Soseki refers to in the second section of 'Letter from London' ('The other day I was invited to a certain place and tea with the lady there').

Probably wondering whether they were making any progress, Mrs Edgehill asked Soseki whether he prayed, and when Soseki replied ironically that he knew no God worth praying to, Mrs Edge-hill burst out crying and declared it terrible that he did not know this 'great comfort'. To pacify her Soseki said he would try to pray, and Mrs Edgehill repeatedly made him promise to read his Bible.

Even when Soseki arrived at his fourth and final boarding-house he discovered that his landlady Priscilla Leale and her sister Elisa-beth Leale (referred to in 'Bicycle Diary') were, as daughters of a Wesleyan Minister, deeply religious types who urged him to go to church. He finally remarked in his notes that the English think that 'one size suits all, and being born in England they know nothing outside of England and no religion apart from Christianity. They think the entire world will feel the same when they hear a church bell, or become tearful when they hear a sermon, or have a feeling of ecstasy when they hear an organ. But the bell actually sounds like a fire alarm; the sermon like a platitude; and the organ gives out noth-ing more than a vast amount of meaningless noise.'

p. 14 *Regrettably, he received little correspondence in return*: Soseki's wife Kyoko was not somebody who enjoyed writing. She also had two young children to look after and found herself desperately short of money in Soseki's absence. The Japanese government provided her with only a tiny allowance of twenty-five yen a month to live on. She and her children lived rent-free in a small house provided by her father, but any further financial assistance was made impossible when her father was forced to resign as Secretary General to the House of Peers and suffered heavily through imprudent investments – all developments back home that were not properly understood by Soseki while abroad.

倫
敦
塔

p.21 *At the heart of this drama*: 'The Tower of London' has a distinctly dramatic quality, which Soseki reminds us of by emphasizing that each scene is being played out on 'the stage of imagination'. As Japanese critics have observed, the narrator's journey is closely similar to that of a Noh play in which a traveller encounters a mysterious figure from the present whose identity is only gradually revealed to be the ghost of a tragic historical figure. However, the story is also clearly indebted to the ghosts that appear to Richard III in Shakespeare's play.

p.26 *a subtle symbolism*: This observation, together with many others in this introduction, is purely my own and has not been detected by any critical analysis in Japanese.

p.32 *It would appear from a letter*: See letter of 9 February 1901 to Yamakawa Shinjiro and Suga Torao in *Soseki Zenshu* (Soseki's complete works).

p.37 *Soseki was a 'literary name'*: The name Soseki was first used by Natsume Kinnosuke when he was a student at the First Higher School. It is derived from a Chinese phrase, *Soseki Chinryu*, meaning 'To rinse one's mouth with stones and take a river for one's pillow'. This somewhat bizarre expression was a corruption of 'To have a stone for one's pillow and drink from the river', which meant abandoning the city to go and live at one with nature. However, the Chinese characters had over time got jumbled up by the Chinese themselves and produced a completely different expression which alluded to someone who would keep going in their own obstinate way no matter what the circumstances. Soseki's literary name, therefore, referred to qualities of stubbornness and tenacity.

Similarly, Masaoka Shiki, the haiku poet and Soseki's close friend, had chosen the literary name Shiki, his real name being Masaoka Tsunenori. *Shiki* meant cuckoo, and he had chosen this name because a cuckoo was said to be a bird that so loved to sing that it would continue singing even if it was to bring forth blood. While still a student at the First Higher School, Shiki was diagnosed with tuberculosis and advised by his doctor to convalesce. Instead, Shiki threw himself into his literary endeavours and chose his literary name in order to express his determination to compose poetry and write come what may. In 1897 the literary magazine *Hototogisu*, which was an alternative word for cuckoo, was founded by Shiki's literary circle and this was the magazine in which Soseki's first works would be published.

Soseki in London

p.47 *Charles Freer Andrews*: One of the most intriguing encounters of Soseki's time in England was that with Charles Freer Andrews (1871–1940) in Cambridge in November 1900. In 1904 Andrews was sent as a missionary to India, there becoming close friends with both Mahatma Ghandi and Rabindranath Tagore, and also becoming a leading figure amongst those who spearheaded the dissolution of the British Empire on the Indian subcontinent. It was largely through his efforts that Indian indenture was abolished in 1920.

In 1900 he was vice-principal of Westcott House, a seminary college associated to Cambridge University. As a graduate of Pembroke College he knew Mrs Nott's son Percy, also a clergyman and a graduate of the college. During the two days Soseki spent in Cambridge he was shown around by a Japanese student called Tajima, who had entered Pembroke College in 1898. Tajima was from a wealthy family and seems to have enlightened Soseki to the high costs of studying there. Soseki also later remarked that he had neither the time, money nor temperament for a lifestyle that consisted of 'showing up for two or three hours of lectures in the morning, spending two or three hours doing outdoor exercise after lunch, visiting someone for afternoon tea and then all going to college to dine together in the evening'. Thus the plan to study at Cambridge was abandoned and Mrs Nott's plan to entrust Soseki to Andrews's ministry failed.

Ironically, a week after the outbreak of the First World War, Andrews himself ceased his missionary work, later claiming that Jesus had been influenced by Hinduism and Buddhism.

Letter from London

倫
敦
塔

p. 53 *Letter from London*: 'Letter from London' was published in the literary magazine *The Cuckoo* (*Hototogisu*) in May 1901. The piece is derived from three letters sent by Soseki to Masaoka Shiki and Takahama Kyoshi, two of the greatest haiku poets of the modern era, both of whom were friends of Soseki and founders of *The Cuckoo*. Soseki's first letter was sent on 9 April 1901, followed by two more on 20 and 26 April. Shiki edited out the beginning of the first two letters, added the title 'Letter from London' and published the letters as one piece divided into three sections.

In November 1901, Shiki wrote to Soseki asking that he write another piece for the magazine, but Soseki failed to respond to the request, saying that he was too busy with his research in London. It was the last opportunity Soseki would have to write anything for his friend. Shiki died the following year from tuberculosis. Never having had the opportunity to see Shiki again, and having failed to respond to his encouragement, was a source of lasting regret. When in 1904 Soseki began writing *I Am a Cat*, he declared that the longstanding debt to Shiki was at last discharged.

p. 53 *How nonchalant and self-satisfied our gentlemen are!*: This outburst appears to have arisen out of indignation against the other Japanese in London who were invariably from rich families and affluent companies or else were civil servants on generous pay and able to indulge themselves in dissipation and luxury while Soseki struggled in relative poverty. Soseki noted in his correspondence that Tanaka Kotaro, the other Japanese boarder at the house in Camberwell, talked about little else but visiting London's prostitutes.

p. 54 *written in the style of the diaries solicited by* The Cuckoo: In July 1900, *The Cuckoo* had invited readers to contribute diaries describing their lives during a week in September 1900. The feature continued in subsequent editions of the magazine.

p. 54 *It might be interesting to say I lost Ann on Oxford Street*: Soseki is alluding to an episode in Thomas De Quincey's *Confessions of an English Opium Eater* (1822).

p. 54 *The husband and wife here*: In December 1900 Soseki had moved from the boarding-house at 85 Priory Road, West Hampstead, to 6 Flodden Road, off Camberwell New Road, in south-east London. His new landlord and landlady were Harold Brett and his wife Sarah. Harold was twenty-five and his wife forty at the time, and they had just married the previous September. They lived with Sarah's younger sister, Catherine Sparrow (aged thirty-six), and a former student turned lodger named Isabel Roberts.

p. 54 *Tanaka*: Tanaka Kotaro (1872–1950) travelled to Europe in 1901 to study commercial practice and shared the same lodgings with Soseki for a while.

p. 54 *the maid, Penn*: According to the 1901 census, Annie Penn was twenty-three.

p. 54 *the first gong of the day*: A gong was often the signal for mealtimes in such boarding-houses.

p. 55 *my bottle of Carlsbad salts*: Mineral salts from Carlsbad (now in the Czech Republic), taken to improve digestion. Soseki had chronic stomach problems.

p. 55 *Dodsley*: Robert Dodsley (1703–64), poet and publisher. Dodsley published many of Samuel Johnson's works and edited some notable multi-volumed collections of poems and plays.

p. 55 *Roche's*: A bookshop near Tottenham Court Road Station.

p. 56 *Warton's* History of English Poetry: Thomas Warton (1728–90). *The History of English Poetry* (1774–81) was published by Dodsley.

p. 56 *Kalthoeber*: British bookbinder active at the beginning of the nineteenth century.

p. 56 *I am getting up at the hour of the gong*: A Japanese pun. Getting up at the hour of the tiger (4 a.m.) was a phrase used to express a hard-working lifestyle. The Japanese word for gong (*dora*) is here punningly substituted for the word for tiger (*tora*).

p. 56 *Johnson's Dictionary*: Samuel Johnson (1709–84); *A Dictionary of the English Language* (1747–55).

p. 58 *the Aquarium*: The Royal Aquarium, now the Methodist Central Hall opposite Westminster Abbey. Despite its name, the Aquarium

倫
敦
塔

was actually a kind of music hall used for a variety of entertainment purposes. The building was purchased by the Methodist Church in 1903.

p. 58 *Irving*: Sir Henry Irving (1838–1905), famous Shakespearian actor. This production of *Coriolanus* was to be his final acting appearance.

p. 58 *Tree's* Twelfth Night: Sir Herbert Beerbohm Tree (1853–1917), Shakespearian actor. Soseki's diary records that he and Tanaka went to see *Twelfth Night* on 23 February 1901. Tree played Malvolio.

p. 58 *Nikki Danjo*: Famous Kabuki villain, who in one play makes his appearance by slowly rising up out of a hole in the walkway (*hanamichi*) leading to the stage.

p. 59 *ten Japanese sen*: The sen was a now obsolete unit of Japanese currency. One hundred sen made one yen.

p. 60 *'The wise man knows no greater pleasure'*: Soseki is alluding to a passage in Confucius' *Analects*, in which Confucius' disciple Gankai is praised for enduring poverty in order to follow the Confucian way.

p. 60 *My rank at home*: The Japanese Civil Service had a ranking system similar to that used in the armed forces. As a civil servant working for the Japanese Ministry of Education, Soseki's rank was equivalent to that of a major.

p. 61 *herds of women walk around like horned lionesses with nets on their heads*: An allusion to the contemporary ladies' fashion for wearing hats with veils covering the face.

p. 62 *least-poor Chinese*: This phrase appears in the original in English – 'least-poor' presumably refers to the fact that Soseki's appearance was much less impoverished than the Chinese coolies seen in London at this period.

p. 63 *we may go to heaven and pass the future with toads on lotus leaves*: According to some Buddhist sects, the virtuous were reborn in paradise seated on lotus leaves.

p. 64 *This house was originally not a boarding-house. Until last year it was a girls' school*: In 1891 Sarah Sparrow had been working as a governess at a small school for girls at another house on Flodden Road. This school had eleven boarders aged between five and sixteen. From around 1894 Sarah and Catherine rented the house at 6 Flodden Road and set up a similar type of small school giving a rudimentary education to girls, but in 1899 sickness spread through the pupils and forced the school to close. After Sarah married Harold Brett in September 1900, their home was used as a boarding-house, the sisters preferring Japanese lodgers as they were quiet and paid their rent on time.

Soseki thought that because the sisters used to run a school they would be able to provide the kind of cultured company he was looking for, but was to be greatly disappointed by Sarah Brett's empty chatter and self-important airs.

p. 64 *the pretty women*: Soseki is making a pun on the Japanese word *karen*, meaning both pitiful and pretty.

p. 64 *Not being on speaking terms with any god worth praying to*: An allusion to the ironic response Soseki gave when asked by Mrs Edgehill whether he prayed.

p. 65 *That Japanese fellow finally ran off*: When on 13 April 1901 Soseki's fellow Japanese lodger Tanaka Kotaro moved north of the Thames to the wealthy area of Kensington, the Bretts were unable to maintain a boarding-house with just two lodgers (Soseki and Isabel Roberts) and Soseki found himself moving with them from 'the notorious slum Camberwell' down to the even more unappealing area of Tooting Graveney. This pattern repeated itself. The following month the brilliant scientist Ikeda Kikunae arrived in England after studying in Germany, and on 5 May 1901 came to stay with Soseki at the house in Tooting Graveney. In the weeks that followed, Soseki found Ikeda's ideas hugely stimulating, but on 26 June Ikeda also moved to Kensington. For Soseki this was the last straw, and on 20 July he, too, left the Bretts and moved to his final boarding-house near Clapham Common.

p. 65 *Edokko*: someone born and bred in Tokyo: Edo was the old name for Tokyo; *ko* means child.

p. 66 *talked with the lady there*:: Mrs Edgehill. For the background to this see note to 'Mrs Nott and her consorts' in the Introduction. Mrs

Edgehill would later publish a series of devotional works including *Woman's Crown and Other Sacred Songs* (1909), *Is It Well with Child? A Book for Mothers and Speakers to Mothers* (1912) and *Ideals and Realities* (1914).

p. 66 *there is another old woman*: Mrs Nott; see note to 'Mrs Nott and her consorts' in the Introduction.

p. 67 *I am unable to because there is no room*: Soseki returns to this subject in 'Professor Craig'.

p. 69 *David Copperfield living with Micawber*: In Charles Dickens's novel *David Copperfield*, David, after suffering the death of his mother, is sent by his abusive stepfather to work in a factory in London where he lodges with the Micawbers. Mr Micawber, although always in debt, is a warm-hearted soul; when the Micawbers are sent to debtors' prison David has to search for a new home.

p. 73 *The old agent's eye is on the husband's own belongings*: Harold Brett had married Sarah Sparrow the previous September, so the owner's agent clearly saw this as an opportunity to make him pay his wife's longstanding rental arrears.

p. 76 *It is just a picture of a nude girl*: In his diary entry for 1 January 1901 Soseki had noted that he had asked Harold Brett about paintings of nudes, only to be told that nudes were rare in Britain. The morality of the nude was a much-discussed topic of the period. The provision of this nude painting therefore appears to have been a thoughtful gesture by his landlord towards Soseki. Nor were such acts of kindness out of character. On 2 February 1901 Harold Brett had accompanied Soseki to Hyde Park to watch the funeral procession of Queen Victoria. Because of Soseki's short stature and the huge crowds he could see nothing until physically raised up on to Brett's shoulders to watch the procession, an incident alluded to in Soseki's 1916 novel *Light and Darkness*.

p. 76 *Russia and Japan keep on trying to make war*: This line was subsequently revised to 'Russia and Japan are trying to make war and trying not to make war'.

Bicycle Diary

p. 77 *On a certifiable day in a certifiable month:* In September 1902 Soseki was staying at his fourth boarding-house, run by a Miss Leale at 81 The Chase, Clapham Common, London SW. Soseki was by now suffering from severe mental health problems owing to constant confinement in his room, and it was recommended by a doctor, his landlady and other Japanese boarders at the same house that he take up riding a bicycle as a form of outdoor exercise which would help to assuage his mental problems.

p. 77 *My coach and teacher is Mr X:* Inuzuka Takeo, who happened to be staying at the same boarding-house as Soseki, noticed his mental breakdown and encouraged him to take up cycling. Inuzuka had travelled to England as a companion to Count Ogasahara Nagayoshi (1885–1935), who later attended Cambridge University for three years and became, in 1918, a member of the Japanese House of Peers.

p. 80 *The bicycle brays . . . autumn approaches:* A play on lines from a Chinese poem, 'A horse brays, the day closes, my sword rings as autumn approaches.'

p. 84 *Haiku poets of the Japan School:* Masaoka Shiki's group of poets, who, in the newspaper *Japan*, sought to modernize the haiku form. Shiki joined the newspaper in 1892 and edited the haiku column.

p. 84 *a certain young count:* Count Ogasahara Nagayoshi. See note above.

p. 85 *if one shows respect to one's lord one fails to show filial piety to one's teacher:* A parody on a famous episode in Japanese history in which the warrior Heike Shigemori laments having to choose between loyalty to his tyrannical father Kiyomori or loyalty to the emperor Go-shirakawa, here transferred to Soseki's dilemma whether to collide with his coach or his aristocratic friend. The parody continues with Soseki's references to falling off his bicycle like a warrior falling from his horse and wishing he could reverse his bicycle in the same way that in a famous episode in *The Tale of Heike* (which recounts events from the Genpei War of 1180–5) members of the Minamoto clan discuss installing oars at the front and the back of their boats in order to change direction easily.

倫
敦
塔

p. 85 *Whether to perform this commissioned smile the policeman received six-pence or a shilling*: The proverbial laughing policeman. According to contemporary Japanese accounts of London, all the policemen were tall, moustachioed figures who looked strangely similar whether walking the beat or loitering in one place. In contrast to the generally brusque man in the street in London, the policemen were reported to be unfailingly polite, saying 'please' and 'sir' even when rebuking someone, and often accompanying someone asking directions in order to show them the way. In return for such civility, it was said to be necessary to press a few coins into the helpful policeman's palm.

p. 86 *'The story continues tomorrow!'*: An allusion to the custom of pro-fessional storytellers in Japanese theatres of breaking off at an apparently crucial point to encourage listeners to come back again tomorrow.

p. 87 *Chin Chin Chinaman*: In 1896 the musical comedy by Sidney Jones called *The Geisha* premièred at Daly's Theatre, Leicester Square, and became a huge hit running for 740 performances. 'Chin Chin Chinaman' was the title of one of the songs from the show.

p. 88 *her younger sister, a seven-stone old woman*: The boarding-house was run by Priscilla Lealle together with her sister Elizabeth.

p. 88 *Since being subjected to torment by these two old women*: In reality, the landlady and her sister were surely not interested in spying on Soseki but simply concerned about his mental health. Soseki's belief that he was being made fun of and ill-treated acutely illustrates his sense of paranoia at the time.

The Tower of London

p. 91 *I went there shortly after arriving*: According to Soseki's diary, he visited the Tower of London on 31 October 1900, three days after arriving in London.

p. 91 *a Gotenba rabbit suddenly let loose in the heart of Nipponbashi*: Gotenba is a country district in the foothills of Mount Fuji, while Nipponbashi is in the bustling centre of Tokyo. The contrast conveys the impression of being utterly bewildered by one's surroundings.

p. 91 *Max Nordau's* Degeneration: A hugely influential book of the period, Max Nordau's *Entartung* (1893; translated into English as *Degeneration* in 1895) heaped scathing criticism on contemporary artists and writers such as the Pre-Raphaelites, Ibsen and Nietzsche, for their 'degenerate' tendencies. Not a work to be taken over-seriously, the topic of 'degeneration' was, nevertheless, highly topical and would occur repeatedly in Soseki's later works.

p. 93 *A single boat goes along . . . this, too, hardly moves*: Soseki appears to have based this scene on a picture contained within the photographic collection *Tower of London – Exterior Views* found in his personal library.

p. 93 *Kudan Yushukan*: A museum belonging to the Yasukuni Shrine in Tokyo, displaying armour and war trophies from Japan's victories in the Sino-Japanese (1894–5) and Russo-Japanese (1904–5) wars. A Western-style brick building, it was opened in 1881.

p. 94 *Through me you pass . . . ye who enter here*: The words written over the entrance to Hell in Canto III of Dante's *Divine Comedy*.

p. 94 *This is called the Middle Tower*: This is actually the Byward Tower; the Middle Tower is on the other side of the moat.

p. 95 *Sometimes they ring it fervently . . . they would have rung it*: These lines contain playful adaptations of Zen riddles (*koan*) encouraging one to devote oneself single-heartedly to attaining enlightenment. The second line is based on the aphorism 'If you meet a holy man, kill him; if you meet a Buddha, kill him', which reminds the Zen acolyte that enlightenment is to be found within oneself not in the adoration of others. Here Soseki employs the sayings to denote the single-minded earnestness with which the tower bell is rung.

p. 96 *Archbishop Cranmer*: Thomas Cranmer (1489–1556), Archbishop of Canterbury. Leading Protestant reformer under Henry VIII, sent to the Tower in 1553 after the accession of the Catholic Queen Mary I and burned at the stake three years later.

p. 96 *Wyatt*: Sir Thomas Wyatt (1521?–54), son of the famous English

倫
敦
塔

poet. He raised an insurrection in Kent and attempted to occupy London but was defeated and beheaded.

p. 96 *Raleigh*: Sir Walter Raleigh (1552?–1618), soldier, explorer and author. Knighted by Elizabeth I, but, with the accession of James I in 1603, he was imprisoned in the Tower and finally beheaded. During his long years of confinement he wrote *The History of the World* (1614), poems and political essays.

p. 97 *because they are brothers*: The famous 'Princes in the Tower', Edward and Richard, the sons of Edward IV. After their father's death they were imprisoned and supposedly murdered by their uncle Richard III. Soseki based this 'vision' on the painting by Paul Delaroche, *The Princes in the Tower* (1831), although Soseki has swapped the position of the two princes: in Delaroche's painting it is Edward V, the elder brother, recognizable by his royal chain, who is sitting on the bed with a book on his knees, and his younger brother Richard who is reading. This is a typical piece of improvisation by Soseki, who while finding inspiration from various sources, was loath to follow slavishly the precedent set by others, and would frequently rearrange details in this way..

p. 97 *Happy are those . . . goes before God*: Lines from *The Imitation of Christ* by Thomas à Kempis.

p. 98 *From inside the moat a dabchick floats to the surface*: The narrator previously crossed the 'empty moat', so by this small detail we are made aware that we have been transferred to a different historical epoch.

p. 100 *Richard II*: 1367–1400, the last Plantagenet king. The son of Edward the Black Prince, his tyrannical actions in the latter part of his reign caused him to be deposed by the armies of Henry Bolingbroke, Duke of Lancaster, and later assassinated.

p. 100 *Henry*: Henry IV (1367–1413). As Henry Bolingbroke, Duke of Lancaster, he was exiled to France by his cousin Richard II but raised an army, defeated Richard and deposed him.

p. 100 *Exton*: Sir Pierce of Exton, the murderer of Richard in Shakespeare's *Richard II*.

p. 101 *Henry VI*: 1421–71, of the House of Lancaster and embroiled in the War of the Roses with the House of York. He was captured but managed to regain the throne, only to be captured again and murdered in the Tower.

p. 101 *The most surprising thing is how enormous it is*: This is actually the armour of Henry VIII.

p. 101 *Art School*: The Tokyo Art School, founded in 1890. The uniform was in the style of ancient Japanese dress.

p. 101 *Ainu people*: The aboriginal people of Japan, now very few in number.

p. 101 The Chronicle of the Three Kingdoms: A Chinese historical novel written in the fourteenth century by Luo Guanzhong, it describes the wars between the states of Wei, Shu and Lu between AD 221 and 265.

p. 102 *Charles II*: 1630–85, exiled after the English Civil War but assumed the throne with the Restoration in 1660.

p. 103 *Edward III*: 1312–77, son of Edward II, claimed the throne of France, thereby starting the Hundred Years War.

p. 103 *countless memorials . . . on the surrounding walls*: Soseki based this section on the booklet *A Short Sketch of the Beauchamp Tower, Tower of London and also a Guide to the Inscriptions and Devices Left on the Walls Thereof* by W.R. Dick. The names and inscriptions that follow are as they appear in this booklet.

p. 104 *the inscription of a priest called Paslew*: According to *The Short Sketch of the Beauchamp Tower*, 'MY HOPE IS IN CHRIST' is 'an inscription by "Walter Paslew", dated 1569 and 1570'. As for who Walter Paslew might be, the guidebook notes, 'In 1537, we read of a John Paslew, Abbot of Whalley, in Lancashire, being apprehended for his part in the rebellion called "The Pilgrimage of Grace", and executed March 12th,1537.'

p. 104 *Since fortune hath chosen that my hope . . . my planet being ever sad and unpropitious*: This inscription bears the signature 'William Tyrell, 1541' and is written on the wall of the Beauchamp Tower in Italian. The guidebook suggests that William Tyrell may have been an English Knight of the Order of St John of Malta.

倫敦塔

p. 104 *Honour all men . . . Honour the King*: The words to this inscription are taken from the First Epistle of St Peter. The name and date have been cut away and lost.

p. 108 *The one doing the sharpening starts to sing at the top of his voice*: The contrast between the jocular air of the executioner and his grim work of sharpening the axe is, as Soseki records in the afterword, derived from Ainsworth's novel *The Tower of London*. It was particularly significant to Soseki as an example of contrast in narrative content and mood and is cited again in Soseki's monumental *Bungakuron* (*Theory of Literature*; Section Four, Chapter Six).

p. 110 *Yow that these beasts . . . serche the ground*: The Short Sketch of the Beauchamp Tower speculates that this inscription is incomplete and the third line may be finished with 'there may be found'.

p. 110 *Jane Grey*: 1537–54, granddaughter of Henry VII. Beautiful and scholarly, she was versed in Greek, Latin, Hebrew, Italian and French. She married Guildford Dudley, son of the ambitious Duke of Northumberland, who contrived, after the death of Edward VI, to place her on the throne. However, within a mere nine days, facing popular unrest in favour of Edward VI's sister Mary, she was arrested and later beheaded together with her husband.

p. 111 *the tender age of eighteen*: Jane Grey was born in October 1537 and died on 12 February 1554, and so, by Western means of counting age, was sixteen at the time of her execution.

p. 111 *Ascham*: Roger Ascham (1515–68), humanist, first taught Greek at Cambridge University then was appointed by the Court as tutor to Elizabeth I and Latin secretary to Edward VI and Mary I.

p. 111 *they move closer and suddenly stop*: Soseki seeks not just to reproduce the content of Delaroche's picture but also its effects. In the same way as the viewer of Delaroche's picture is drawn into it (almost feeling culpable in the act), Soseki's narrator, too, finds the space between the scene and himself suddenly contracting to a few yards, so that, at the moment of execution, he fears his trousers will be specked with blood.

p. 112 *'Is my husband Guildford Dudley already gone to the kingdom of*

God?': Not historically accurate. According to a contemporary account, on the morning of 12 February 1554 Jane saw Guildford being taken to execution on Tower Hill and his carcass being brought back. Jane herself was executed that same afternoon on Tower Green.

p. 112 *'Do you wish to enter into the true faith?'*: Jane's powerful father-in-law, John Dudley, architect of the plan to put Jane on the throne, had converted to Roman Catholicism the day before his execution.

p. 112 *If my husband be first, I follow. If after, I beckon*: Soseki considerably romanticizes the union between Jane Grey and Guildford Dudley, which was in fact a political marriage forced on Jane by her own parents and Guildford's father, the powerful Lord of Northumberland. Jane strongly disliked Northumberland, protested about the proposed marriage to Guildford – stating that she was already promised to Lord Hertford – and would later complain of Guildford's ill-treatment of her.

p. 112 *Guy Fawkes*: 1570–1606, responsible for attempting to carry out the Gunpowder Plot of 1605. Gunpowder was installed in an underground room of the Houses of Parliament with the intention of blowing up James I, but the plot was discovered and Fawkes executed.

p. 114 *Shakespeare employs a direct style . . . to describe the scene indirectly*: See *Richard III*, I iv, and IV iii, for the two contrasting styles.

p. 114 *Ainsworth's novel* The Tower of London: William Harrison Ainsworth (1805–82), English historical novelist. Born in Manchester and educated at the grammar school there, he moved to London, became a writer and magazine editor and published thirty-nine works. *The Tower of London*, a historical novel about Lady Jane Grey's imprisonment in the Tower, was published in 1840.

p. 115 *Queen Anne*: Anne Boleyn, second wife of Henry VIII, beheaded in 1536.

p. 115 *Salisbury's countess*: The Countess of Salisbury, Margaret Pole (1473–1541). According to some fanciful accounts of her execution, she was said to have run around the scaffold pursued by her executioner and had no limbs left by the time she was beheaded.

p. 115 *Queen Catherine Howard*: fifth wife of Henry VIII, beheaded in 1542.

p. 115 *I thought about translating all this*: The song appears in English in the original.

p. 115 *Delaroche*: Paul Delaroche (1797–1856), French history painter in a combined romantic and classical style. *The Princes in the Tower* exists in two versions, one from 1830 is kept at the Louvre in Paris, and one from 1831 in the Wallace Collection, London. *The Execution of Lady Jane Grey* (1833) is in the National Gallery, London.

The Carlyle Museum

p. 117 *In a corner of the park*: Speakers' Corner in Hyde Park.

p. 117 *Aren't you Carlyle?*: Thomas Carlyle, although scarcely read today, was held in immense reverence in the mid-Victorian era. Born the son of a poor stonemason in Ecclefechan, Scotland, by the time of his death his ideas and fame had spread across the globe. His principal works are *The French Revolution* (1837), *The Life and Letters of Oliver Cromwell* (1845) and *Frederick the Great* (1858–65).

p. 117 *sage is a bird's name*: The reference is to such birds as the sage grouse and sage sparrow, so called because they live amongst, and eat, sagebrush.

p. 117 *The deep fog so characteristic of London*: This description of fog by the river near Chelsea has been linked by Japanese critics to scenes of the Thames in fog by Whistler (e.g. *Nature in Blue and Gold – Old Battersea Bridge*, 1872–7) and Monet. Until the advent of Impressionism, these critics have noted, fog was not considered to add mystique and beauty to a scene in this way.

p. 117 *I head back to my boarding-house*: Soseki's fourth and final boarding-house, at 81 The Chase, Clapham Common.

p. 118 *After Carlyle's death some public-spirited men decided to bring together the furniture, personal effects and books Carlyle had used during his life*: The original catalogue to the Carlyle House contains information regarding the creation of the museum. In April 1894 George Lumsden, a passionate admirer of Carlyle's works, visited the site of Carlyle's former home. He discovered that 'all was dirty and dingy, the windows particularly manifesting those signs which one normally associates with an empty, neglected house'. He walked back towards the city indignant, regarding 'the discrepancy between the splendour of living mediocrity, and the squalid neglect of the modest old house which had been the abode of greatness'. After discovering that the house might be coming up for sale, he came back for an internal inspection with a friend and found that 'all was waste, desolation, and dirt, gas fittings half torn down, no furniture whatever visible'.

On 6 September 1894 Lumsden published a letter in the *Standard* newspaper, and subsequently reproduced in many other newspapers, announcing the formation of a subscription list to raise the £1750 necessary to buy the house. The response was lukewarm. One writer caustically commented:

Some well-meaning people are attempting to acquire, and to set apart for ever, as a national possession, the house in which Carlyle died. There is also talk of making a Carlyle Museum – of what? The slippers he used to wear? The pipe he used to smoke? A portion of his last blotting pad? Echoes of the old man's grumblings? I do not think that we want a Carlyle Museum, and I have great doubts on the subject of buying the house unless some rich man comes forward. Of course, we ought to keep all the houses of all the great writers; but it seems hardly likely that a people who a few years ago suffered Milton's house to be pulled down will concern themselves to preserve Carlyle's. Moreover, I understand that the younger generation does not read Carlyle. He was a mighty power in the land forty years ago; all men over fifty, and a great many over forty, can bear witness to the influence of Carlyle's writings upon their own mind . . . In those days the younger and more generous souls revelled in the teachings of Carlyle. But, is his teaching still a source of inspiration for the young men? I doubt it . . . He is lying on the shelf, unread.

Nevertheless, a committee was gradually formed. Mary Carlyle Aitken, Carlyle's niece, promised a considerable number of articles of old furniture, and hundreds of subscription letters were circulated. The German Emperor himself pledged £100, and further committees were created in New York and Glasgow. By May 1895 the house was purchased. It was immediately renovated, and on 26 July it opened to the public. In October the Carlyle's House Memorial Trust was formed to administer the property.

p. 118 *Thomas More*: English statesman (1478–1535), humanist and Lord Chancellor to Henry VIII between 1529 and 1532. He opposed the annulment of Henry's marriage to Catherine of Aragon and refused to recognize the Act of Supremacy, for which he was executed on a charge of treason. Canonized by the Roman Catholic Church, his *Utopia* (1516) expounds his concept of the ideal state.

p. 118 *Smollett*: Tobias George Smollett (1721–71), Scottish writer of picaresque novels including *Roderick Random* (1748), *Peregrine Pickle* (1751) and *Humphrey Clinker* (1771).

p. 118 *Leigh Hunt*: James Henry Leigh Hunt (1784–1859), poet, essayist and founder of *The Examiner* (1808). One of the first critics to promote the works of the Romantic poets Keats and Shelley.

p. 118 *Eliot*: George Eliot (1819–80), real name Mary Ann Evans, English novelist.

p. 118 *If I say hermitage it has an antiquated feel*: The word 'hermitage' conjures up to the Japanese images of the kind of simple wooden huts found in Japanese tea gardens.

p. 119 *It is just as if a large factory chimney had been cut off at the root*: In his lecture 'The Philosophical Principles of the Literary Arts', delivered in 1907, Soseki gives the odd example of the sight of black smoke rising from the tall chimney of a factory as something which gives rise to a feeling that is 'akin to that felt with regard to the expression of will'. He goes on to say that will is expressed in literature by means of characters with imposing personalities, who, when they conform to some moral ideal, exemplify the noble quality called 'heroism'. Soseki's description here of Carlyle's 'smoke-like life' within a house shaped like a factory chimney, therefore, seems to allude to Carlyle's heroic stature in Soseki's eyes.

Indeed, in a much earlier piece called 'My Friends in the School', written in English by Soseki when he was only twenty-two, Soseki describes an encounter with Carlyle's ghost. Despite being warned by Carlyle that it is dangerous to copy him, the narrator admits to reading the great man's works, loving his good sense and admiring his talent. Carlyle is 'the hero of my piece', he concludes.

p. 119 *from the north country*: Craigenputtock, the remote Scottish farm which had been the Carlyles' home for six years before they came to London in 1834.

p. 119 *turned to his wife*: Jane Welsh Carlyle (1801–66). Recognized in her lifetime as a woman of considerable wit and strength of character, her stature was further elevated after her death by the publication of her letters.

p. 120 *it is even known that the canary the maid was carrying chirped in its cage while they were moving in*: Carlyle gives in the *Jane Welsh Carlyle*, written immediately after his wife's death in 1866, the following account of the journey: 'We proceeded all through Belgrave Square hither, with our Servant, our looser luggage, ourselves and a little Canary bird ("Chico", which she had brought with her from Craigenputtock); one hackney coach rumbling on with us all. Chico, in Belgrave Square, burst into singing, which we took as a good omen.'

p. 120 *turned down a pension recommended by Disraeli*: This precedent was perhaps in Soseki's mind when he himself turned down a Doctor of Letters degree conferred on him by the Japanese government in 1911.

p. 120 *She eventually brings out what looks like a register and says, 'Write your name please'*: Item Four on the list of 'Rules and Regulations for the Admission of Visitors' at the Carlyle House states: 'Visitors shall be requested to sign the Visitors' Book.'

p. 120 *I recall having entered this house four times and recording my name four times in the register during my sojourn in London*: In reality, Soseki's own name appears in the visitor's book only once, on 3 August 1901, when he was accompanied by another distinguished individual, the chemist Ikeda Kikunae, whose name appears alongside his own.

p. 120 *I must be the first Japanese to have come here*: Not actually correct; there are previous Japanese visitors recorded in the visitors' book.

p. 120 *The woman says, 'This way'*: Item Eleven on the list of Rules and Regulations states, 'No Visitor or Visitors shall be left alone in any part of the premises.'

p. 121 *Apparently there were no gold medals*: The House Catalogue lists no gold medals in the contents but records that Carlyle, on his eightieth birthday on 4 December 1875, had 'an address and a gold medal presented to him'.

p. 121 *the Prussian decoration Bismarck sent to Carlyle*: The Prussian Order of Merit.

p. 122 *Above them, like a patient with a sick stomach, hangs only a leaden sky*: Both Carlyle and Soseki had chronic stomach disorders. In the early work 'My Friends in the School' (1889) the narrator even suspects that his dream of being visited by Carlyle's ghost is the product of indigestion.

p. 123 *green curtains silently hang over it*: The curtains are actually red, a slip perhaps caused by Soseki's misreading of the House Catalogue, 'This was not a "red bed", but a green one, although in later years Mrs Carlyle supplied new curtains, etc. of her favourite red colour, and they are the ones now on the bed.'

p. 127 *Mrs Aitken*: Carlyle's sister.

p. 127 *Kant has written a treatise . . . strong texture of their brain tissues*: Soseki is quoting, with a few modifications, the opening to Schopenhauer's essay 'On Noises' from *The Essays of Schopenhauer*, translated by Mrs R. Dircks (1897).

p. 128 *On 12 October 1844 when the famous poet Tennyson first visited Carlyle*: Not historically accurate; according to the House Catalogue's

'Chronology of Events', Carlyle noted in his diary on 12 October 1844 that 'Tennyson came the other day', so the meeting must have been before this day. Furthermore, nearly two years earlier, on 28 December 1842, Carlyle had recorded, 'Last night we had a Poet here, a very clever man called Alfred Tennyson.'

Short Pieces for Long Days

p. 133 *The first place I took lodgings*: Soseki had arrived in London on 28 October 1900 and stayed for the first two weeks at a house at 76 Gower Street, near the British Museum. This house was called Eva Stanley Apartments and was somewhere to which many of the Japanese in London at the time, including Japanese naval officers, made their way upon first arriving. Although cheaper than a hotel and centrally located, it was, however, still expensive, costing twelve shillings a day. Soseki's entire monthly salary from the Japanese government was fifteen pounds a month, so, even excluding all other expenses, he could not afford to stay there for long. Soseki spent these first two weeks looking for a suitable boarding-house by inspecting the register of foreign students at the Japanese Embassy and perusing newspaper adverts. However, as the few Japanese in London were a tightly knit group, networking between them often led to introductions to boarding-houses where other Japanese people were staying. It was for this reason that there were other Japanese lodgers present in all the houses that Soseki stayed in London.

After Soseki took the decision to stay in London rather than study in Cambridge or elsewhere, he was introduced to a boarding-house at 85 Priory Road, West Hampstead. It is this boarding-house that is referred to in 'Lodgings'. A Japanese businessman called Hirao Hachisaburo had first come across this house in 1898 and had lived there for nearly two years. Hirao recalled that, including embassy staff, there were probably hardly more than thirty Japanese in the whole of London in the late 1890s. When Hirao returned to Japan another prominent Japanese businessman called Nagao Hanpei

倫
敦
塔

('Mr K' in this story) took over these rooms. It seems likely that another Japanese living nearby, called Kadono Jukuro, introduced Soseki to this residence.

In a fascinating memoir written from a hospital bed in Buenos Aires in 1935, Hirao gives an intriguing account of this house at 85 Priory Road. In contrast to the 'dark hell' described by Soseki, Hirao recorded pleasant memories of an elegant house where the family running it were not simply interested in extracting profit from their boarders but where the whole family got dressed up and threw a party for Hirao on his birthday, even toasting him with champagne. Hirao even recalled that the family always had his socks and trousers warmed up on the stove for him to change into when he came home on winter days. The head of the house, Frederick Milde, never having met a Japanese person before and at first believing Hirao to be Mexican, even borrowed library books about Japan to get on better terms with his lodger.

Like everything else in *Short Pieces for Long Days*, then, this household undergoes a dreamlike transformation. We can understand how this differed from the reality by tracing the history of the family living there.

When Hirao lived at 85 Priory Road in 1898, the family consisted of Frederick Milde, a Prussian-born tailor, his wife Julie and two of her three children from a first marriage, Antonia and Edmund. In 1899 Julie Milde died, meaning that when Soseki moved in the following year Frederick Milde was living with his two stepchildren. The 'old maid' character in 'Lodgings' was based on the stepdaughter Antonia Doring, who was aged forty-one in 1900. Her brother Edmund was aged forty-two and their stepfather Frederick Milde was sixty-eight.

According to Hirao, in the 1860s Frederick Milde had worked as a tailor at the court of Napoleon III in France. He appears to have moved to London just before the Franco-Prussian war and in 1869 opened a tailor shop, Salanson and Milde, at 55 Conduit Street in the West End. In 1877 he married Julie Doring (née Lange), who was also German, having been born in Breslau. She appears to have married her first husband Frederick Doring, also a tailor, in 1856 or 1857, and they moved to England in 1858, but this husband had died in 1875. Her three children from this first marriage – Antonia, Edmond and Alice – were all born in London.

There are, therefore, a number of significant differences between the real family who lived at 85 Priory Road and the sinister family group described in 'Lodgings'. First, the landlady reveals to the narrator that 'she was not British but French', yet Antonia Doring was, in fact, born and reared in London. According to Nagao Hanpei's recollection of the house, Antonia 'was of German descent and could speak German and a little French'. So she was certainly not French. Then, although Edmond and Antonia were in fact full brother and sister, in 'Lodgings' the landlady's brother is the son of the head of the house and hence her stepbrother. In reality Frederick Milde had no natural children. Further, we are told that 'the landlady had lost her mother a long time ago', but in reality Edmund's and Antonia's mother had died only the previous year. Finally, although the landlady is clearly described in terms of being a middle-aged woman, we are told that her 'mother had, some twenty-five years ago, married a certain Frenchman and produced this daughter', meaning that the landlady could not be more than twenty-five years old.

Writing eight years later about a household in which he only spent a month or so, it is unlikely that Soseki would recall the precise details of the family members, but there is no question that the fictional elements in these short pieces were carefully conceived. The landlady in 'Lodgings' becomes an isolated figure like the narrator himself, alienated and without true family in a foreign land. Rather than the reality of a middle-aged landlady of northern European stock, we are presented with a young woman from a warm Mediterranean country upon whom the effect of London's cold has been to cause her to become unnaturally shrivelled up and aged.

Into this already sinister household is then added the secret

倫
敦
塔

concerning the child-maid Agnes. As Agnes's face is said to resemble that of the landlady's stepbrother, we must assume that she is either the illegitimate child of this stepbrother or the landlady's stepfather, the former being perhaps the more likely. Japanese critics have had a field day speculating on the consequences of this. An entire history of Agnes's childhood has been imagined – from the landlady's stepbrother getting a seamstress at his father's tailor shop pregnant, having the child raised in Germany (thereby accounting for her being constantly silent) and finally brought back to England to help out with Japanese lodgers. Others have seen the child-maid Agnes as the symbol of a potent sexual threat in a household where the family members are not blood relations. One prominent critic has argued that the landlady uses the Japanese lodgers as a shield against this threat and, being herself the victim of prejudice and repression, in turn piles prejudice and repression on to one in an even weaker position than herself, thereby swirling the entire household into a 'dark hell'. Yet, in fact, the hell of this household surely lies not in the way that the landlady treats Agnes but, rather, in that the one person the narrator recognizes as being a 'real human being' is the one he begins to suspect of being Agnes's father. Yet there is no indication of any fatherly warmth or protection being extended to her.

Whether there really was something deeply sinister about this house is unclear, but certainly Soseki did not refer to it in any of his correspondence of the period. Because of the fictional transformation of other elements of this household, critics have speculated that the character 'Agnes' may have been Soseki's fictional creation also. However, the census of 1901, published in 2002, revealed for the first time that there was indeed a maid called Agnes Bruce (aged fifteen in 1901) living at 85 Priory Road.

It seems probable, however, that the reality of this household had fused in Soseki's mind with neuroses stemming from his own childhood. Soseki himself had been handed out to a foster family when he was a child, and even when he returned to his own family he was raised believing his own mother and father to be his grandmother and grandfather until a young maid came to him one night and whispered the truth. Therefore Agnes's situation not only mirrors Soseki's childhood trauma but connects to the theme running throughout 'Short Pieces for Long Days' of being lost and bewildered by one's surroundings.

Perhaps the most telling comparison, however, is between the portrayal of the forlorn young woman Jane Grey in 'The Tower of London' and the young maid Agnes in 'Lodgings'. In the former story the narrator fled from the sight of the blindfolded Jane being executed, just as the narrator at the end of 'Lodgings' wishes to flee from the piteous eyes of Agnes staring up at him in the doorway. The Tower of London was 'an image of hell', a historical nightmare from which the narrator could escape back into the safety of his boarding-house; yet in 'Lodgings' it is now the boarding-house itself that has become the 'dark hell'. Hell, once seen as something historical and distant, has been internalized into something contemporary, everyday and psychological.

As for the reason why Soseki left this boarding-house, it may have been that Soseki did find the atmosphere of the house unpleasant. However, part of the answer may also be suggested in the first lines of 'Lodgings'. At two pounds a week the house may have been simply too expensive. Soseki had fifteen pounds a month to live on. Paying over eight pounds a month in rent and another pound to his private tutor, William Craig, left Soseki less than six pounds a month for all other expenses. Soseki was obsessed with having enough money to buy hundreds and hundreds of second-hand books to take back to Japan. His next boarding-house in Camberwell (described in 'Letter from London') cost only twenty-five shillings a week, allowing him an extra three pounds a month to spend on books. This was surely at least part of his motivation for moving

p. 133 *Mr K*: See note above.

p. 134 *She asked me if I spoke French*: Having spent a week at the 1900

World Fair in Paris before arriving in England, Soseki showed a strong desire to improve his French. In 1901 he even wrote to a friend to sound out the Japanese Ministry of Education on the possibility of extending his stay abroad to include four or five months in France.

p. 134 *Kruger*: Paul Kruger (1825–1904), Boer statesman and president of the Transvaal Republic (1883–1900). His resistance to British imperialists such as Cecil Rhodes – who were intent on seizing the gold and diamond wealth of the Transvaal – and his denial of political rights to the Uitlanders (foreign workers in the Transvaal) led to the Second Boer War (1899–1902). As the war turned against the Boers, Kruger fled to Europe, and on 22 November 1900 (ten days after Soseki moved into the house at 85 Priory Road) arrived in Marseilles to a rapturous reception. Kruger subsequently began a tour of Europe to try to drum up support and financial aid for the Boer cause but was denied access to the Kaiser and died in exile in 1904.

p. 135 *He had opened a tailor's shop in the West End*: The shop that Frederick Milde had opened at 55 Conduit Street changed its name in 1877 to Milde and Pyne and again in 1887 to Frederick Milde and Son. The shop was introduced in *Modern London* (1889) as a distinguished 'Military Tailors and Outfitters' that enjoyed the patronage of many prominent lords and dukes and one that had a special connection to the Egyptian court and the Khedive's Minister of War. It relates that 'The selection of patterns in various materials exhibited in the firm's handsome Conduit Street showroom is one of the most choice and elegant in the West End . . . Military uniforms are a speciality . . . Mr Milde is himself a cutter of conspicuous skill and the best experience, as well as a thorough master of the tailoring art in all its details and generalities.' In 1898 the shop moved to 3 George Street, Hanover Square.

p. 137 *About two weeks before I left this boarding-house K returned from Scotland*: Three days after moving into 85 Priory Road, Soseki noted in his diary spending all day talking with Nagao Hanpei, so in reality it was clearly not two weeks before he left the house that Soseki was introduced to his fellow Japanese lodger. Rather, just as the 'warm dreams of distant France' in 'Lodgings' anticipate the Mediterranean scene of 'A Warm Dream', so K returning from Scotland and injecting the house with sudden warmth anticipates the triumphant outburst of warmth and brightness discovered in Scotland in 'Long Ago'. And it is when K is about to cross 'to the other side of the Mediterranean' that the narrator, sensing that the house will again lose its warmth, takes his leave.

p. 138 *K said enough is enough and lent me the money*: In his semi-autobiographical novel *Ramblings* (*Michikusa*, 1915; translated as *Grass on the Wayside*) Soseki repeats much of this material about Mr K, indicating just how much of an impression his fellow Japanese lodger and his comfortable room and luxurious clothing made on him. He also goes on to reveal his distress at being asked to refund the loan (£10 in *Ramblings*; £20 according to Nagao Hanpei) once the two men had returned to Japan. Soseki appears to have assumed that, given the apparent wealth of his fellow lodger, the loan would never need to be repaid. Nagao Hanpei recalled the matter differently and claimed that he never pressed Soseki for its return.

p. 138 *Keio period*: Lasted for only three years, 1864–67. Soseki was born in 1867, the third year of the Keio era.

p. 139 *the smell of my past boarding-house, which in the last three months I had forgotten*: In reality, the month after leaving this house, on 12 January 1901, Soseki wrote in his diary, 'went to see Nagao Hanpei', indicating that this scene of the narrator confronting the piteous figure of Agnes at the doorway after being away for several months was probably fictional.

p. 141 *I flee into one of the houses*: Her Majesty's Theatre, where Soseki saw Herbert Beerbohm Tree in *Twelfth Night* on 23 February 1901. Soseki refers to this in 'Letter from London'.

p. 142 *a dream of warm Greece*: *Twelfth Night*, the play that Soseki saw at Her Majesty's Theatre is set in Illyria, the Greek and Roman name for the land on the east side of the Adriatic Sea.

p. 143 *the house*: Soseki is describing his first impressions of London and therefore this 'house' must refer to the apartments he first stayed at on Gower Street. See note to 'the first place I took lodgings'.

p. 143 *The colours of these buses . . . are red, yellow, green, brown, blue*: the different colours of the buses signified which route they took. These are of course horse-drawn buses. Motor buses were still in their infancy in Britain at this time but were rapidly to replace horse buses in the years leading up to the First World War. In 1914 horses were requisitioned for military use, and horse-drawn buses practically disappeared from London's streets.

p. 143 *I am suddenly conscious of having drowned in a human sea*: Soseki was caught in huge crowds in the centre of London the day after his arrival, 29 October 1900, because of a victory parade given for the Civic Imperial Volunteers, troops returning from the Boer War. Britain had announced the incorporation of the Transvaal Republic into the British Empire on 3 September 1900, but the Boers had decided to continue a guerrilla war. The 'Khaki Election' of 16 October 1900 handed a landslide victory to the Conservative Party supporting the war, but demonstrations against the war led to large numbers of troops and police being mobilized to maintain order in London on this day, and disturbances left two dead and thirteen injured. This is the unspoken background to the swirling mass of humanity in 'Impression'.

p. 144 *There are two lions . . . with a thick copper column in the centre*: There are actually four lions in Trafalgar Square, and Nelson's Column is made of stone not copper, but the objective here is to convey the impression not the reality.

p. 146 *the neighbourhood*: On 24 July 1901 Soseki moved to his fourth and final boarding-house at 81 The Chase, off Clapham Common.

p. 149 *The Vale of Pitlochry*: In October 1902, shortly before returning to Japan, Soseki, suffering from severe depression in London, accepted the invitation of John Henry Dixon, a prominent lawyer and Japanophile, to pass some time at Dixon's home in Pitlochry in the Scottish Highlands.

How Soseki became acquainted with Dixon is unclear, but it may have been through a connection with Glasgow University where Japanese students had started to come to study engineering. The university entrance examination required knowledge of a language other than English, so Japanese was permitted as an acceptable second language and Soseki was appointed to write examination questions. Dixon, who was living in Pitlochry, may have heard of Soseki through this connection and invited him to stay.

p. 151 *When the Highlanders and Lowlanders fought at the Pass of Killiecrankie*: In 1689 the Jacobites defeated William III's forces but lost their leader, Viscount Dundee, at this pass in central Scotland.

p. 152 *Professor Craig*: After initially attending the classes of Professor Ker at London University, Soseki was introduced to an Irish scholar of English literature called William Craig. Born in Londonderry in 1843 and educated at Trinity College, Dublin, Craig had been a professor of English at University College, Aberystwyth, in 1876, but had resigned only three years later in order to move back to London and devote himself to research on Shakespeare, eventually becoming one of the leading Shakespeare scholars of the day. On 22 November 1900 Soseki called around to his chambers with a view to employing him as a personal tutor. He attended one-hour lessons with Craig every Tuesday until October 1901.

p. 153 *Satsuma*: Present-day Kagoshima prefecture in the extreme south of Japan, notorious for its difficult accent.

p. 154 *Swinburne*: Algernon Charles Swinburne (1837–1909), English poet and critic.

p. 154 *Rosamund*: *Rosamund, Queen of the Lombards: A Tragedy* (1899).

p. 155 *Atalanta*: A drama in classical Greek style. *Atalanta in Calydon: A Tragedy* (1865), a drama in Classical Greek style.

p. 155 *Watson*: Sir William Watson (1858–1935).

p. 155 *The boarding-house I was in became extremely irksome to me*: See Soseki's reference to this in 'Letter from London'.

p. 158 *Schmidt's* Shakespeare's Lexicon: Alexander Schmidt (1816–87), a German scholar of English, published *Shakespeare Lexicon: A*

Complete Dictionary of all the English Words, Phrases and Constructions in the Works of the Poet.

p. 158 *Dowden*: Edward Dowden (1843–1913), English literary historian and Shakespearian scholar.

p. 159 *I am already fifty-six*: Craig was actually fifty-seven in 1901.

The Yellow Lodger

p. 163 *those Shakespearian lines*: 'Be bloody, bold and resolute. Laugh to scorn / The power of man, for none of woman born / Shall harm Macbeth.' [Second Apparition to Macbeth in Shakespeare's *Macbeth*, IV, i.] 'Macbeth shall never vanquished be until / Great Birnam Wood to high Dunsinane Hill / Shall come against him.' [Third Apparition to Macbeth in *Macbeth*, IV, i.]

p. 163 *my literary knowledge is practically zero*: Despite Watson's observation in *A Study in Scarlet* that Sherlock Holmes's knowledge of literature is nil, Holmes actually alludes to *Macbeth* itself in this, his very first adventure. 'If a man can stride four and a half feet without the smallest effort, he can't quite be in the sere and yellow,' he says, alluding to *Macbeth* V, ii, 'I have lived long enough. My way of life / Is fall'n into the sere, the yellow leaf.'

p. 164 *nestled himself like a swallow on a certain third floor of Homer Street*: A reworking of 'Professor Craig is nestled like a swallow on the third floor,' Soseki's famous introduction to his short sketch of Professor Craig. The following section carefully works in elements of Soseki's description of Craig, including the appearance of his flat and housekeeper, and the rambling nature of his conversation. Craig's actual address was not Homer Street but 55a Gloucester Place, Portman Square, close to the Baker Street Underground.

p. 164 *the ciphers of "The Dancing Men" case*: 'The Dancing Men' case, in which figures of dancing men appear as encoded letters of the alphabet, appears in *The Return of Sherlock Holmes*.

p. 164 *Thomas Carlyle*: In *A Study in Scarlet*, Watson demonstrates that Holmes's literary knowledge is 'nil', by observing that 'Upon my quoting Thomas Carlyle, he [Holmes] enquired in the naïvest way who he might be and what he had done.' Shortly afterwards, however, Holmes manages to quote flawlessly an epigram of Carlyle's, 'They say that genius is an infinite capacity for taking pains.'

p. 165 *'You are amazed . . . when I lived with Whitman for a while'*: An almost exact reproduction of Soseki's own account of his conversations with Professor Craig.

p. 165 *slight pockmarks*: Soseki's nose was disfigured with pockmarks which were caused by an attack of smallpox when he was a small child. It was something he was extremely self-conscious about throughout his entire life. According to one anecdote, long after establishing himself as Japan's leading literary figure Soseki was engaged in an innocent discussion about love with one of his young friends when he suddenly exploded into anger and raged, 'Don't think I don't know about love just because I have pockmarks!'

p. 165 *Japan . . . which even tomorrow might conclude an offensive and defensive alliance with the British Empire*: The Anglo-Japanese Alliance was concluded the following year, on 30 January 1902.

p. 166 *he has been named Hirohito, I believe*: The Showa emperor (1901–89; reigned 1926–89), better known in the West by his given name Hirohito.

p. 166 *'Jujube . . . or "Natsume' as they say in Japanese"*: Futaro here uses the Chinese character for 'jujube', which is different to the two used in Soseki's surname but also has the reading 'natsume', to effect a pun.

p. 166 *suddenly withdrew his hand and abruptly turned the other way*: An allusion to Soseki's own account of his awkwardness regarding shaking hands as described in 'Professor Craig'.

p. 167 *Klopman*: In Conan-Doyle's short story 'His Last Bow', set at the outbreak of the First World War and thus chronologically the final Holmes adventure, Holmes informs the German agent Van Bork, 'It was I also who saved from murder, by the Nihilist Klopman, Count Von und Zu Grafenstein, who was your mother's elder brother. It was I –.' The name Klopman appears as equally preposterous as the nonsense German title Count Von und Zu Grafenstein ('Von und

Zu' meaning 'from and to', and 'Graf' itself being German for 'Count').

p. 168 *Greuze*: Jean Baptiste Greuze (1725–1805), French genre and portrait painter, cited by Soseki himself in his novel *Sanshiro* (1908), where the heroine Mineko appears as the very embodiment of Greuzian 'voluptuousness'.

p. 169 *'And I see that you have also been to China'*: The following exchange about Holmes's deductive methods is typical of all the classic Holmes stories but appears to be in particular a playful homage to the opening section of 'The Red-Headed League' in *The Adventures of Sherlock Holmes*. Holmes's opening line to Klopman is also reminiscent of Holmes's famous introductory line to Watson in *A Study in Scarlet*, 'You have been in Afghanistan, I perceive.'

p. 170 *'Well, it was Wednesday, April 10th'*: That is, the day after Soseki began writing 'Letter from London'.

p. 171 *Inspector Lestrade*: The perennial foil for Sherlock Holmes first appears in *A Study in Scarlet*, set in 1881, and frequently appears in subsequent cases.

p. 173 *Shinwell Johnson*: Appears in only one Sherlock Holmes story, 'The Illustrious Client', from *The Case-Book of Sherlock Holmes*. His character is quite different from that of Dr Watson, as he is a reformed criminal, acting as an agent for Holmes in the London underworld.

p. 173 *Carlsbad Spring*: See note to 'Letter from London'.

p. 174 Don Quixote: Soseki's entire personal library of around 2,400 books, many with fascinating marginalia and underlinings, are carefully preserved at Tohoku University Library in the northern Japanese city of Sendai and continue to provide invaluable reference material to scholars. Many of the books were bought by Soseki in London and shipped back to Japan. *Don Quixote* appears amongst them. Soseki recorded in his diary that he purchased the book on 5 February 1901.

p. 174 *a swarthy Italian was playing the violin while a young girl of about four years dressed in a red hood danced*: In his diary entry for 14 April

1901 Soseki records seeing on the street that day a blind man playing the organ and a swarthy Italian playing the violin, while a four-year-old girl in a red dress and red hood danced along to the music.

p. 174 *the Russian army would not withdraw from Manchuria*: The tension between Japan and Russia over Manchuria is referred to at the close of Soseki's 'Letter from London'. The following section makes liberal use of that material in its depiction of Soseki's third boarding-house and the maid Penn – although, strictly speaking, her presence would be impossible, as Soseki relates that she was dismissed after the family moved to the new house.

p. 174 *heavily bearded coachmen, looking rather like Professor Craig, raised their fingers*: A combination of the description of the cabmen in the opening lines of 'A Warm Dream' in *Short Pieces for Long Days* and Soseki's observation in 'Professor Craig' that Craig looked like a cabman who had lost his whip.

p. 175 *a dubious district of ill-repute not to my liking*: An allusion to the areas of prostitution that Soseki passed on his way back to the boarding-house in Camberwell.

p. 175 *'Hey, Mr Detective . . . Did you think the ha'penny suspicious?'*: This episode is based on some famous anecdotes related by Soseki's wife, Kyoko, in her memoirs of Soseki, written after his death in 1916. Coming close to nervous breakdown on several occasions, both while he was in England and after returning to Japan, Soseki became obsessed that small tricks were being played on him. Kyoko relates how on one occasion, while suffering from severe neurosis in England, Soseki became convinced that a small coin he discovered in the toilet of his boarding-house was the same coin he had earlier given to a beggar on the street and that his landlady was following him and had retrieved the coin, leaving it in the toilet to taunt him.

Delusions of such tricks would provoke entirely unpredictable violent outbursts from Soseki towards his family after his return to Japan also. In 1903 Soseki was to be put under great strain again from having to teach for twenty hours a week at the First Higher

倫
敦
塔

School and six hours at Tokyo Imperial University, while all the time wanting to proceed with his research for his massive *Theory of Literature*. One of the most humorous manifestations of his otherwise disturbing behaviour at this time was his becoming obsessed with the idea that a student living in the house next door was actually a detective shadowing his every movement. Soseki would apparently shout out to him every morning before setting off to work, 'Hey, Mr Detective, I wonder what time you will be going out today then', to the student's total bemusement. This type of bizarre happening became the source material for the high comedy of Soseki's first novel, *I Am a Cat*.

p. 178 *He's here on strange terms, you see*: Mysterious lodgers such as this appear in two original Holmes stories, 'The Red Circle', in *His Last Bow*, and 'The Veiled Lodger', in *The Case-Book of Sherlock Holmes*.

p. 189 *literary research, where the emphasis lies on 'why'*: This idea that the emphasis in science lies in 'how' while the emphasis in literature lies in 'why' forms the central argument of section three of Soseki's *Theory of Literature*.

p. 191 *My graduation thesis at university was on Lao-tzu*: Soseki published an essay called 'The Philosophy of Lao-tzu' in his penultimate year as an undergraduate at the Imperial University in 1892.

p. 191 *Ku Klux Klan*: Sinister letters containing nothing but the mark of the Ku Klux Klan and importing the impending death of the recipient feature in the story 'Five Orange Pips' in *The Adventures of Sherlock Holmes*.

p. 192 *There had been, even before now, cases . . . where the case had been left unsolved*: In the opening of 'Thor Bridge', from *The Case-Book of Sherlock Holmes*, Dr Watson alludes to three unsolved cases:

> A problem without a solution may interest the student, but can hardly fail to annoy the casual reader. Amongst these unfinished tales is that of Mr James Phillimore, who, stepping back into his own house to get his umbrella, was never more seen in this world. No less remarkable is that of the cutter *Alicia*, which sailed one spring

morning into a small patch of mist from where she never emerged, nor was anything further ever heard of herself and her crew. A third case worthy of note is that of Isadora Persano, the well-known journalist and duellist, who was found stark staring mad with a match box in front of him which contained a remarkable worm, said to be unknown to science.

Translator's Afterword

The inspiration for producing this collection of translations came to me on a train in Korea in 1997. As an American companion slumbered beside me, and the landscape raced by outside, I clawed my way through the dense, complex beauty of each sentence of Soseki's 'Tower of London' and soon found myself, from Pusan to Seoul, drifting in space, detached from the present world and borne back into the past of Victorian London, of the Renaissance, of the Middle Ages and beyond.

Further bewitched by Soseki's account of 'The Carlyle Museum', two years later I was in London, dragging a bemused overseas guest, visiting the UK for the first time, around not the usual sights but, rather, to Chelsea and the Carlyle House. No century has demonstrated the force of the passage of time more starkly than the twentieth. London, the world's first industrial megacity, was blitzed, cleared of slums, electrified, de-fogged, linked by telephone and internet, stripped of horses and filled with cars. Yet on my visit in 1999 the Carlyle House in Chelsea remained exactly as Soseki described it in 1901, 'just as it always did', an unchanging, timeless monument to a dead sage.

So moved was I by Soseki's description – as redolent today as it was a hundred years ago – that I thought to translate this story and lodge it in a little magazine somewhere. Having translated it, I belatedly realized that there was probably no magazine to publish it in. So I concluded that perhaps I should translate all Soseki's London stories and publish them together as a book.

By coincidence, this collection was being prepared exactly one hundred years after Soseki himself had lived in London. Soseki's arrival in London in October 1900 is one of the defining moments in world literature. Without the intense maelstrom of cultural dislocation and loneliness precipitated by Soseki's two years in London, it is impossible to imagine the explosive emergence of his literary genius.

Yet, as is the way with these things, the centennial anniversary of Soseki's arrival in London, commemorated by a stream of articles in the Japanese press, passed off entirely without note in the United Kingdom. Bizarrely, Japan's most important literary figure was not somebody that the Japanese government seemed to think needed to be introduced to the British public even during the year-long 'Japan 2001' festival.

So acute had the situation become that I began to wonder whether there was any publisher who would be interested in an author who was – in the United Kingdom at least – almost completely unknown. In the 1960s and 1970s Peter Owen had published a variety of well-regarded English translations of Soseki's novels. Yet, somehow or other, one by one these had drifted out of print, and that generation of translators had disappeared. By 2003 only one novella (*The Three-Cornered World*) was still being published by Peter Owen. One publishing old hand gloomily told me that, although Soseki was clearly a most remarkable writer, establishing him in the English-speaking world would be a 'Herculean endeavour'. It seemed as though my goal of promoting Soseki to the very forefront of world literature might remain unfulfilled.

In July 2003, however, I published a book in Japanese on Soseki which proclaimed that not only had Soseki been misunderstood by the Japanese but that Soseki was the 'King of the Novel' and a finer writer than Tolstoy, Proust or Joyce. The Japanese had always revered Soseki, but, once having turned him into a national treasure, not even a small fraction of the enormous amount of research and criticism written about him ever reached the outside world. A foreigner telling the Japanese that their national author had not only been misunderstood but also that he was not their 'national author' at all was therefore something new. Features on the book appeared throughout the Japanese press and sparked interest about the continued state of obscurity in which Soseki languished in the English-speaking world.

Meanwhile, a chairman of a leading Japanese company, having read about my aspiration to re-establish Soseki in the West, contacted me and offered his full patronage. I was invited up to Tokyo, put up at a top hotel and treated royally. Suddenly it was obvious that there were enlightened Japanese who realized how important it was that the rest of the world should be introduced to Soseki's works. Partially thanks to this spur of activity, it has been possible not only to release this collection of Soseki's London stories but to re-release classic translations of Soseki's novels with new critical introductions.

I would like to extend my sincere thanks to all those who have sustained me through this project.

Charming companions who patiently listened to me enthuse about Soseki were Anne Gaske and Anna Wilson. When illness brought everything to a halt in 2002, Rina Monchka was my greatest support. In Japan Ono Hiromi, Sue Yoshiki, Sven Serrano, David and Sachiko Jack and my Japanese editor Mizukoshi Kenji urged everything forward; Yamamura Yuka did the proofreading; while in Hong Kong Karen McCann was my constant muse. 'W' – the above-mentioned patron – not only provided assistance when needed but, more importantly, added a certain pizazz to what had always seemed like a resolutely solo endeavour. My sister Geraldine offered much useful advice, while Soseki scholar Senkoku Takashi helped out with knotty problems of translation.

I would also like to thank Yamada Keiko, widow of the late Yamada Futaro, whose desire to open the eyes of the world to Japanese literature was such that she allowed 'The Yellow Lodger', one of her husband's many excellent stories, to be translated without royalty. In London, the Japan Foundation and Sasakawa Foundation have also been generous with their support.

In tracking down illustrations, my gratitude is due to Elisabeth

Stacey at the National Trust, Melanie Oelgeschlager at the Wallace Collection and Henry Firmin at the Tower of London. I would particularly like to acknowledge Akiyama Yutaka, editor of Soseki's collected works (*Soseki Zenshu*) at Iwanami Shoten in Tokyo, for his many kindnesses.

I am also delighted that both this book and the re-releases of the other classic Soseki novels are adorned with the calligraphy of the Kobe-based artist Kosaka Misuzu, who not only enthusiastically accepted the commission to draw the Japanese titles for the front covers she also transformed them into superb works of art for the frontispiece of each book.

All of this would have been impossible if the staff of Peter Owen Publishers had not understood my desire to reintroduce Soseki to the West and done the hard work of turning vision into books.

Lastly, I would like to thank my mother, Ellen Flanagan, who broke the habit of a lifetime by reading this book and marked my errors with a pencil. Thanks. This book is dedicated to her.